PRAISE FOR JEFF EDWARDS NOVELS

"Jeff Edwards has created a superb thriller that grips the reader from beginning to end. Brilliantly executed."

> — **CLIVE CUSSLER**, International bestselling author of *'RAISE THE TITANIC'* and *'THE ROMANOV RANSOM'*

"Flies off the page and into your face. Hopefully, it will remain fiction!"

> — **LARRY BOND**, New York Times bestselling author of *'DANGEROUS GROUND'* and *'CAULDRON'*

"A taut, exciting story by an author who knows his Navy — guaranteed to keep you turning pages well into the night!"

> — **GREG BEAR**, New York Times bestselling author of *'KILLING TITAN'* and *'DARWIN'S RADIO'*

"Jeff Edwards spins a stunning and irresistibly-believable tale of savage modern naval combat."

> — **JOE BUFF**, Bestselling author of *'SEAS OF CRISIS'* and *'CRUSH DEPTH'*

"Brilliant and spellbinding... Took me back to sea and into the fury of life-or-death combat. I could not put this book down."

> — **REAR ADMIRAL JOHN J. WAICKWICZ, USN (Retired)**, Former Commander, Naval Mine and Anti-Submarine Warfare Command

"Edwards wields politics and naval combat tactics with a skill equal to the acknowledged masters of military fiction."

> — **MILITARY PRESS**

"Smart and involving, with an action through-line that shoots ahead ... fast and lethal. I read it in one sitting."

> — **PAUL L. SANDBERG**, Producer of *'THE BOURNE SUPREMACY'* and *'THE BOURNE ULTIMATUM'*

THE
DAMOCLES
AGENDA

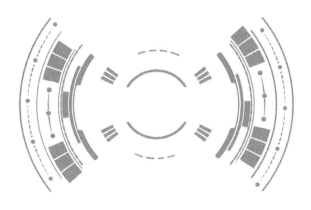

THE
DAMOCLES
AGENDA

Jeff Edwards

Braveship
BOOKS

Aura Libertatis Spirat

THE DAMOCLES AGENDA
Copyright © 2021 by Jeff Edwards

Braveship Books
www.braveshipbooks.com

Aura Libertatis Spirat

Cover Artwork & Design by Rossitsa Atanassova

Selected graphic elements licensed from 123RF.com

ISBN-13: 978-1-64062-131-2
Printed in the United States of America

**To Brenda, who finds magic in
everything I do.**

ACKNOWLEDGMENTS

I'd like to thank the following people for their assistance in bringing this book to life:

Former Space Shuttle Commander, Joe F. Edwards, Jr. (Commander, USN, Retired) for nudging my descriptions of space flight in the general direction of reality and for helping me get at least part of the astronaut stuff right; Abolfazl Shirazi Ph.D Fellow, Astrodynamics & Machine Learning, for creating detailed simulations to answer my questions about orbital patterns of the ISS; Thomas A. Mays (Captain, USN) for casually performing space probe acceleration calculations that would make my head explode; Dr. William Radasky (*Commission to Assess the Threat to the United States from Electromagnetic Pulse Attack*) for providing insight into the risk of EMP to commercial electronics and critical national infrastructure; career airline pilot Captain Scott Redford for walking me through a certain in-flight emergency scenario for an Airbus 320; Ian Kharitonov for help with the Russian language; Karl Kruger for suggesting a much subtler and more interesting panic reaction than the one I'd had in mind; and Kevin Miller (Captain, USN, Retired) for alleviating some of my ignorance on U.S. Navy flight deck procedures.

Any errors or exaggerations that have found their way into this novel are entirely of my own creation.

I'd also like to thank my all-star team of advance readers, proofreaders, second-guessers, nitpickers, and literary busybodies. Somehow, you've done it again—made me seem like a better writer than I am.

And most of all, my wife, Brenda, for believing and for keeping the world at bay long enough for me to write this book.

Damocles, a courtier in the retinue of Dionysius II, spoke with envy about the wealth of his master and the splendor of his royal palaces—maintaining that no man was ever happier than the great ruler.

Dionysius, having heard the remarks of his underling, called the envious man to his side. "As this kind of life pleases you, have you a desire to partake of it yourself?"

When Damocles said that he should like that very much, Dionysius ordered the courtier to be laid upon a bed of gold with the most beautiful covering, embroidered with the most delicate work, and he dressed out a great many sideboards with silver and embossed gold. He ordered servant girls, distinguished for their surpassing beauty, to wait at the feet of Damocles and lavish the lucky man with whatever delights he fancied.

There were ointments and garlands. Perfumes were burned, and tables ladened with the most exquisite meats. Kisses, caresses, and all forms of earthly pleasure were his for the asking.

Damocles thought himself happy indeed.

But, in the midst of the courtier's merriment, his master ordered for a long sword to be hung from the ceiling, suspended by a single horsehair, so that the bright and deadly blade dangled above the head of the blissful man.

After this, Damocles did not cast his eye on the beautiful servant girls or delight in their affections. Nor did he touch any of the delicacies on his plate. At last, he entreated the tyrant to give him leave to go, for he had no further interest in the luxuries enjoyed by his master.

"Now you know what it means to sit in my place," said Dionysius. "For all the freedoms of my station, there can be no peace for he who lives in the shadow of the sword."

— Cicero, *The Tusculanae Disputationes*, 45 BCE

There is a tendency in our planning to confuse the unfamiliar with the improbable. The contingency we have not considered looks strange; what looks strange is therefore improbable; what seems improbable need not be considered seriously.

— Thomas C. Schelling, in Roberta Wohlstetter's
Pearl Harbor: Warning and Decision
Stanford University Press, 1962

PRELUDE

Akademgorodok District
Novosibirsk, Russia

It was the perfect spot for a discovery that would shatter the balance of international power.

The *Laboratoriya fiziki dvizheniya Altshulera* (Altshuler Propulsion Physics Laboratory) was situated in the Akademgorodok district of Novosibirsk, one of more than three dozen research facilities hidden among the pine and birch trees of southwestern Siberia.

Built in the half-decade following the Cuban Missile Crisis, this strange amalgam of city, military compound, and university campus had gotten its start as the Soviet Union's ultra-secret crucible for cutting-edge science. A citadel of Cold War physicists, biologists, chemists, engineers, and mathematicians—all laboring in seclusion for the glory of the motherland.

Because of the extreme secrecy that shrouded the site in its early years, the world will probably never know how many discoveries took hold and flourished in the intellectual Petri dish of Akademgorodok. Some of the resulting innovations were no doubt suppressed for contradicting the principles of dialectical materialism. Others were co-opted by the KGB or the Soviet military. An unknown fraction of the unsuppressed discoveries may have edged humanity a few centimeters (or a few kilometers) closer to extinction.

But nothing coming out of the place had ever resembled the kind of revolutionary technological advantage that the Russian Politburo had hungered for. No radical breakthrough had given them the hammer they needed to pound the West into submission.

So, there's a certain dark symmetry to the fact that—long after the fall of the Berlin wall and the collapse of the USSR—the no-longer-secret Russian research center would finally become what its founders had envisioned.

In hindsight, it would have been hard to find a more appropriate site for an innovation that would alter the course of human events.

Even the building housing the laboratory was suitably ominous. Brutalist architecture, over-built and Stalinesque. A squat assembly of raw concrete slabs that resembled a bomb shelter yanked out of the ground.

The people who worked in the lab were not searching for a tool of global domination. They had something quite different in mind.

What happened can best be described as an accident, but it was the kind of accident that changes everything.

Afterward, there could be no going back.

ONE

Altshuler Propulsion Physics Laboratory
Novosibirsk, Russia

It wasn't supposed to be about money.

Doktor Yevgeny Koltsov steered his brown Lada hatchback into the parking structure and chose a slot at random. There was no shortage of vacant spots this late in the evening; the usually crowded ground floor of the garage contained only a handful of cars.

Most people were home with their families by now, enjoying dinner, relaxing, preparing for bed. Koltsov's team was just getting started on what was likely to be another long night. Those were getting to be a habit.

His team (if you could still call it that) was up against a deadline. Not a project goal or a contractual delivery date. Nothing so respectable as that. The time limit was financial. The lease on the lab facility was up at the end of the month, and Koltsov couldn't afford to renew it.

Money again.

He shut off the engine, set the parking brake, and reached for the white paper bag on the passenger's seat. Six *pirozhki* stuffed with sugared apples, from that bakery shop on Morskoy Prospekt. The aroma of warm dough and candied fruit permeated the air of the little hatchback.

To Koltsov, the scent was pleasant for obvious physical reasons, and distasteful for less obvious intellectual ones. The grant money had run out, and none of the potential investors were willing to commit funding without more positive indicators of a successful outcome. Koltsov couldn't pay Uri and Svetlana for the extra hours. He was reduced to bribing them with pastries and hopes of better times to come. Even the pirozhki made a dent in what was left of his budget.

Climbing out of the car, he closed the door harder than he intended. The Lada was another measure of the downward spiral in his research. His ambitions. His life.

He'd traded the Mercedes a month ago, in exchange for the Lada and enough cash to (barely) keep the lab running for another few weeks.

The Mercedes had been several years old but still magnificent. Elegant lines, the famously precise German machine work, and fawn-colored leather upholstery as soft as a baby's cheek. A trophy from bygone and better days.

Now he had the Lada. A little brown turd of a hatchback that wheezed and groaned as badly as Koltsov himself did after three flights of stairs. If things didn't turn around, it too would have to be sold before long. Assuming that anyone would buy the ugly thing.

Walking toward the exit of the parking structure, he kept his jaw muscles carefully loose. He'd taken to grinding his teeth lately, hard enough that he was worried about breaking a crown. He didn't need a dental bill on top of everything else.

This wasn't supposed to be about money. It was supposed to be about discovery. Pushing back the borders of human ignorance by some small but significant amount. Only it turned out that grand dreams and noble intentions didn't pay the bills.

He'd watched his resources dry up one by one, his laboratory staff get siphoned off by competitors who could make payroll on a reliable basis, and his standing in the academic community erode away to practically nothing.

It was *always* about money. Rubles. Euros. Dollars. Whatever. You might sneak some science in there somewhere, but not without first abasing yourself before the altar of the money gods.

He stalked out of the garage and turned toward the lab building. Automatically, his face tilted upward, eyes lifting to the darkened evening sky where the first stars were becoming visible against the curtain of infinity.

The sight fired his imagination, as it had since he was a boy. There were inconceivably vast resources up there. Abundant energy. All the minerals that humanity could ever need. Iridium, tungsten, iron, cobalt, nickel, titanium, manganese, molybdenum, aluminum, phosphorus, antimony, zinc, tin, and copper—along with enough platinum, gold, and silver to appease the greediest of the money gods. Bountiful hydrogen, oxygen, and ammonia to support settlers, asteroid miners, and explorers as Man finally spread beyond the planet of his birth.

The energy shortages and dwindling resources of the human race could be reduced to distant and unpleasant memories. All we had to do was get up there. *Out* there....

Which was, at least in part, the real point behind all the frantic last-minute laboratory work.

Koltsov and his team had built a functioning—or nearly functioning—prototype of an electromagnetic propulsion engine for use in spacecraft. What the international press had taken to calling an "EmDrive" system.

The core design was similar to a concept invented by British engineer Roger Shawyer, and which was currently under experimental development by America's NASA. But Koltsov—with his tinkerer's mind—was taking the idea in a different direction.

Training and professional credentials aside, he was more engineer than scientist, a leaning which brought him disdain in academic circles. He accepted the jibes of his purist brethren as the cost of doing work that fascinated him. Work that might actually matter to the future of his species.

He pushed through the front doors of the building into the foyer and tapped the elevator call button. He should be taking the stairs, one flight at least. A man of his age and state of health needed more exercise and less pastry, a fact of which neither his wife nor his cardiologist ever tired of reminding him.

But he'd look ridiculous arriving in the lab out of breath with a sack of goodies clenched in one sweaty fist. The image was as absurd as it was undignified.

He banished it from his mind as the lift doors opened and he rode up three floors. There would be time for the stairs tomorrow.

Tonight was for more important things. His team had been edging toward a breakthrough for weeks. They were close now. Koltsov could feel it.

When he let himself into the outer office, the television was playing but no one was in the room. Svetlana again. She was forever turning the thing on, watching for two minutes, and then walking away without turning it off again.

Also true to Svetlana's habits, the channel was set to Rossiya 1, the state-owned news and entertainment network. On the screen, President Polichev was making a statement—justifying yet another escalation of Russian military forces in Ukraine. Something about Ukrainian attacks against pro-Russian citizens in Donetsk and Horlivka.

Maybe there had been such attacks, and maybe there hadn't. More likely, some local toady favored by Moscow had tripped over his own bootlaces and given himself a bloody nose.

Polichev knew how to make an elephant out of a fly. The man was beginning to make Vladimir Putin look reasonable and level-headed by comparison. Incredibly, Polichev seemed nostalgic for the bad old days, when the Warsaw Pact had played at nuclear brinksmanship with the United States and the rest of NATO.

The television remote was in its usual place. Koltsov picked it up and flicked the off button. The screen went dark as a column of Russian infantry carriers and T-14 battle tanks were surging across the Ukrainian countryside.

He dropped the remote on a chair and continued through into the lab. As he walked in the door, Svetlana looked up from calibrating the phase controls for the stator rings and smiled. Tired, but cautiously optimistic about the upcoming test.

She spotted the bakery bag and her smile widened by a couple of centimeters.

When she spoke, it was in a passable imitation of the baritone actor who had dubbed William Shatner's voice for the Russian release of the original *Star Trek* series. "Captain's log… Stardate: Wednesday evening, just about dinner time. These are the voyages of the Starship *Pirozhki*. Its ongoing mission to seek out laboratory technicians who are willing to work for treats—"

"You're mixing up the intro with the commercial break recaps," said Uri. "And speak for yourself. *I'm* not willing to work for treats. I want vodka and a nice foot rub."

He was checking over the vacuum pump as he spoke. A Swiss-built rotary vane model rated at 1×10^{-3} pascals. Uri (a tinkerer, like Koltsov) had modified the pump to exceed the manufacturer's specifications. When the thing behaved itself, it could pull 1×10^{-7} pascals of vacuum. Far from absolute vacuum, but adequate for the parameters of the test.

"I may be able to help you with the vodka," said Svetlana. "There used to be a half bottle of Putinka somewhere in my kitchen. Might still be there. You'll have to figure out the foot rub thing on your own."

Their friendly back-and-forth gave Koltsov a minor sense of comfort. If Svetlana and Uri had some playfulness left in them, their morale couldn't be totally depleted.

He unrolled the bakery bag and doled out a pirozhok to each of his two remaining lab workers, and one for himself as well. He'd hold the other three pastries in reserve, either for celebration or for commiseration, depending on the results of the evening's test event.

It took the better part of another hour to complete the pre-test preparations and ensure that the setup and conditions were scrupulously documented.

Finally, comfortable that all was in readiness, Koltsov spent a moment looking over the EmDrive itself.

The prototype was mounted to a low-thrust torsion pendulum suspended at the center of a cylindrical polycarbonate vacuum chamber. Any movement of the pendulum would be monitored and recorded by optical displacement sensors and mechanical deflection gauges, each independently capable of measuring thrust down to the single-digit micronewton level.

Koltsov—who didn't believe in unnecessary reinvention—had

adapted the design from a NASA technical paper published in the *Journal of Propulsion and Power*. He'd made a few modifications to fit the specific needs of his drive prototype, but the essential elements of the design were unchanged.

Seen through the transparent walls of the vacuum chamber, the drive was a conical brass shape swaddled in a rat's nest of colored wiring. The second stage was recognizably descended from Roger Shawyer's resonant cavity thruster concept, but the architecture of the first stage was a radical departure from all other known designs.

In place of the usual RF amplifier and phase-locked loop antenna, Koltsov's prototype employed a non-explosive flux compression generator, configured to fire electromagnetic pulses into the RF cavity of the second stage.

Like the torsion pendulum and cavity thruster, the compression generator was based on existing technology. In this case, a selection of components from the French *Centre d'Etudes de Gramat's* research in the field and U.S. Patent Number 8,723,390 B2 (filed—strangely enough—on behalf of the United States Secretary of the Navy).

What the Americans called "prior art" was a wonderful thing. Koltsov didn't have to invent the technologies that he wanted to experiment with. He merely needed to license them. He had done that: submitted the requisite paperwork and paid the necessary fees.

The licensing payments had cut heavily into the lab's budget, but it was vital to ensure that his work was both legal and ethical in all respects. If... no, *when*... he demonstrated a fully functional EmDrive design, he would not be mired in court battles or allegations of intellectual property theft.

The drive had already proven itself to a degree. They'd blown a power supply during the previous test, but the thrust output had been up to nearly 170 micronewtons when the component had failed. Slightly better than NASA's prototype. Adequate for proof of concept, but not enough to show that his approach to the first stage was fundamentally superior. Certainly not sufficient to attract new funding.

Besides, he wasn't after a superior test article. He wanted a practical drive system. Something that could be developed and improved upon until it was ready for use in actual spacecraft.

His private target—a goal he'd never shared with even Uri and Svetlana—was one millinewton or better. Not just a few points more powerful than NASA's drive. Ten times more powerful.

If they could break the millinewton mark, the grant money would come pouring in. When that happened (and Koltsov was sure that it *would* happen), he'd be able to reward Svetlana and Uri for sticking with him. For believing in his dream.

Uri made a subtle throat-clearing sound, perhaps a gentle reminder that it was time to be getting on with things.

Koltsov nodded and leaned over the laptop that served as the drive system's primary control interface. "Everyone ready?"

"Ready on my end," said Uri.

Svetlana reassumed her faux baritone Captain Kirk voice. "Warp factor six, Mr. Sulu."

Koltsov smiled and tapped the activation icon on the laptop screen.

Two things happened at once. The lights went out in the laboratory, and Koltsov felt something akin to an explosion just below his left collarbone. A tearing, burning, white-hot agony, like nothing he had ever experienced before.

Clutching his chest, he collapsed to the floor of his lab and lay convulsing in the darkness.

The area of effect was just under two kilometers in diameter. Within that sphere, an electromagnetic pulse of unknown (but massive) intensity surged through every power line, electrical wire, antenna, conduit, ground strap, and electronic device—destroying microchips, erasing magnetic media, and burning out electrical components.

Koltsov's research team had predicted a maximum field strength of approximately 5 milliteslas, roughly equivalent to the force of a typical refrigerator magnet. The pulse generated by their EmDrive prototype was many orders of magnitude more powerful.

Propagating at the speed of light, the electromagnetic wavefront killed electronic ignition systems in vehicles, fried computers, devastated cell phones, and cooked every circuit more complicated than a battery and flashlight bulb.

Certain types of electronic components in close proximity to the source of the pulse suffered catastrophic structural failure: especially assemblies containing liquid dielectrics, fluid-based electrolytes, and any compound subject to outgassing under conditions of extreme overvoltage.

The autopsy of Doktor Yevgeny Koltsov would establish the cause of death as massive internal hemorrhage, secondary to laceration of the left subclavian vein, actuated by the explosion of a lithium/silver vanadium oxide battery in the victim's Thoracigenix Sync III cardiac pacemaker.

The results of the autopsy were immediately classified by Russian military intelligence. All associated files and documents were expunged, and the pathologist of record was placed under continual surveillance by agents of the GRU.

Koltsov's prototype was about to receive more funding than its inventor ever imagined, for purposes that had nothing at all to do with the dead man's dream.

THREE YEARS LATER

TWO

International Space Station

Lieutenant Commander Sarah Keene touched the screen of the Guidance, Navigation, and Control panel, calling up the top-level management display. "Dogs before an earthquake," she mumbled.

Soft though her voice was, Dmitri Ivchenko flinched at the sound. As cringes went, it was a small one and quickly suppressed. But in microgravity, the sudden movement was enough to start the unanchored cosmonaut on a slow roll to clockwise.

He reached for a handhold and absorbed his momentum to stop the roll. "Pardon me?"

Sarah tabbed down to the Tier 2 GNC interface menu, bringing up the control protocols for the Beta Gimbals that adjusted the angular positions of the solar power arrays. She grimaced. "Sorry, D! Didn't realize I said that out loud."

Dmitri's eyebrows drew together. "Dogs and earthworms?"

"*Earthquakes*," said Sarah. "The last few days, you and Anya have been acting like dogs before an earthquake. Both of you have got this quiet-nervous thing going on. Like something bad is about to happen and you can feel the pre-tremors."

"You've been in orbit too long," said Dmitri with a grin. "Imagination is getting the better of you."

Only it wasn't his usual grin. There was something beneath it. A strained quality, at odds with the Russian's normally cheerful personality.

Whatever had gotten into Dmitri, Anya had it too. She'd always been more reserved than her male counterpart, but her laughs were quick and warm. Or they *had* been. Because Anya's sense of humor had been noticeably absent for a while. If the cosmonaut had so much as chuckled in the past week, she had done it in private.

Sarah checked the time readout on the GNC screen—still a few minutes until she needed to move the arrays. "I'm not the only one who's noticed. Larry and Rutger have picked up on it too."

As if summoned by the sound of his name, Dr. Rutger Braam came drifting in through the hatch from the Destiny Module—silver foil pouch of drinking water in hand. "Picked up on *what*?"

"On whatever's bothering Dmitri and Anya."

"Nothing is bothering us," said Dmitri. "We're the same as always."

Rutger fiddled with the valve on the stem of his drinking pouch. "If you say so…. But I just beat Anya at chess, and it was *not* a close game. I don't know where her brain was, but it certainly wasn't on the board."

The last bit might have been the Dutch astronaut's notion of a joke. He and Anya played with an imaginary chessboard. The pieces were real, positioned carefully in mid-air, but the board existed only as visualized in their minds.

Sarah had tried it once and abandoned the attempt about eight moves into the game. The extra effort required to track spatial relationships between the various pieces subtracted from brainpower that she needed for strategy and planning. Also, it wasn't easy to park the pieces with sufficient precision to keep them in place. The slightest residual inertia could send your knights or pawns wandering off in weird directions.

Anya and Rutger were the only people aboard the station who had enough surplus intellectual capacity to play air chess without blowing a gasket. And—of the two—Anya was the better player by a fairly significant margin. Rutger managed to beat her about one game out of seven, but she never made the victory easy.

If he truly had just mopped up the "board" with Anya, the woman's head must be way off in the Russian equivalent of La-La Land.

Sarah laid a hand on Dmitri's elbow. "Something's eating you, D. *Both* of you. I'm guessing it's either Moon Song or the augmentation crew."

Moon Song was *Lunnaya Pesnya*, the unofficial nickname of the electromagnetic drive prototype that Dmitri and Anya had been assembling in the station's Nauka Module over the past several weeks. With construction complete, the Russian space agency, Roscosmos, was sending up an augmentation crew: three additional cosmonauts with specialized training for a series of EmDrive experiments.

The Soyuz carrying the new arrivals was now on final approach. If nothing exploded and the laws of orbital mechanics remained constant, the spacecraft would dock with the ISS in a little less than an hour.

That had to be the source of Anya and Dmitri's growing discomfort. Otherwise, the timing was too much of a coincidence.

Possibly, they were anxious about someone in the augmentation crew. Maybe one of the arriving cosmonauts had a reputation as a prima donna.

Sarah had worked for a couple of temperamental jerks during her Navy days, and one or two more after she'd moved over to NASA. Probably every organization had at least a few of the type. Self-entitled perfectionist egomaniacs who were nightmares to deal with. Screaming assholes, known for hoarding credit, deflecting criticism, and sabotaging the careers of anyone unfortunate enough to attract their ire.

Then again, the source of apprehension could be the drive itself. Dmitri and Anya might be worried that their assembly work would be blamed if the prototype failed to perform as expected.

Either way, she was sure that the rising tension among the Russians had something to do with the approaching Soyuz.

Sarah checked the time readout again. Coming up on the mark now. She tapped a series of soft keys on the GNC screen.

Outside the pressure hull, the Beta Gimbals began turning the station's massive solar arrays away from the sun, rotating them to an orientation parallel to the velocity vector of the incoming vehicle.

The procedure—known as 'feathering' the arrays—was a precautionary measure to prevent damage from the maneuvering thrusters of the docking spacecraft. As the PHALCON (Power, Heating, Articulation, Lighting, and Control) Officer, Sarah was tasked with managing the solar panels and all electrical systems aboard the ISS. In addition to feathering the arrays, she was responsible for cycling the primary power systems offline during docking and undocking maneuvers.

Because the solar arrays were no longer angled to intercept the sun's rays, their collective energy output fell to nearly zero, leaving the station on battery power. Sufficient to operate life support and lighting, but far too little for scientific payloads and other nonessential operations.

As Sarah completed the transition to battery backups, a buzzer sounded from a Caution and Warning panel mounted to the bulkhead next to the GNC control screen. The 'FIRE,' 'ΔP' (Loss of Pressure), 'ATM' (Atmospheric Contamination), and 'WARNING' lamps were all dark. Only the nonspecific 'CAUTION' light was flashing, signaling an unspecified change to the operational status of the ISS: in this instance, loss of primary electrical power to major systems.

The buzzer and flashing light were being repeated on every C&W panel throughout the station, but no one would be reacting to the "emergency." The power reduction was a planned event, and Sarah had initiated the transfer to battery backups right on schedule.

She navigated through the screen displays to the Cautions and Warnings menu and canceled the alert.

Her immediate tasks now out of the way, Sarah logged off of the GNC panel and turned back to Dmitri. "You sure there's nothing you want to tell us?"

The Russian cosmonaut opened his mouth and hesitated. Then he gave his head an almost imperceptible shake. "Everything is fine."

"If you say so," Rutger said again. "Just remember that you can talk to us, D. We're your friends."

"Yes," said Dmitri. "Friends...."

Before anyone could respond, he pushed off from his handhold and soared through the open hatchway of the Destiny Module toward the Russian end of the station.

Forty-five minutes later, Sarah made her way to the Zvezda Service Module. She was early but the expedition commander, Colonel Lawrence Winfield, was already there, chatting with Rutger when she arrived.

No surprise for either man. Rutger had the stereotypical Dutch fetish for punctuality and Larry liked to pretend that his Air Force Academy background gave him a military bearing superior to that of any officer trained by the Navy.

Sarah didn't mind conceding the man a few meaningless victories. She could afford to be magnanimous. After all, she was a *Super Hornet* pilot, while poor old Larry was stuck flying the F-16 *Falcon*, or *Chicken Hawk*, or whatever that single-engine single-tailed lawn dart was called.

(If that was the Air Farce's idea of a fighter plane, no wonder all the real aviators flocked to the Navy.)

Inter-service rivalries notwithstanding, Larry was a top-notch astronaut. He was also a good guy and not a bad expedition commander, despite his poor judgment in having joined the Air Scouts.

Sarah drifted to casual conversation range and latched on to a cable junction to check her inertia. "What's up, kiddies?"

Rutger looked at her and grinned. "Larry's practicing his welcome speech for our visitors. Rather good if you ask me."

"All right," said Sarah. "Knock me out with some of that Air Force elocution."

Larry cleared his throat with a theatrical rumble. "Welcome aboard...."

Sarah waited, but he showed no sign of continuing. "That's all?"

"Don't want to overdo it," said Larry.

"Well then," said Sarah, "mission accomplished." She glanced around. "Where are Anya and Dmitri?"

"No idea," said Rutger. "Maybe they're off making themselves presentable for their countrymen."

It was traditional for the entire ISS crew to greet new expedition members as they first entered the station. Russian vehicles attached to the Universal Docking Module, so the customary gathering place was the adjoining Zvezda Service Module, which was less claustrophobic.

Such events were rare enough to be cause for a minor undercurrent of celebration. After a few months cooped up in an orbiting aluminum can, even the faces of good friends could become too familiar.

The arriving Soyuz would bring an infusion of new personalities, new voices, and new energy—subtly (or not-so-subtly) transforming the tempo and culture of life aboard the ISS.

So, it was a bit odd that Dmitri and Anya were not present to meet their fellow cosmonauts.

They couldn't possibly have duties elsewhere in the station. With the solar arrays feathered, there was no power available for scientific work or maintenance, and telemetry and docking for the incoming Soyuz were being handled by Mission Control Center Moscow. It was standard operating procedure for MCC-M to control all Russian vehicle approaches and departures, just as Mission Control Houston managed telemetry and docking for all U.S. spacecraft.

A communications headset floated loosely around Larry's neck, tethered to a control unit on his belt by a short length of cable. He moved the headset into place, got the earpiece settled properly, and swung the little plastic arm up to put the microphone in front of his mouth. He clicked the channel selector on his belt unit to 'Internal Public Address' and keyed the transmit button. When he spoke, his words came out of every speaker aboard the ISS.

"This is your friendly expedition commander speaking. All Russian cosmonauts are cordially invited to get their butts to the Zvezda Module A-S-A-P. The Baikonur Express is about to dock."

He released the transmit button but continued speaking in the same voice, as though continuing his announcement. "Cleanup on Aisle 9. We need a cleanup on Aisle 9."

Sarah grinned. "That ought to bring 'em running, Boss."

But the missing Russian crew members still didn't appear.

After several more minutes, Rutger sighed. "I'll go find out what's keeping them."

As he was turning to go, there was a low thump and a nearly inaudible scraping noise—the sound of the docking probe aboard the Soyuz vehicle sliding into the cone-shaped drogue socket built into the station's Universal Docking Module.

There followed a short series of metallic bangs as the probe was pneumatically retracted, pulling the hatch ring on the nose of the Soyuz into the matching collar on the station side. Then came the snap of the latches engaging.

The Russian augmentation crew had arrived.

There was another half-minute of mechanical sounds as the hatches were opened and moved out of the way. And then the guest cosmonauts came floating up through the exit of the Universal Docking Module. All three of them were male, as expected.

Larry made eye contact with the first man, presumably the leader, and smiled. "I'm Colonel Larry Winfield, the expedition commander. Welcome aboard the International...."

It took Sarah a second or so to realize why Larry had stopped in mid-sentence.

Then, she saw it too.

The arriving cosmonauts were armed. Each of them carried an automatic pistol in one hand, a short brutish-looking knife in the other, and a military-grade Taser strapped to his belt.

Sarah recognized the guns as the type of 9mm Makarov carried in the emergency survival kit of every Soyuz. Russian spacecraft routinely landed in wilderness areas of Kazakhstan, where the weapons were sometimes useful for signaling search parties or as defense against wild animals.

Sarah had handled and practice-fired a Makarov as part of her pre-mission training. There were not yet enough Crew Dragons or Starliners in the rotation to guarantee the presence of an American spacecraft for emergency escape. U.S. astronauts were still training to operate the Soyuz, just in case.

Makarovs were a regular part of the Russian manned space

program. So common as to seem unremarkable—beyond the absurd and distant notion that Sarah might one day have to shoot a wolf or a bear during the post-landing recovery phase of an emergency return flight.

Only these Makarovs were no longer pieces of survival equipment with abstract (and vaguely ludicrous) purposes. They were suddenly real weapons again. Instruments of domination and death.

Larry's attention was fixed on the lead man's pistol. "What the hell? You can't bring—"

The Russian cut him off. "I am Colonel Pavel Sergeivich Volkov. I am taking command of this station on behalf of the Russian Federation. All personnel and resources aboard are now under my direct control."

"Not funny," said Sarah. But she knew before the words came out of her mouth that this was no joke. The truth was written in the hard eyes of the intruders.

She turned and was not surprised to find that Anya and Dmitri had finally joined the party. They were also armed with 9mm Makarovs, minus the knives and Tasers.

Their faces were determined, but their eyes seemed more resigned than hard. Neither of them would have chosen this path, whatever it was. Sarah was certain of that. But they were throwing in with the intruders; friendships and international laws be damned.

Three unprepared astronauts against five armed Russian cosmonauts. The odds were not good, but Sarah's brain automatically tripped into tactical mode: calculating angles and estimating distances to her various adversaries. Trying to decide who might be more vulnerable—the three new arrivals, whose bodies and reflexes would still be adapting to microgravity—or Dmitri and Anya, both of whom seemed less than overjoyed with the unfolding situation.

If Sarah made a grab for one of the weapons, would Anya shoot her? Would Dmitri?

"Your guns are no good here," said Rutger. "Pull the trigger one time and you depressurize the module. Then we're all breathing vacuum."

"We are not idiots!" Anya snapped. "Our engineers have prepared for this. Frangible ceramic ammunition and reduced propellant charges. Rounds that shatter on impact with hard surfaces."

"My compatriot is correct," said Colonel Volkov. "These bullets are the result of long experimentation. They will shred human tissue, but the risk of penetrating the hull is low."

"Low," said Rutger. "*Not* zero."

"True," Volkov conceded. "But we have other weapons as well."

Larry shook his head. "Think about what you're doing! This is an act of war. You have no *idea* what—"

Volkov interrupted him again. "Political and legal ramifications are not your concern. You will now order your personnel to do exactly as I say."

"Kiss my ass!" muttered Larry. He flicked the channel selector on his belt unit to the far-left position: 'NASA Mission Control,' and jabbed at the transmit button. "Houston—ISS! Emergency! We are under…."

It happened so fast that Sarah could barely register the movements.

Volkov's knife hand snapped up, and the blade launched itself free from the handle, a blur of flying steel that took Larry just above the Adam's apple.

Warning transmission only half delivered, Larry's fingers jerked away from the transmit button and went to his throat—where his other fingers were struggling (and failing) to remove the handleless dagger from the wound.

He thrashed in midair, gurgling, mewling, and spraying spherical globules of blood.

The scene was both hideous and surreal. A convulsive and dreadful ballet of arching spine and gyrating limbs that could not have been duplicated in any significant fraction of gravity.

There was probably a point near the height of the commotion when Sarah could have made a move. An optimal moment when a lunge toward one of the Russians might have given her a reasonable opening to grab a weapon. If such an opportunity occurred, she was too dazed and too horrified to recognize it.

The unheralded assault on the station. Anya and Dmitri siding with the murderous newcomers. Larry flailing his life out as she watched in sickened fascination.

So, the golden instant had passed. Or *had* it? Maybe it wasn't too late. Maybe there was still a chance....

She felt her muscles tensing of their own accord, the back of her tongue going bitter with surging adrenaline. Her body readying itself for a lunge toward the nearest Russian, mind already picturing the opening moves of her attack.

A millisecond before she sprang, her brain registered a new bit of tactical information. Anya and Dmitri were not distracted by Larry's death spiral. Both of their Makarovs were pointed directly at Sarah's face. If she moved now, it would be the last thing she ever did.

She willed her muscles to relax and tried to imagine her tissues reabsorbing the unneeded adrenaline. Store it. Save it for later.

There would come a time. Sarah knew that instinctively. There *would* come a time. And she would be ready.

Larry's spasms were petering out now. Energy draining from his musculature as he surrendered the last inches of his life.

Somewhere in the tumult, his headset had come off. It floated at the end of its cable tether, bobbing and jerking with every twitch of the dying man's body.

Through the earpiece came the crackling sound of a human voice over radio. "ISS—Houston. Say again your last! ISS—Houston. Say again your last!"

THREE

**Johnson Space Center
Houston, Texas**

Director of Flight Operations Irene Harper tossed the briefing folder onto the conference table and stared across at the man who was trying so assiduously to pump sunshine up her butt. She gestured in the direction of the projector screen. "Shut that thing off for a minute, please."

Her unexpected interruption drew the eyes of everyone seated around the table. The only person standing, NASA Financial Officer George Sherman, paused with his mouth open—the remote control for the projector clutched to his chest like a priceless relic. "Off? I have more...."

"I'm sure you do," said Director Harper. "Your briefing slides are simply breathtaking, George. I mean, who doesn't enjoy a good candlestick chart? Am I right? But you know what strikes me as funny?"

With an expression of supreme reluctance, Sherman clicked the power button on the remote and the projector went dark. "These aren't the numbers you were hoping for, Irene. We realize that. We just can't give you money that's not in the budget."

"I'll tell you what's funny," said Harper. "Your charts are calling for a decrease in funding at the same time they're showing an increase in mission tempo. Do you have a slide in there somewhere that tells me how we're supposed to make that happen?"

"I don't create the budget," said Sherman.

Harper gave him a sardonic smile. "And I don't create the principles of economics. When you work people more hours, they can be downright pissy about wanting to get paid for it."

She pushed the briefing folder closer to the center of the table. "You know who else likes to get paid? Suppliers. When we burn through more resources, the vendors expect us to pay for what we use. Maybe that's unreasonable, but it seems to be how those guys do business."

Sherman lowered the remote. "I can't perform miracles, Irene."

"Then stop asking *me* for miracles," Harper snapped. "If you want to peddle your *do-more-with-less* routine, go talk to the unmanned programs. When they cut corners, we don't end up with dead astronauts on CNN."

The Financial Officer's reply was preempted by a tap at the door.

Lloyd Etheridge, one of Harper's assistants, poked his head into the conference room. "Sorry to intrude. I need to borrow the director for a minute."

Harper followed Lloyd out into the hall. "I wish somebody would make these pencil pushers study physics. If that bonehead understood the concept of boundary conditions, he'd know there are a limited number of...."

She took a breath and waved a hand to dismiss her uncompleted sentence. "Never mind. What have you got?"

"We've lost comms and telemetry with the ISS," said Lloyd.

Harper nodded, her thoughts back in the conference room with Mr. PowerPoint. "Our end, or their end?"

"Theirs."

"Estimated time of repair?"

Lloyd swallowed. "It's not a technical casualty. We think it might be...."

Harper stopped herself in mid-nod, her attention finally shifting from budgetary politics to the current conversation. "Whatever it is, spit it out."

"Mission Control received a partial transmission at 14:08 local, a few minutes after the incoming Soyuz docked with the station. Based on voice characteristics, we believe the call came from Expedition Commander Winfield."

"And...."

"He began by signaling an emergency. Then he said something like 'We are under....'"

"Under *what*?"

"That's where the transmission chopped off. Telemetry dropped out about five minutes later."

"So, there's no message traffic coming out of the ISS? Not even automated sensor feeds?"

Lloyd didn't respond.

Harper raised her voice a notch. "What is it that you're trying so hard not to tell me?"

"We *are* picking up message traffic from the station."

"Okay," said Harper, "now, you're confusing me. Either the ISS is communicating, or it's not."

"It's communicating," said Lloyd, "but not with us."

"What exactly does that mean?"

Lloyd shrugged. "All radio traffic out of the ISS is now encrypted, and it's not any schema that our techs are familiar with."

"Someone up there is talking to somebody else, and they've cut us out of the conversation?"

"It sure seems that way."

"You're telling me the International Space Station has been hijacked?"

"Figuring out the answer to that question is waaaaaaaaaay the hell and gone above my pay grade," said Lloyd.

"Holy sheep shit..." whispered Harper.

"Yep," said Lloyd. "I think that just about sums up the situation."

**White House
Washington, DC
(22 Minutes Later)**

President James Roth was scrawling corrections on a draft of the Sierra Club speech when Clayton Forrester let himself into the Oval Office.

As White House Chief of Staff, Clayton was one of the few people with full run of the Oval. Even the president's personal secretary, who'd been with him since his days in the Pennsylvania Legislature, would stand at the doorway of her office vestibule and wait to be invited inside.

Clayton, in keeping with the dictates of his position, did not wait for invitations. He wafted in and out like the wind—quietly appearing with status updates, emerging information, or important reminders—then disappearing to transform the president's ideas and orders into plans of action.

A sudden (and unsummoned) visit from Clayton could signal anything from a casual check-in with the boss, to a natural disaster, to an attack on a U.S. embassy.

When he breezed in through the side door, it usually took him four or five seconds to cross the carpet to the famous HMS *Resolute* desk. The path he took to get there had become a reliable clue to the urgency of his errand. If at all possible, Clayton avoided stepping or standing on the presidential seal in the center of the carpet: a custom he'd followed from his very first moments in the West Wing.

When he swung around the ellipse of furniture and took the longer route to the president's desk, the news or reminder that he carried was either low priority or not time-critical. When he took a shortcut across the center of the room, whatever update he brought was guaranteed to be red-hot.

This time, he went straight up the middle of the carpet, walking right across the seal without hesitation. Not a good omen.

He stopped a couple of feet from the desk. "Mr. President?"

The president capped his pen. "I know that look. My first quiet afternoon in weeks, and you're about to screw it up."

"Regretfully so, sir."

"Don't keep me in suspense...."

"The Sit Room is putting together a briefing," said Clayton, "but the quick and dirty is that Russian operatives may have taken over the International Space Station."

"*Taken over?* Are you saying it's been captured?"

"That's the preliminary assessment from NASA and the NSA. Could be a while before we get confirmation."

"Somebody's misreading the tea leaves," said the president. "Polichev is unpredictable, but he's not crazy."

Clayton said nothing.

President Roth tossed his ink pen onto the desk blotter. "Continue."

"A little over a half-hour ago, a Soyuz spacecraft carrying three Russian cosmonauts docked with the ISS. Shortly afterward, NASA Mission Control received a partial distress call from the station commander. His message was chopped off in mid-sentence. Approximately five minutes after that, all transmissions from the ISS ceased. Now the station's back on the air and broadcasting radio traffic again, but they're not talking to NASA. According to a preliminary analysis from the National Security Agency, all communications in and out of the station are being encrypted by Russian military ciphers."

"We're sure this is not a technical glitch?"

"Not yet, Mr. President," said Clayton. "We don't have positive confirmation, but the signs lean toward a hijacking scenario."

"Let's say you're right about that. We're looking at a hostage crisis aboard the ISS?"

Clayton nodded. "Presumably, sir. If the Dutch astronaut is siding with our personnel, it's three of them against five Russians. If the Dutch guy is in with the Russians, our people are outnumbered six to two. Unless...."

"Unless *what*?"

"Our astronauts could already be dead."

The president spent half a minute digesting the idea before he spoke again. "What are the Russians saying?"

"Not a thing, Mr. President. NASA Mission Control has hotlines and priority radio circuits from Houston to Mission Control Center Moscow, but the Russians are refusing to answer. First time that's ever happened."

"Diplomatic channels?"

"That part's even stranger, sir. State just got a call from the Russian Embassy. Their ambassador is requesting a face-to-face meeting with you."

"You mean with Sec State."

"No, Mr. President. Ambassador Ulanova wants to talk to *you*."

That tidbit of news was nearly as surprising as all the other craziness that had suddenly dropped out of the sky.

Apart from the initial ceremony in which he accepted their diplomatic credentials, the president seldom met directly with ambassadors. Matters of foreign affairs, including meetings with diplomats, fell to the Secretary of State.

When one of the rare direct meetings did occur, it was scheduled at the request and the convenience of the president. His privilege and his prerogative. For an ambassador to ask for such a meeting was a major diplomatic faux pas.

President Roth nodded slowly. "If they really *have* captured the ISS, I guess the niceties of protocol go out the window as well."

"Apparently so, sir."

"You think I should take the meeting?"

"Frankly, Mr. President, it may be the quickest way to find out what the hell they're up to."

"All right. Tell State to make the arrangements."

The chief of staff turned to go. "Yes, sir."

When the man was halfway to the door, the president spoke again. "Clayton?"

"Sir?"

"When you decide to screw up my afternoon, you don't settle for half measures."

Russian Embassy
Washington, DC

Holding the secure cell phone tight against her left ear, Ambassador Natalia Ulanova stepped past the saluting sergeant and tucked herself into the rear seat of the black Cortege limousine. The car was a thing of beauty. New, powerful, stylish, and superbly engineered and appointed.

She had ridden in the limo only six or seven times since its delivery, taking private delight in every kilometer along the way. It was the kind of vehicle traditionally reserved for princes and heads of state. But her usual sense of wonder for the luxurious machine was suddenly missing.

The rich smell of leather, the whisper-quiet engine, and the meticulous coachwork were entirely lost on her—dispelled by the sharp Russian voice on the other end of the scrambled cellular call.

"You have the documents?"

She touched the sealed leather document attaché on the seat next to her, tactile reassurance of what she already knew. "Yes, of course. I'm not a complete *durachit'*."

"No one is calling you a fool," said the voice. "But this meeting is of utmost importance. Everything must go according to plan."

Natalia signaled for the driver to proceed. "You have told me that many times already."

"You must be brutally clear with the Americans," said the voice. "This is not a diplomatic discussion. It's an ultimatum."

The driver pulled through the opening steel gates and turned right onto Wisconsin Avenue.

"I understand my orders," said Natalia.

But that was only half true. She understood what she was being ordered to do, and she knew how to carry out her instructions. What she didn't understand was *why*.

And—for the first time in the memory of her ever-inquisitive mind—she didn't want to know.

FOUR

Cape Canaveral, Florida

He finished his homework first.

Those were the rules, and eleven-year-old Terry Watts followed them. Well, he followed *that* one anyway. He wasn't quite as good with some of the others, like keeping his room neat or staying away from certain websites.

But school was something Terry took seriously. His mom was all the proof he needed that education was important.

She was sleeping now. Catching a few hours between her day job at Subway and her night job slinging drinks at Rocky Rockets. She spent half of her life smelling like salad oil and cold cuts, the other half smelling like beer and tobacco smoke, and *all* of it exhausted—just to pay rent and keep food in the fridge.

Not that she complained. Mom would tell you straight out that she had created most of her own problems. Blowing off high school. Hooking up with the fast-talking assclown who'd gotten her pregnant. And by the time she realized how much the world pisses on people without educations, she'd been alone with Terry to care for.

One of these days, Terry was going to fix all that. He had it all figured out. Keep his grades up, finish high school at the top of his class, and sign up for every academic scholarship he could find. Then college and a good job. He hadn't decided what kind of job yet, but something that brought in real money.

He'd buy Mom a condo or maybe even a house. Take care of her. Let her rest a bit, without struggling to pay the electric bill—and no fending off drunk guys who thought their lousy tips entitled them to cop a feel.

She didn't think Terry knew about that part. He could see it in her eyes, though. And sometimes she came home with bruises on her arms, where somebody had grabbed her a little too hard.

One time, she'd come home with her right hand in a bag of ice, two knuckles swollen after she had rabbit punched some bozo who didn't understand that *no* means *no.*

That was why homework came first. *Always.* Before hanging out with friends. Before TV or internet. Before playing games.

But homework was finished now. Carefully rechecked and packed up, all ready for tomorrow morning. He'd totally put a shine on the English essay. Mr. Papadakos could be generous with extra credit if he saw you were working at it.

Now, with the important stuff out of the way, it was time to kill some aliens.

He plugged the PlayStation 2 cable into the television's Aux port and made sure he had his earphones jacked in. Mom had found the gaming console at a yard sale for about three bucks. It was older than Terry, and the graphics weren't all that, but it worked okay.

The disc was left in the drive from his last gaming session. A bootleg copy of *Singularity War,* ported from a Steam knockoff to the old PS2 format by somebody on one of the torrent sites. Probably illegal three different ways, not that he cared about crap like that.

He checked the earphone jack again (no sense waking Mom up), put the buds in his ears, and sat down on the carpet in front of the TV. Seeing that everything was set up properly, he hit the power button on the old television.

There was a quick flash of a news report, something about the International Space Station, before he flipped the channel selector to Aux. The Sony Computer Entertainment intro did its usual boot-with-disc animation, ending with the PlayStation 2 logo in white against a black background.

Then the display froze and a pair of gnarly looking cartoon rats scampered across the screen to begin gnawing bite-shaped chunks out of the PS2 logo.

Each rat had the number '3.1415926' painted or tattooed on its back. Kind of a stupid joke, but the *pi-rats* had been smart enough to crack Steam's DRM *and* port a new(ish) game to a console built when people still lived in caves, so they couldn't be too dumb.

The *pi-rats* intro was replaced by the opening credits of *Singularity War*: that badass cutscene where the Krevax mother ship fires a singularity beam into the core of the earth and the planet implodes into a swirling black hole.

The mother ship was the game's final boss. Terry hadn't gotten anywhere close to it yet. He was still dinking around in the city defense scenarios, trying to work his way up to the off-planet campaigns.

There were pay-to-win options in the uncracked version of the game, where you could use real money to upgrade your weapons and shielding to level-up faster. But that stuff didn't work on the PS2, and he couldn't have paid for it anyway. Besides, you could get most of those things by grinding through, if you didn't mind putting in the extra time.

When the menu screen opened, Terry toggled down to his most recent saved game and tapped the 'Load' icon. He was rewarded with the game's call to action—a male movie star voice shouting, "All pilots to your planes!"

All right! Time to kick some alien butt!

Ten seconds later, he was flying over the skyline of Tokyo, his manta-shaped starfighter launching plasma missiles at the Krevax marauder ship that was firing destructive energy rays into the streets below.

"Yeah..." he whispered as he pounded out another round of shots. "Eat *that*, slug boys!"

Nauka Module
International Space Station

At the center of the module, in a motorized cradle at the junction of crossed aluminum I-beams, rode a device that the late Doktor Yevgeny Koltsov would have recognized. In appearance, it resembled a greatly scaled-up version of the late scientist's EmDrive prototype, but this alternative incarnation of the dead man's dreams would never reach for the stars.

Cosmetic similarities aside, the design had been modified far beyond even Koltsov's extensive tinkering. The conical second stage was significantly elongated and much more heavily built than the original model; the first stage was almost entirely hidden behind curved plates of meshed copper Faraday shielding, and the lab-grade Metrix power supply had been replaced by five cascaded arrays of brick-sized supercapacitors. With no need to establish the integrity of test conditions, the enclosing vacuum chamber had been eliminated.

As a result of these (and other) changes, the device had an ominously purposeful look that had not been present in the cobbled-together assembly of its predecessor.

It was in pursuit of that purpose that Volkov and his two men, Lieutenant Boris Levkin and Captain Mikhail Syomin, now labored.

Levkin was assigned to sequence the capacitor banks online, bringing them up to full charge and readying them for operation.

Syomin was tasked with giving the entire device a final once-over, checking cable connections, examining status readouts from the various assemblies, and verifying that all units had been properly installed and configured. This task was technically redundant. He had already scrutinized the results of low-power tests and diagnostic evaluations performed by the two installers. By all indications, everything was functioning according to design specifications.

Still, a good soldier never went into battle without checking his weapons. Syomin considered himself an *exceptionally* good soldier.

Volkov was at the master control screen, waiting for the last tattletale on the left edge of the display to blink from amber to green.

The majority of his screen was given over to a shaded

topographic map enclosing the circle of Earth within the station's line of sight. The map scrolled in locked synchronization with the orbit of the ISS, always showing the geographic territory within the station's visible footprint.

At the current orbital altitude, that footprint was approximately 3,200 kilometers in diameter, making the region within the circular map a shade under 8,100,000 square kilometers—an area roughly 4/5 the size of the United States. Which (not coincidentally) happened to be the particular landmass sliding into view on the display.

Volkov used a small integral joystick to maneuver a targeting reticle around the map. The device at the center of the Nauka Module moved in unison with every shift of the reticle, motorized cradle humming briefly with each change of position.

All three cosmonauts performed their duties with the confidence of familiarity. They had practiced extensively on a detailed mock-up of the device in the underground facility at Mount Yamantau. Except for the absence of noticeable gravity, operating the real thing didn't seem measurably unlike operating the training replica. It felt different to be floating rather than standing or walking, but the arrangement of the mock-up had provided a high-fidelity preview of the actual experience.

It *wasn't* the same, of course. This was not an inert model of the device; it was the real thing, and they were about to unleash its power on the unsuspecting planet below.

With a rising squeal, the capacitor banks ramped up to maximum charge and the final tattletale on the master control screen winked to green.

The Eastern Seaboard of the United States came scrolling into view right on schedule.

Volkov centered the target reticle on the designated coordinates and locked them in. The software took over and the reticle was now slaved to its assigned target, moving on the screen as the ISS footprint shifted in real-time. The device moved in precise coordination, keeping itself pointed toward the location under the crosshairs.

At the top of Volkov's screen, a rectangular icon began pulsing in red, at its center the word "GOTOV" (READY). He looked around the module, catching the eye of first one man, and then the other.

"Levkin?"

"Go!"

"Syomin?"

"Da!"

He extended his trigger finger and touched the flashing icon.

The lights in the module dimmed as the banks of supercapacitors discharged and the weapon fired.

Cape Canaveral, Florida

By any reasonable measure, the pulse was invisible. Only the tiniest fraction of the transmitted energy crossed over into the 390 to 700 nanometer range of the visual spectrum, and the duration was less than a microsecond—well shy of the briefest interval perceptible to the human brain.

If anyone saw the pulse at all, it might have registered as a flare of light at the back of the eyeballs, so flicker-fast as to seem imaginary. In contrast, the effects of the invisible wavefront were not difficult to recognize.

Uncounted kiloteslas of electromagnetic force slashed through the atmosphere like an unseen sword—wiping out microchips, transistors, digital storage devices, and electronic circuits of all kinds. In an instant, Cape Canaveral—and the surrounding areas of Cocoa Beach, Rockledge, Port St. John, Titusville, and Patrick Air Force Base—were stripped of every necessity of modern existence.

Every building, vehicle, and piece of infrastructure within the effective area of the EMP attack suffered an immediate and all-encompassing electrical power blackout.

In strict chronological terms, the passengers and crew of American Airlines Flight 1547 were first to be affected. En route from Baltimore to Miami at 35,000 feet, the Airbus A321 was struck by the pulse about 31 microseconds before anyone at ground level.

(Another interval so brief as to have no meaningful referent in the human mind.)

The aircraft was equipped with state-of-the-art glass cockpit electronics and multiple-redundant systems, not one of which provided the slightest degree of protection against the pulse.

Every display screen, instrument, and indicator lamp in the cockpit went dark. Deprived of its haptic feedback signal, the fly-by-wire control stick was reduced to an ergonomic lump of metal and plastic in the pilot's hand. The wail of the twin CFM56 turbofan engines spun down to silence, along with every ventilation blower, actuator, and electrically powered component on the aircraft.

The instant it was touched by the electromagnetic wavefront, the Airbus ceased to be a flying machine. It became a hurtling assemblage of unresponsive parts that no longer held the ability to challenge gravity.

Captain Stanley Griffith felt the rush of panic that comes with any unexpected life-threatening emergency. Like any good pilot, he swallowed his fear and fell back on his training—reaching for the checklist with one hand while hitting the manual deployment button for the Ram Air Turbine with the other.

The RAT was a propeller-driven generator, designed to pop out of a hatch on the underside of the fuselage like an inverted jack-in-the-box, where several hundred knots of airflow would spin the prop hard enough to supply emergency electrical power to the aircraft's flight control systems.

If the RAT had been functional, a status lamp would have illuminated when the little turbine generator came up to speed. But the electronic components in the emergency power device had also been wiped out.

Griffith knew nothing about the pulse, and he didn't have time to wonder why the RAT wasn't doing its job.

He went on resetting circuit breakers and toggling battery backup switches while he searched for any emergency procedure that might actually help. He'd been in bad situations before, and he knew that keeping his head straight was the only hope of getting through this.

As he worked the checklist, his copilot tried to go out over the radio. "Mayday! Mayday! This is American 1547, flight level three-five-zero over Titusville. Lost engines. Lost electrical power. Flight controls out! Mayday! Mayday!"

But the radio was as dead as the instrument panel. So were the alternate power busses, the emergency battery system, and everything else that depended upon electricity.

The computer-assisted fly-by-wire system had only electronic backups, all of which had been cooked by the pulse. There could be no heroic "Sully" moment, where cool-headed aviators manually steered their stricken aircraft down to a safe landing area.

Griffith and his copilot had no control whatsoever. Their plane could not glide. It could only fall.

Back in the passenger section, the cabin lights were dark; the ventilation system had exhaled its last breath, and the whine of the engines had been replaced by the rising shouts of terrified human beings.

There were no calming announcements from the flight deck when the nose of the plane pitched downward and commenced a roll to starboard.

Clouds streaked past the windows at a dizzying rate as the loss of altitude accelerated and the g-forces began to mount. The handful of passengers not shrieking their lungs out fumbled with the screens of unresponsive cell phones, trying (and failing) to make final calls to loved ones.

Down at ground level, cars, trucks, motorcycles, and busses coasted to stops as computer-controlled engines and ignition systems failed. Electric power lines smoked and shorted out. Distribution transformers arced themselves into slag.

A WFTV Channel 9 News helicopter tumbled out of the sky into the wooded area of the Hidden Oaks housing development, killing everyone aboard and setting fire to the trees.

Amid the growing chaos, American Airlines Flight 1547 came down on a shopping center south of Florida State Road 405, blasting through the roof of a Verizon Wireless store like an impromptu cruise missile, plowing through walls into Marshalls and Target. Exploding fuel, shrapnel, and kinetic overpressure wiping out passengers, shoppers, and any bystanders unfortunate enough to be in the path of destruction.

Seventeen miles to the southeast, Terry Watts regarded the black television screen and cursed under his breath. It wasn't just the TV. The power light on the PS2 console was out and the window fan had stopped turning. In the sudden quiet, he noticed that the low grumble of the refrigerator was also missing.

Must be a blackout.

There were two rumbling booms in the distance that sounded like thunder. Probably one of those summer storms that came out of nowhere. Another lightning strike on a power pole, maybe. If that was the problem, it could be hours before the electricity came back on.

So much for Singularity War.

He got to his feet and went to the window, peeking out between the curtains. The sky was blue, and the few clouds were white and fleecy. Not like storm weather at all.

Then he noticed the ribbon of rising smoke.

Something was burning a few blocks up the street, and all the traffic seemed to be stopped. People were getting out of their cars and looking around—some of them popping hood latches and staring into engine compartments.

That didn't seem right. A lightning strike shouldn't mess up people's cars. Something weird was going on.

Terry didn't know it, but thousands of other people in the surrounding area were having variations of that same thought.

Throughout the circular zone of effect, microprocessors were fried; credit cards were slicked; hard drives were erased. Electronic systems of all kinds had suffered catastrophic failures, taking out cell phones, landlines, radios, video games, traffic lights, gas pumps, smoke alarms, elevators, water pumps, and every electrical device within the invisible footprint of the EMP beam.

Fires were springing up from the aircraft crashes and other accidents, but no firetrucks would be coming. No ambulance or police sirens could be heard. The switchboard and computer station of every 911 dispatcher was fried. Firetrucks, patrol cars, and ambulances were just as dead as the rest of the machines.

Situated squarely within the target zone, Kennedy Space Center was slammed just as hard as the nearby communities. Not a single piece of electronic equipment was spared.

With one fleeting pulse of energy, the heartland of the American space program had been driven into the dark ages.

FIVE

Johnson Space Center
Houston, Texas

Irene Harper looked around as Eleanor Moseley strutted into Mission Control like she owned the place. As (acting) Deputy Administrator of NASA, Moseley was entitled to a certain amount of proprietary conceit. But there was such a thing as carrying it too far.

Harper didn't actively dislike the Deputy Administrator. It was just that Moseley never stopped politicking long enough to do anything useful. Harper had little patience for people who valued upward mobility over accomplishing the mission.

Everyone had their moments, when the importance of a particular advancement opportunity seemed to overshadow the substance of the job itself, but such descents into self-promotion were supposed to be rare exceptions. For Eleanor Moseley, they appeared to be the default mode of operation.

So, Harper wasn't overjoyed to see Ms. All-About-Me barging into Mission Control with three notebook-carrying flunkies in tow. Moseley's presence was more or less guaranteed to interfere with efforts to attack the current problem, and there was a roughly one hundred percent chance that she would contribute nothing toward finding a solution.

Nevertheless, the woman *was* the Deputy Administrator. Or at least the acting one, until (and unless) her political contacts could weasel the Senate into confirming her nomination. Better not to antagonize her if that could be avoided.

Harper started to utter some sort of polite greeting, but Moseley spoke first. "How are we doing with troubleshooting comms with the ISS?"

The '*we*' in the question implied a level of involvement that existed nowhere outside of the Deputy Administrator's mind. Harper let the allusion pass without comment.

"We're not actually troubleshooting. We're—"

Moseley cut her off. "What are you waiting for?"

The shift in pronouns did not escape Harper's attention. If there was progress being made, Moseley counted herself among the '*we*' who were accomplishing the work. At the barest suggestion that forward motion might be lacking, Harper and her team became '*you*' and Moseley instantly detached herself from the group of underperformers.

This was the sort of tactic that gave Irene Harper an occasional urge to reward Ms. All-About-Me with a quick haymaker to the jaw. Instead, Harper mentally counted to three. "We're not troubleshooting because the cause is not a technical malfunction. This is not a failure of hardware or software that can be repaired. We're dealing with a deliberate act by hostile—"

The word was not completely out of her mouth when about a third of the video displays in Mission Control turned blue and began showing the words "SIGNAL LOST" in large block letters.

Harper caught the change out of the corner of her eye and stopped speaking. "What was that? What just happened?"

There was no immediate answer as several flight controllers began checking over their respective consoles.

Harper raised her voice. "Will somebody kindly tell me what just happened?"

One of the controllers responded without looking up from his console. "We lost Kennedy."

"What?"

"Kennedy Space Center," said the flight controller. "They just dropped completely offline."

At that same moment, approximately 60,000 miles away (and continually increasing in range), four Magnetospheric Multiscale Observation satellites were on the outbound leg of their elliptical orbit—headed toward the trailing edge of the *magnetotail*: that portion of the Earth's magnetosphere most distant from the sun. Part of NASA's Solar Terrestrial Probes program, the quartet of MMO sats were designed to observe interactions between the solar winds and the planet's magnetic field.

Octagonal in shape, the main body of each satellite was about 11.5 feet across, with four 197-foot sensor booms in the spin plane, two 41-foot sensor booms in the axial plane, and a pair of 16-foot magnetometer antennas. The spread of these booms, added to the width of the main body, gave each satellite a physical sensor diameter of more than 400 feet, but the effective diameter was much larger.

The satellites flew in a tetrahedral formation that altered in size and alignment as they moved through the various stages of their orbit. (Their respective positions had been meticulously calculated to achieve optimum geometry just as they crossed the outer boundary of the magnetotail.)

Current spacing between the satellites was almost exactly five miles, and the readings from all four units were merged and processed as a single array. This gave the formation an effective sensor area of over 43 square miles, with correspondingly high sensor acuity.

The MMO sats were primarily intended to study the microphysics of three fundamental plasma processes: magnetic reconnection, energetic particle acceleration, and turbulence—all of which are best observed at the boundaries where the solar wind interfaces with the Earth's magnetosphere. As a result, the majority of their work occurred at the magnetopause on the sunward side of the planet, and the magnetotail on the night side.

Not that the satellites were inactive during the other parts of their orbit. They took measurements ceaselessly throughout their transit, even when they were far from the two areas of major activity— transmitting the results back to NASA via an S-band radio link with the Tracking and Data Relay Satellite System.

Except for an occasional minor perturbation, the transmitted results remained almost entirely within predicted statistical limits.

Almost.

Accounting for the speed of light lag, approximately 0.322 seconds after all signals out of Kennedy Space Center ceased, the field strength readings observed by all four satellites went from the statistical norm to some value completely off the measurement scale of the MMO instruments.

The electromagnetic spike reached an intensity far beyond anything anticipated by the architects of the MMO program, and then vanished as quickly as it had appeared.

If the satellites had been capable of curiosity, they might have wondered why the point of origin for the surge did not coincide with any of the expected locations for major EM events. The source of the pulse was not the magnetotail, or the magnetopause, or even the sun. Oddly, the lines of maximum signal intensity all converged on a locus in low Earth orbit, from which no such electromagnetic anomaly had ever before been recorded.

The processors aboard the MMO satellites made no judgment regarding the anomaly. They merely transmitted the data back to NASA and continued without pausing in their outbound orbit.

White House Situation Room
Washington, DC

Chairman of the Joint Chiefs of Staff, U.S. Air Force General David Christopher, suppressed an urge to pace up and down the Sit Room. He hated this part: the early moments of a crisis, when your instincts were screaming for you to take decisive action, but you didn't have a clear enough picture to act intelligently.

Right now, the picture was as clear as mud. *Something* was happening in eastern Florida, but no one could agree on the exact location of the problem, much less the specific nature or cause.

Reports were trickling in of widespread power failures, missing aircraft, and communications outages. The available information (what there was of it) seemed to be coming from locations around the perimeter of the trouble zone. Nothing at all out of the affected area; not cellular or landline calls, satellite relays, radio broadcasts, internet, or even vehicle traffic. Unless some of the reported sightings of smoke were attempts to signal or summon help, all forms of contact had been suddenly and thoroughly chopped off.

To all appearances, a half-dozen cities and towns had dropped out of the grid at the exact same time, along with Kennedy Space Center, Patrick Air Force Base, and God alone knew what else.

How many critical infrastructure failures would it take to trigger a communications blackout of that magnitude? How many separate and redundant types of technology would have to simultaneously stop working? General Christopher didn't know, and—for the moment—neither did anyone else.

His instinct was to start barking orders. Mobilize troops and equipment to the scene of action. But he didn't know where to send them, or what to expect when they arrived on site.

Homeland Security was ramping up an investigation; Florida Highway Patrol was dispatching cars into the affected area, and Orlando PD was diverting a couple of high-altitude surveillance drones for a flyover. Until somebody relayed back at least a little information, there was nothing Christopher could do. And he wasn't all that good at doing nothing. So, he was ready for the diversion when a young Navy lieutenant interrupted the useless circling of his thoughts.

"Sir? Message from the Signals Office. The NASA Director of Flight Operations is holding on a secure line."

General Christopher nodded. "Let's hope it's an update about the ISS." The unconfirmed hijacking of the space station was the *other* crisis on his plate, and nobody had much information about that one either.

In a less intimidating setting, the lieutenant might have shrugged. Instead, he maintained a neutral expression. "The call was routed from Delta 9 at Space Force, to the Space Operations Branch of STRATCOM with top priority, and STRATCOM is passing it to us, also at top priority. That's all I know, sir."

The young officer reached for one of several Secure Terminal Equipment phones in the middle of the conference table and slid a Fortezza Hyper-X encryption card into the slot. Roughly the dimensions of a standard size cell phone memory card, the small wafer of circuitry contained the latest NSA Type 1 cryptographic algorithm. The phone bleeped, and the word 'SECURE' appeared in the rectangular LCD window.

The lieutenant slid the phone across the table to a position within easy reach of the general. "Ready, sir."

Christopher picked up the handset and waited for the rapid warble of audio tones as the phones on both ends synchronized their encryption. "Situation Room, General Christopher speaking."

The voice on the other end of the line was female and oddly modulated by the digital gymnastics of the crypto software. "General, this is Director Harper at Mission Control Houston. As I just explained to someone at U.S. Strategic Command, our MMO satellites have detected a high-intensity electromagnetic energy pulse from the ISS. The field strength was off the scale of our satellite instrumentation."

Christopher hesitated before responding. "Director, I'm not sure why STRATCOM routed your call to me. If there's been some kind of accident aboard your station...."

"It wasn't an accident," said Harper. "The timing of the surge coincided perfectly with the loss of communications out of Canaveral. I think the Russians have deployed an EMP weapon aboard the ISS."

General Christopher frowned. "Would you repeat that, please?"

But he wasn't listening when she said it again. He'd understood her words the first time around. His brain was busy combining the two emergencies into a single crisis with a common cause. The picture was suddenly becoming a lot clearer.

President Roth straightened his necktie and nodded to his chief of staff. "Okay, Clayton. Let's bring her in."

Shortly afterward, the Russian Ambassador was escorted into the Oval Office by the State Department's Deputy Assistant for European and Eurasian Affairs.

The deputy assistant hardly looked old enough to have graduated from college, and the president couldn't remember having seen the man in the West Wing before. Either a newcomer to State, or someone who had (so far) been able to fly under the radar.

The man's youth was clearly no barrier to self-assurance. He made the traditional announcement with absolute aplomb. "Mr. President, I present Natalia Ulanova, ambassador extraordinary and plenipotentiary from the Russian Federation to the United States of America."

The president reached to shake the ambassador's hand, but his usual smile was notably absent. "Good afternoon, Ambassador."

He did not follow up with the polite expressions of welcome that were common coin in meetings of state.

The ambassador returned his handshake with an equally somber expression. "Thank you for seeing me, Mr. President. It's a breach of protocol; I know, but it will greatly simplify matters."

As Ambassador Ulanova spoke, Clayton Forrester ushered the deputy assistant to the door. This meeting would be limited to the president, his chief of staff, and the ambassador—not counting the pair of Secret Service agents who stood with their backs toward the curved north wall.

Under ordinary circumstances, the president might have invited his visitor to take a seat in the clutch of armchairs and sofas at the foot of the presidential seal. But these were not ordinary circumstances, and he wasn't feeling any inclination to make the Russian Ambassador comfortable.

He walked behind the *Resolute* desk and settled into his chair, leaving the ambassador on her feet.

When Clayton returned, he instantly spotted the implications of the arrangement. It was a geometry of power familiar to any child who's ever been called into the principal's office.

Clayton took up a standing position to the right of the desk, within arm's reach of the president.

The imbalance of authority was further emphasized by the historical import of the desk itself. Franklin D. Roosevelt had led the U.S. through the Second World War from behind this desk. Harry Truman had sat there when he'd signed the order to drop atomic bombs on Hiroshima and Nagasaki. John F. Kennedy had given his Cuban Missile Crisis television address seated in the very spot where President Roth was sitting now.

If Ambassador Ulanova was intimidated by her surroundings or the seating arrangement, she did an excellent job of concealing it. She broke the embossed seal on her leather attaché and opened the flap.

Perhaps she didn't notice the subtle changes in posture as both Secret Service agents shifted weight to the balls of their feet— muscles readying automatically for action.

The attaché was not a diplomatic pouch. It wasn't exempt from inspection by x-ray, ion-spectrometer, infrared scans, or millimeter-wave imaging—all of which had been employed discretely but thoroughly when the ambassador had passed through West Wing security. It contained only papers, none of which gave off trace molecules consistent with explosives or toxins.

The Secret Service knew with a high degree of confidence that the attaché held nothing that could be used as a weapon against the president. Even so, no agent is ever comfortable watching an untrusted person reach into a bag, a parcel, or a pocket. Too many dangerous articles could be pulled from such enclosures, and it was always possible that an entity hostile to the U.S. had produced some novel weapon capable of slipping past the current generation of screening measures.

Both agents were on high alert when Ambassador Ulanova reached into her attaché, and neither of them completely relaxed when she drew out nothing more than the expected sheaf of papers.

She held out the document to the president. "A copy is on its way to your State Department, but my instructions are to deliver the original directly to you."

The president reached across the desk to accept the papers, then immediately handed them to Clayton. "You've made your delivery. Now, perhaps you can tell us why you've hijacked the International Space Station."

"We would not characterize it as a hijacking," said Ulanova, "but I won't quibble over semantics. I'm here to issue an ultimatum on behalf of my government."

She took a breath before continuing. When she spoke, something in her voice suggested that she couldn't quite believe the words coming out of her mouth. "By now, you are receiving reports of the power and communications outage in Florida. What you probably *don't* know is that the effects are not temporary. As you'll soon discover, all electronic components in the target zone have been destroyed by a high-intensity electromagnetic pulse. Except for paper records, every scrap of stored data has been thoroughly erased."

President Roth sat up straighter. Whatever he'd been expecting, this was not it. "You're telling me that Russia has conducted a deliberate attack on American citizens?"

"A low-power demonstration," said the ambassador. "Approximately one-quarter of the weapon's full capacity. And also, a warning."

The president stood up so quickly that his chair nearly went over backward. "You threaten us?"

Ulanova shook her head. "Not a threat, Mr. President. A demand. The United States will completely dismantle its nuclear arsenal and agree to a permanent state of nuclear disarmament."

She gestured toward the document that the president had passed so carelessly to Clayton. "It's all there in writing. Russian military inspection teams will be allowed to enter any and every U.S. missile silo, weapons installation, ballistic missile submarine, ammunition dump, and nuclear fuel repository, without warning and without restriction. Our inspectors will personally supervise the demolition of every warhead, taking possession of all fissionable nuclear materials as the weapons are dismantled. Furthermore, we will maintain permanent observation teams in every American nuclear power plant and laboratory, to guard against any future attempts to produce weapons-grade materials."

Clayton couldn't contain a snort. "That's insane! You can't dictate terms to the United States!"

"Actually, we can," said the ambassador. "And we *are*. As we speak, President Polichev is making the announcement to journalists from Reuters, TASS, and Agence France-Presse. The story will reach your media in the next few minutes, and your citizens will learn what I'm telling you now. You have seventy-two hours to go before the American press and publicly accept our demands."

The president's voice was nearly a growl. "Or *what*?"

Ambassador Ulanova checked her watch. "Seventy-two hours from this moment, the ISS will commence a northwest-to-southeast pass over U.S. territory. At one minute after the deadline, we begin wiping out your military command and control, your missile silos, and your technological and industrial base. Our experts estimate that the first pass will take down seventy-five to ninety percent of your national power grid. By the second pass, there won't be an electric light burning anywhere on American soil. You'll be left trying to feed nearly 400 million people without tractors, trucks, cars, aircraft, trains, phones, radios, or running water. Not quite the Stone Age, but certainly an end to civilization in any meaningful sense."

President Roth blurted out the first words that came to mind. "This is an act of war!"

For the first time since her arrival, the Russian Ambassador smiled. It was a rueful expression, signaling regret and trepidation rather than happiness or goodwill.

"No, Mr. President. An act of *peace*. The United States will merely be the first nation to lay down its nuclear weapons. We are inaugurating a future that you yourself have spoken of with great eloquence. A world in which no nation fears nuclear annihilation at the hands of its enemies."

"I see," said the president. "I didn't realize that it was anything so noble. I guess that means you'll be dismantling your own nuclear arsenal as well?"

Ambassador Ulanova did not respond.

Groping for the arms of his chair, the president sat down again.

"So, this freedom from fear doesn't apply to enemies of Russia?"

He leaned back in the seat and let his eyes travel over the presidential sigil molded into the ceiling. "A Pax Russica... Leonid Polichev with supreme military power over every nation of the Earth, and all roads lead to Moscow...."

This brought a one-shoulder shrug from Ulanova. "We can hardly do worse than your Pax Americana, can we? And perhaps the world is ready for a different country in the seat of global power."

On the last word, she pivoted and strode toward the door.

By the rules of protocol, it was a deadly insult to walk out on a national leader without being properly dismissed.

The Secret Service agents watched her as she departed. Their job was to defend the president from physical threats, not to avenge diplomatic slights.

After a few seconds, the door closed behind the Russian Ambassador and she was gone, leaving the president and his chief of staff in the silence of disbelief.

SIX

The *Corvus* was imagination made real. Beauty given physical shape.

From the design phase, through modeling, prototyping, and assembly, Paul Keene had seen the sleek black spaceplane in a hundred different permutations—beginning from the image in his mind and the first rough concept sketches on his digital drawing tablet. But familiarity (and his own role in the creation process) had done nothing to blunt his appreciation for the graceful shape of the vehicle.

There was utilitarian engineering and there was aesthetic perfection. To Paul's eye, the *Corvus* was both: a seamless melding of function and form.

He stood at his office window, looking down onto the assembly floor where the object of his admiration dangled beneath a bridge crane. The five cables of the lifting harness were so slender that it was easy to lose track of them under the bright hangar lights.

The cables (like the *Corvus*) were an invention of Apogee Launch Systems. And (also like the *Corvus*) they seemed far too delicate for their intended purpose.

They were *not* too delicate, of course. Cables and fuselage were spun from an advanced composite that Handsome Dan Conway had dubbed the 'secret sauce.' A product of Apogee's material sciences team, the proprietary substance fused graphene nanotubes with meshed Kevlar threads and a specially formulated laminate to create a strength-to-weight ratio well above industry standards.

The application used in the fuselage was necessarily different from the one created for the cables, but both were derived from the secret sauce. Licensing fees for the ultra-lightweight material were, so far, Apogee's primary source of revenue.

Paul shifted his focus from the *Corvus* to Handsome Dan, down on the hangar floor, supervising the mounting procedure.

Dan circled the *Corvus* and the delta wing ferry jet over which it hung; his spectacularly unhandsome face tight with concentration, his piggy eyes narrowed to slits behind John Lennon glasses.

Satisfied that everything looked good, Dan signaled to the crane operator, and the electric winches began slowly unspooling cable. The *Corvus* inched downward toward its mounting cradle on the back of the much larger aircraft.

Nicknamed the '*Kickstart*' (another title bestowed by Handsome Dan) the ferry jet was powered by four F110-GE-132 afterburning turbofan engines. Between them, they produced sufficient thrust to carry the *Corvus* to 52,000 feet at a hair under Mach 2.5. From that speed and altitude, the aerospike rocket engines aboard the *Corvus* could catapult the spaceplane into low Earth orbit, or so the computer models alleged.

That part of the system was untested. The *Corvus* had not yet been granted a space flight worthiness certification—a legal requirement for all civilian spacecraft.

Thought of the elusive certificate brought Paul's mind reluctantly back to his assigned task for the afternoon. While Handsome Dan was down on the assembly floor doing the fun stuff, Paul was schmoozing with the rep from the FAA's Office of Commercial Space Transportation.

Trouble was, the FAA guy wasn't very schmoozable. He was your basic bean-counting government bureaucrat: self-important, obsessed with regulatory minutia, and ignorant of the laws of aerodynamics. The kind of guy who could quote obscure government directives from memory but couldn't change a spark plug.

Paul turned away from the window and trudged to his desk. Beancounter would be back from the head any time now.

By long habit, Paul avoided looking at the "brag wall" on the far side of his office. It was the sort of self-aggrandizement that he despised. Framed copies of his diplomas and major awards were interspersed with plaques and photographs from his days as a Navy *Tomcat* pilot and his subsequent career with NASA. The centerpiece was the official PR photo for shuttle mission STS-136: Paul, Handsome Dan, and Mission Specialists Yamada and Foley in their pumpkin-colored Advanced Crew Escape Suits; pressure helmets tucked under their arms, with a night shot of the *Endeavour* in the background, gleaming under the floodlights of Launch Pad 39A.

Below that, in a position only a smidge less prominent, hung a framed copy of a magazine cover: the issue of *Aviation Week* with Paul's face on the front, accompanied by a headline comparing him to Burt Rutan.

The whole collection struck Paul as silly and faintly embarrassing. If you were any good, there was no need to advertise. You did your job and didn't blow your own horn.

But this wasn't the Navy, and it wasn't the Astronaut Corps. He was in the private sector, now. Out here in the real world, you damned well *did* need to advertise. Either that or you went broke in dignified obscurity.

As Handsome Dan never tired of reminding him, investors need to think they're backing a winner. Between his decorations as a fighter jock, his reputation as a clever engineer, and the gravitas of being the last shuttle commander, Paul was the best marketing hook that Apogee had to offer.

So, he tolerated the brag wall, paid it no attention most of the time, and tried not to squirm when some visitor paused to study the various exhibits.

As far as he could tell, the wall was more effective as a Paul Keene museum than it was as a marketing tool. The investors had not exactly been lining up outside Apogee's door.

It wasn't having much effect on Beancounter; that was for sure. The FAA man had either failed to notice the shrine to Paul's magnificence, or he was choosing to ignore it.

If it was the latter, that counted as a point in the man's favor, even if the guy was a doctrine-quoting paper-shuffler.

Continuing to avert his eyes from the preposterous ego wall, Paul allowed himself to enjoy a different collection of photos: the small cluster of framed snapshots near the corner of his desk. There was a shot of Sarah at seven or eight, her grin no less exultant for the lack of upper front teeth, hands clutching a fighter jet that she'd built out of LEGOs. Slightly lopsided and a little off in the proportions, the LEGO jet was recognizably an F-14 *Tomcat*.

Sarah was about fourteen in another photo, standing with careful nonchalance by the cockpit door of the old Aeronca Champion trainer plane that Paul had taught her to fly in.

The next picture had been taken on Sarah's sixteenth birthday, a few minutes after her first solo flight, her face glowing with pride and self-assurance.

There were more recent photos of her tucked away in a drawer somewhere. A shot of her graduation from Annapolis. Another one from the day she had received her Naval Aviator Badge—the coveted Navy wings of gold. Her ISS mission photo was in there someplace too: Sarah and the rest of the expedition crew floating in one of the larger modules of the station—each crewmember in a different orientation from the others—visually emphasizing the weightless environment.

A lot of great photos, but somehow Paul never found time to have them framed. For the four-hundredth time, he mentally added that to his list of things to do.

He checked his watch. Where the hell was Beancounter? Had the man gotten lost on his way back from the toilet?

As if in answer, the FAA rep opened the door and strolled into the office. Without pause or greeting, he dropped into the chair opposite Paul's desk and resumed speaking as if there had been no interruption. "Title 14, Chapter III, Subchapter C, Part 437."

Paul's jaw muscles tightened. This again.

Title 14 was the Aeronautics and Space section of the U.S. Code of Federal Regulations. Part 437 dealt with the issuing of permits for experimental spacecraft.

As a general concept, that was fine, but the rules had been written with suborbital vehicles in mind. The language imposed restrictions that simply could not be applied to an orbital flight.

Which did not stop Beancounter from clinging to his precious regs. "The requirement is quite clear," he said. "An unproven space vehicle must constrain its flight path to transit over sparsely populated areas, and all legs of the routing must be approved in advance by the FAA. It's remarkably simple, Mr. Keene. Lay out a flight plan that avoids population centers. After we verify that your plan is compliant, we'll issue a permit."

"No, it's *not* simple," said Paul. "It's not possible to orbit the planet without flying over populated areas."

"We can't issue a permit until you submit a compliant flight plan. You'll have to figure something out."

Paul reminded himself that strangling the idiotic bastard would not result in the issuance of a certificate. "Nobody can figure it out. What you're asking for violates the laws of orbital mechanics."

Beancounter smiled. "I'm asking you to submit a flight plan. Surely you can file a routine piece of paperwork without disrupting the fabric of space-time."

"I know how to file a flight plan," said Paul with a calm that he was most assuredly not feeling. "But I *can't* bounce around like Ricochet Rabbit to avoid populated areas. No spacecraft could carry enough fuel for that kind of maneuvering."

"If you have a problem with fuel efficiency—"

Paul cut him off. "You're trying to apply suborbital flight restrictions to an orbital spacecraft. That's just flat out ridiculous. Like forbidding a submarine to go under water because maritime law was written for surface ships."

Beancounter's response was forestalled by the clanging of an alarm bell. It was the "all stop" alert, signaling an immediate halt to operations in the hangar area.

Paul reached the window in two long strides, automatically examining the assembly area for signs of an emergency. All work on the hangar floor had stopped, and every eye was pointed back in his direction.

The door flew open and Handsome Dan came bursting in, still moving fast from his dash up the stairs. "See if you can get CNN on your phone!"

The demand took Paul by surprise. "What?"

Dan brushed past Beancounter like the man wasn't there. "Your phone! We just got word. Some kind of attack at Kennedy Space Center. And the Russians have hijacked the ISS."

SEVEN

International Space Station
(Expiration of Deadline: 71 Hours / 23 Minutes)

Sarah Keene waited in the Quest Airlock to receive the remains of Larry Winfield.

The body bag drifted in through the open hatchway, clearing the coamings neatly. Rutger's aim had been careful, a measure of both the Dutch astronaut's respect for a fallen colleague and his ingrained tendency toward precision.

Sarah reached out and accepted the sad burden, allowing her elbows to bend as her hands grasped the incoming mass, absorbing inertia to slow the cocooned form to a stop.

There wasn't much room in the airlock, and the presence of the body created a sensation of crowding that only intensified when Rutger hauled himself inside. Dmitri remained in the adjoining Unity Node, a respectful distance away, but close enough to keep watch on the proceedings, and to intervene or call for backup if the astronaut prisoners tried anything funny.

The body bag was a frosted white color that was not completely opaque, making parts of Larry's body disturbingly visible, along with large dark swaths where the inner surface of the plastic was coated with the dead man's blood. The sight made Sarah a little queasy, but she overrode her instinct to look away. She owed it to her friend to accept the reality of his murder.

So, she hardened herself to this bit of unpleasantness. It was a first step toward preparing herself for worse things that were yet to come.

Trying to keep her lips motionless, she spoke in a low voice, pitching her volume below the quiet hum of the airlock's ventilation fan. "If you can hear me, don't say anything; just nod."

Rutger gave a nod so understated that it bordered on the imaginary.

"Can you recite the Lord's Prayer and listen at the same time?"

A flicker of hesitation, followed by another minimal nod from Rutger, this one less confident.

Sarah peeked past his shoulder toward Dmitri, who watched them from the adjoining module. "Good," she said quietly. "Make it loud enough for our friend to hear you."

Rutger drew breath and began intoning the famous litany from the Gospel of Matthew. "*Our Father who art in heaven, hallowed be thy name....*"

Sarah took a breath of her own. "We have to destroy the station."

She saw her words register in the Dutch man's expression, and— for a terrible instant—she worried that he was going to drop the thread of the prayer. But Rutger kept going, despite the shock he must have been feeling.

"No choice," Sarah said. "We've got to stop them, and they'll never let us get near the weapon."

"*Give us this day our daily bread....*"

"I don't have a plan yet. I just need to know if you're with me."

"*...lead us not into temptation but deliver us from evil....*"

Rutger digested her message and repeated his nearly subliminal nod one final time.

With the pact sealed, Sarah joined in softly for the last verse of the prayer. "*For thine is the kingdom, and the power, and the glory, forever and ever. Amen.*"

When news of Larry's death eventually got out, his family, NASA, and the Air Force would all no doubt want to commemorate his passing. Until then, this pitiful recitation in a crowded airlock was the nearest thing to a funeral that his friends could manage.

Sarah felt no guilt over using the impromptu ceremony as a cover for plotting against the Russians. Larry had died trying to resist the bastards. He'd have been proud to know that, even in death, he was contributing to the fight.

Now that it was over and the decision to destroy the ISS had been ratified by her only co-conspirator, Sarah felt the first tears gathering in her eyes. She touched Rutger's cheek and then squeezed past him to exit the airlock.

There, just on the other side of the hatchway was Dmitri. He had abandoned his respectful distance and coasted silently to within arm's reach of the airlock opening.

Emerging from the hatchway behind Sarah, Rutger made the same unwelcome discovery.

Thankfully, he avoided eye contact with Sarah as she sealed the inner door of the airlock and prepared to eject Larry's remains into the vacuum of eternal night.

Sarah kept her movements calm and measured. How long had Dmitri been lurking there? How much had he overheard?

The cosmonaut watched impassively, offering no clues to his thoughts or intentions. If he'd caught even a hint of what they were up to, Rutger and Sarah were as good as dead.

They'd both be dead before long anyway, of course. The important thing was to stay alive until they could take out the station and end the threat.

Either way, they'd be joining Larry soon enough.

EIGHT

Johnson Space Center
Houston, Texas
(Expiration of Deadline: 69 Hours / 38 Minutes)

Irene Harper held apart two slats of the vertical blinds and peered through the crack at the darkening Texas sky. The lights were coming on down in the parking lot. Pole-mounted sodium-vapor lamps stuttering to life as their photoelectric sensors recognized the arrival of nightfall.

At the table behind her, Lloyd was futzing around with the video teleconference equipment, trying to get re-synced with the VTC system in the White House Situation Room.

Everything had worked fine for the first ten minutes of the telecon, long enough to get the introductions and virtual handshaking out of the way. Then the "bridge" had stopped responding and the connection had failed.

Lloyd knew how to cope with fussy equipment. He'd have things up and running in a minute or two.

In the meantime, the break was not unwelcome. Harper took quiet reassurance from watching each light in the parking lot select its singular moment to illuminate.

The differences in timing would be traceable to a series of

variables. Some photoelectric sensors had accumulated more dust than others. A few sensor apertures were likely covered in bird guano. Certain poles were shielded from the rays of the dying sun by the shadows of buildings. Doubtless, there were inconsistencies in calibration, manufacturing quality, and other disparities.

The technical causes could undoubtedly be identified, if anyone ever cared to investigate. But—to Harper—the unpredictable sequence carried the illusion of deliberate choice, as though each light pole decided for itself when to join in the battle against the gathering darkness.

"Okay, Director," said Lloyd. "I think we're up."

Harper withdrew her fingers and allowed the blind to swing back into place, covering her sliver of visibility into the outside world.

She resumed her seat at the head of the conference table, pausing while the rest of her team shuffled note pads and adjusted chairs. On the wall-mounted flat-screen display at the far end of the table, General Christopher and his staff were making similar adjustments. Red color bars at the top and bottom of the screen displayed the word 'SECURE' in large capital letters.

"We've got our obligatory glitch out of the way," said the general. "I guess we can get down to business."

Harper nodded. "Ready on our end."

"First, a few questions, to clarify the situation. Have you had any luck reestablishing comms with the ISS astronauts?"

"Negative. We've tried every voice, video, and telemetry channel, including emergency freqs. Everything's locked down tight."

"Then we have no idea if our people are alive up there?"

"Unfortunately not."

"And you have no way to take remote control of the ISS maneuvering system? You can't deorbit the station, or bring it down to an altitude where we can reach it more easily?"

"No. Translational burns are controlled from MCC Moscow, or locally from the ISS. That has nothing to do with the Russian takeover. It's by design. Mission Control Houston has never had access."

General Christopher nodded. "Are there any options for disabling the EMP weapon without damaging the station?"

Harper shook her head. "Not that we can think of, General. We've been working the problem nonstop. If there's a way to isolate and disrupt the EMP device, we haven't found it."

The general hesitated. When he spoke, his enunciation was meticulous. He wanted no room for misinterpretation. "Can you offer *any* alternative to a direct attack against the International Space Station?"

Now came Harper's turn to hesitate.

She had years of mental preparation for a crisis in space, but she'd always assumed the cause would be a technical failure. Her generation's version of Apollo 13, or the tragic loss of the shuttle *Columbia*.

The solution to this crisis would not be a brilliant rescue scheme, nor a heartrending vigil by Flight Controllers who were powerless to halt the death spiral of a doomed spacecraft.

Like the *Columbia*, the current crisis was destined to end in tragedy. Not because of a faulty component or accidental damage. This time, the destruction would be intentional. However indirect her role might turn out to be—if she helped the military engineer an attack against the ISS—Irene Harper would have a hand in bringing about the kind of tragedy she had always hoped to avert. That was not an easy thing to wrap her mind around.

Still, it was her job to make difficult decisions. To override her personal desires when it was time to do unpleasant things. And this was a case where a lesser tragedy might be the only way to prevent a catastrophe of global proportions.

She shook her head. "No, General. I can't see any alternatives."

Before she could elaborate, a man in the Sit Room group spoke up. "What about jamming their communications?"

The man (Harper had already forgotten his name) was dressed in a civilian suit and sported a decidedly non-military haircut. Either a member of the National Security Council or one of the president's advisors.

Harper bit back a cutting remark. Did this yahoo think her people would overlook something so obvious?

"If we block all Earth-side signals to the station," said the man, "the Russian government can't issue attack commands. The weapon will be useless until we can find a way to deal with it directly."

Miranda Navarro, one of Harper's Flight Controllers, responded in a more patient tone than Harper would have managed.

As a CATO (Communication and Tracking Officer), Miranda was an expert on ISS comms. "Can't be done," she said, "If the Russians have got two brain cells to rub together, they've leased satellite channels from commercial providers all over the globe. We'd have to jam every frequency on every satellite transceiver in the world."

"Agreed," said General Christopher. "Even if it were technically feasible, jamming would be a no-go. The Russians are sticklers for military doctrine. Those ISS cosmonauts have got a contingency plan for loss of contact; you can bet your last nickel on that. And it includes a prioritized target list if we chop off their comms with Moscow."

The civilian advisor didn't quite manage to conceal his displeasure. He was evidently not accustomed to having his suggestions rejected so quickly and thoroughly.

"I'm not closing the door on non-military solutions," said the general. "If someone comes up with a viable plan for neutralizing the threat without destroying the station, I'll personally take their idea to the president."

Harper nodded, along with most of the people around both conference tables.

General Christopher paused for further suggestions, but none were offered up. "All right," he said, "let's move on to options for attacking the space station. To save time, I've asked Colonel Maxwell to brief us on the possibilities that we've already eliminated."

At the Sit Room table, a rail-thin man in Space Force dress blues leaned forward in his chair. "We can rule out using Ballistic Missile Defense assets. The flight ceiling for our ground-based interceptor missiles is just under 95 miles, and the ISS is orbiting at more than twice that altitude. The RIM-161 Standard Missile 3 carried by the Navy's Aegis cruisers and destroyers has a higher flight ceiling, but still not adequate for this target."

The colonel consulted a folder on the table in front of him. "The Air Force used to have an air-launched anti-satellite missile that might have worked, the ASM-135. Unfortunately, the program was canceled due to technical problems and budget overruns. We've verified that all ASM-135 prototypes were destroyed, and there's obviously no time to restart production. The Delta 9 branch at Space Force is working on a next-generation anti-sat weapon, but we're at least a year away from a functioning prototype."

Colonel Maxwell flipped to the next page in his folder. "We've communicated with STRATCOM about the possibility of launching an Intercontinental Ballistic Missile at the station. There are several variants of ICBMs that can attain the necessary altitude, but the flight trajectories are not compatible with an orbital intercept. STRATCOM estimates nine or ten months to re-engineer the guidance modules, arming logic, and related systems. In summary... ICBMs are not an option."

The civilian advisor held up a finger. "Why is reengineering necessary? If we've got ICBMs that can reach the proper altitude, we get one close to the station and detonate the warhead. Sounds pretty straightforward to me."

There was a pause as Colonel Maxwell considered how to phrase his response. "The ISS is moving at five miles per second," he said finally. "Roughly, ten times as fast as a rifle bullet. An ICBM has a peak velocity about eighty percent that fast and it's on an entirely different flight trajectory—ballistic suborbital versus orbital."

"Nobody has ever conducted a successful intercept at even half that speed. By comparison, shooting a bullet out of the air with another bullet would be a walk in the park."

"It's too risky anyway," said General Christopher. "Russia's early warning networks were specifically built to spot ICBM launches. Their infrared satellites can detect and track any rocket booster powerful enough to reach orbit. The ISS will fry any inbound missile in mid-flight. And on their next flyover, they'll start targeting our cities and military bases."

"What we need," said Miranda, "is a weapon the Russians won't see coming. Something unexpected."

The general nodded. "Exactly."

Someone brought up high-altitude balloons, which led to a conversational tangent about speed differentials, and the distance between so-called "near space" and the orbital plane of the ISS.

Harper was only half listening. Miranda's words had given her the beginnings of an idea.

A weapon the Russians wouldn't see coming....

Something unexpected....

A space launch that didn't *look* like a space launch....

When she put it that way, the answer became obvious. "Wildcats."

General Christopher lifted a hand to silence the balloon discussion. "What was that, Director?"

The pieces were still coming together in Harper's head. "They'll be monitoring all our usual launch sites," she said. "Vandenberg. Wallops. Greely. We have to come at them from somewhere else. Do something they won't recognize as a threat."

The general motioned for her to continue. "Keep going."

"We should be looking at the wildcats," Harper said. "Aerospace startups. Sierra Nevada Corporation. Apogee Launch Systems. Blue Origin. Companies with non-traditional methods of getting payloads into orbit. Find out if one of them has a launch-ready vehicle."

"Sounds like it's worth checking," said General Christopher. "How soon can you get started?"

Harper looked across the table at Lloyd. "We're already on it."

NINE

Apogee Launch Systems
Mojave, California
(Expiration of Deadline: 54 Hours / 30 Minutes)

The convoy came out of the east: a line of eight SUVs silhouetted against the pre-noon sun, dark blue paint jobs gone chalky with the powder-fine Mojave sand.

From his seat in the air-conditioned guard shack, Randy Fleming toyed with his iPhone and waited for the procession of vehicles to roll past. He'd been warned more than once about bringing his phone on the job. According to the rules laminated to the back of the visitor clipboard, the proud security specialists of Sentinel-Pro were supposed to remain constantly alert and monitor the area for suspicious activity.

Proud security specialists. What a joke.

There was never any suspicious activity here, and damned little of the non-suspicious kind. Except for the two main bosses (who tended to come in early and work late), the Apogee people showed up in the morning and left at the end of the day. Sometimes, there was a delivery truck or one of the employees made a run for pizza. The sheet on the clipboard showed nine visitors in the last year. That was the extent of the action around this place.

It wasn't easy to stay alert when nothing ever happened. By messing with his phone, Randy was keeping his brain sharp, like a good "security specialist" was supposed to do. And what did Sentinel-Pro expect for eleven bucks an hour?

He was upvoting a YouTube video of a pit bull on a trampoline when he realized that the convoy hadn't rolled past after all. The SUVs had turned off of State Route 58, and they were barreling up the asphalt connector road toward the gate.

Toward *him*.

There was just time to straighten up and cram the phone into his pocket before the first SUV pulled up in front of the gate. The vehicle's doors flew open and five soldiers in camouflage uniforms popped out, moving with a speed and precision that Randy found both impressive and scary as fuck.

Two of them seemed to be women, but he wasn't interested in finding out at the moment. He was more concerned about the no-nonsense looks on their faces and the short-stocked automatic rifles that each of the soldiers carried.

Sentinel-Pro had equipped Randy with a nightstick, a whistle, and a canister of pepper spray that was supposed to be full but felt empty when you shook it.

None of those things would stop these soldiers from taking control of the guard shack, the gate, or the whole damned Apogee facility.

From his pocket came the muffled audio of the YouTube clip, the pit bull's frenzied barks intermixed with the laughs and shouts of some onlookers. He thought about pulling out the phone to mute the volume but reaching into a pocket might not be the smartest move he could make right now.

Able to think of no better alternatives, he selected his only remaining weapon and stepped out of the guard shack.

He held up the clipboard toward the nearest soldier. "Welcome to Apogee Launch Systems. Can I get you all to sign in, please?"

Paul Keene sat through another repetition of NASA's hold music and fought an impulse to hurl his phone across the office. At some point in the past eighteen or so hours, the supermarket-grade synthetic jazz had crossed the threshold from faintly annoying to pain-inducing.

As the headache behind his eyes grew, he thought about making a list of everyone who put him on hold, subjecting him to another loop of that obnoxious pseudo-music. Later, when all of this was over, he could track them down and spray paint their windshields, or put rabid skunks in their mailboxes, or demonstrate his appreciation in some still more creative fashion.

Lack of sleep was making him cranky, and his desk chair—chosen for its comfortable padding and excellent lumbar support—was starting to do unpleasant things to his lower spine. He'd spent the night in the chair, calling his remaining contacts in the space program; and then the contacts of his contacts; and then *their* contacts, always with the same general lack of results.

The amazing thing was that people had continued taking his calls, regardless of the hour. NASA hadn't gotten much sleep last night either.

Now, he was six or seven removes from anyone he actually knew, and still he couldn't get a simple answer to a simple question.

For Christ's sake, he wasn't asking for fucking nuclear launch codes. Just to find out if Sarah was okay. That wasn't unreasonable, was it?

There was some consolation in knowing that CNN, Fox, MSNBC, and the others weren't having much better luck. One of the Apogee techs had set up a monitor on a side table, so Paul could keep an eye on the news while he played the marathon dialing game.

Even with the sound turned down, it was clear that none of the networks had any real updates to offer. They were tap-dancing their asses off to disguise that fact. Cutting between the capture of the ISS, the aftermath of the Florida EMP attack, and interviews with politicians, pundits, and "experts," none of whom could offer anything better than bald speculation. And each media outlet had its own version of the "doomsday clock," an ingeniously animated countdown of the hours, minutes, and seconds until the Russian ultimatum expired.

Since early morning, the coverage had expanded to include protest rallies of both the *peace-at-all-costs* and the *never-surrender* varieties, intercut with aerial footage of heavy freeway traffic as less courageous city dwellers began to desert the population centers.

If you stripped away the flashy graphics and unsupported opinions, the situation could be boiled down to three basic elements: #1 The Russians had a weapon aboard the space station. #2 The United States had been ordered to surrender its nuclear arsenal or be zapped into pre-industrial oblivion. #3 The American people were scared, angry, confused, or some combination thereof.

Not one of those particulars had changed in a meaningful way since the story had first broken, but the news networks were incapable of acknowledging that. They were locked into repeating the same essential details, just as Paul was locked into repeating the same basic phone conversation, and the NASA call management software was locked into repeating the same goddamned song.

Between the pounding in his head and the chirpy tones of the canned jazz, he didn't immediately notice the murmur of voices filtering up from the hangar floor. By the time the sounds penetrated his consciousness, they were getting louder. He realized they'd probably been going on for a while.

Some of the techs getting rambunctious, maybe? They tended to roughhouse when things were too quiet.

Paul was staring at the photo of fourteen-year-old Sarah when the door opened, and Handsome Dan came into the office.

"I just want to know if she's alive," Paul said. "Why's it so hard to get a straight answer?"

"You can hang up the phone," said an unfamiliar voice.

Paul looked around toward the door.

A man in tiger stripe cammies stood next to Dan. Paul didn't need to see the black star embroidered on each lapel to recognize a flag officer. The stranger was broadcasting the signal on all frequencies.

Here was a person accustomed to the power and responsibilities of high rank, with the easy confidence of one whose metal has been tempered by fire.

"It'll be on the news in about ten minutes," said the officer.

With the door open, the sounds from the hangar were louder. Not roughhousing. Heavy footfalls and raised voices that lacked the tone of friendly horseplay.

The phone still held against his left ear, Paul got to his feet. "What's going on?"

The officer crossed to the desk and extended a hand to be shaken. "General Hiram Byrd, United States Space Force."

Paul returned the handshake automatically while the pallid hold music continued to ooze into his ear.

The general disengaged from the handshake first. "That commotion you hear is my detachment taking control of your facility."

"What?"

"By executive order and in the interest of national security, I am commandeering Apogee Launch Systems and all assets herein for the duration of this crisis."

Paul turned to Handsome Dan, who shrugged. "They rolled in like a SWAT team. No shots fired, but these guys are *not* playing."

General Byrd laid his hand on the back of a guest chair. "Mind if I sit?"

When no one responded, he sat down anyway. "This just became my office, so I don't need permission. Just trying to keep things polite."

Dan plopped onto the sofa with a grunt. "You've got the guns. You don't have to make nice."

"True," said the general. "But I'd rather have your willing cooperation if I can get it."

"What do you know about my daughter?" Paul asked.

"I've just given NASA approval to release the video," said Byrd. "You really *can* hang up the phone."

Paul ended the call and dropped his phone on the desk. "What video? What are you talking about?"

"We got it from the Russians about a half-hour ago. Short clip. Maybe ninety seconds. Lieutenant Commander Keene and the Dutch astronaut, Braam. Obviously under duress, but they don't seem to be injured."

Relief washed over Paul in a wave so powerful that he groped for his chair and collapsed into it. "You're sure it was Sarah? She's okay?"

"As far as we can tell, she and Braam haven't been harmed, but the expedition commander is dead. He resisted when the Russians captured the station."

Paul was surprised by the tremor in his own voice. "When can I see the video?"

"It'll be on television in the next few minutes."

"I'm surprised the pentagon's not sitting on it," said Dan.

General Byrd smiled. "If we don't release the video, Polichev will. It's tailor-made propaganda. Gets their message across in a way that's hard to misunderstand. Go along with their demands and we live. Try to stop them and we die."

"Gotcha," said Handsome Dan. "Moscow is the bogeyman, and their marketing department is shit hot. That doesn't explain why you just overran us with the camo-commandos."

Byrd retrieved a slip of paper from the breast pocket of his cammies. "Commander Paul Xavier Keene, USN Retired. Seventh in your class at Annapolis. Shot down a Libyan MiG over the Gulf of Sidra. Two more confirmed kills during Operation Desert Storm and you flew strike missions over Afghanistan in Operation Anaconda. Three DFCs and a string of lesser medals and citations. You were an instructor at Fighter Weapons School when your transfer to the Astronaut Corps was approved."

The general flipped the paper over. "And then we have Lieutenant Commander Daniel Elwood Conway. Third in your class at the Academy. Top marks in Flight School 'til you got a medical down-check for bilateral astigmatism. Cross-trained as an F-14 Radar Intercept Officer. Flew back-seater in *Tomcats* during—"

"Yeah, yeah, yeah," said Handsome Dan. "Mother Conway's favorite son and butter don't melt in my mouth. What's your point?"

General Byrd looked up from his notes. "We're mounting an operation against the space station. NASA thinks your *Corvus* can get there."

The words seemed to flip a switch behind Paul's sternum. It felt like his heart had resumed beating.

"A rescue? You bet your ass we can get there!"

"We're in!" said Dan. "What's the plan?"

There was a long moment before the general responded. "I believe I've expressed myself poorly. It's not a rescue. We're going to take out the ISS."

"What do you mean 'take it out'?" snapped Paul. "You're going to destroy it?"

"Yes," said the general. "And you're going to help us."

"My daughter is up there!" said Paul.

General Byrd nodded. "Lieutenant Commander Keene is a Navy combat pilot, just like her old man. Sworn to uphold and defend. To give her life in the line of duty."

Paul's headache—nearly forgotten for a few brief seconds of hope—found an entirely new level of intensity. "Not the same," he said. "It's not like risking herself against ground fire or going up against enemy pilots. You're asking me to kill my own daughter."

"It's time for you to stop thinking like a father. I need you to be a fighter pilot, now. Your *country* needs it."

This brought a grunt from Handsome Dan. "You know the interesting thing about the military? Whenever some chair warrior sends your butt into the meat grinder, it's *always* a matter of national security. You fly enough combat missions, and you start to ask yourself how *every damned one of them* can be critically important to the safety and welfare of the American people."

"SECDEF is standing by for my call," said General Byrd. "You're both Category II retirees. Under sixty, not medically discharged, and eligible for recall to active duty in case of national emergency. If *this* doesn't qualify as an emergency, then there ain't no such thing."

Handsome Dan said something in reply but his voice (and that of the general) were fading to unintelligible drones. Merging with a sound from Paul's past: the stuttering rumble of the Aeronca Champion's propeller.

Eyes closed against creeping exhaustion and the relentless throb in his temples, Paul gave himself up to memory, letting his mind and heart carry him back into the cockpit of the old trainer plane.

Inverted and coming out of a five-eighths loop, Sarah reaches the forty-five-degree line and rolls smoothly back into level flight.

From the instructor's seat in the rear, Paul can only see the back of her head, but he knows what her expression will be in this moment. A tiny crease between her eyebrows the only sign of concentration on her fourteen-year-old face.

The kid's getting pretty damned good at this. She's got the Half Cuban-Eight down pat.

Even so, Paul can't stop himself from speaking into the voice-activated intercom. "Pretty good, Sprite. More rudder, less stick. But not bad at all."

He doesn't have to see Sarah's face to know that she's rolling her eyes at the familiar (and unwanted) advice.

She does an admirable job of keeping the exasperation out of her voice. "I've got this, Dad."

Which is true, of course. She's as solid as most pilots twice her age, and she rarely needs his guidance.

But somehow, Paul can't stop trying to teach her things that she already knows.

He does it again without thinking. "Check your trim, Sprite."

"My trim is fine," she says. "Trust me, Dad. I've got this."

She pulls back on the stick and gooses the throttle, starting her climb for another Half Cuban-Eight.

"...a word of it," said a different voice.

Older, male, and authoritarian.

Definitely not Sarah.

Paul opened his eyes and found himself back at his desk, the headache coming on like a tidal wave. "Sorry, what was that?"

"I was throwing down my best shtick," said General Byrd. "Patriotism. Duty. Responsibility to all mankind. Good shit. And you didn't hear a word of it."

"No," Paul admitted. "I didn't."

"Well, I was goddamned persuasive," said the general. "Maybe even eloquent."

Handsome Dan nodded. "Oh yeah. Definitely eloquent. Positively inspiring. Erudite."

Paul stood up and half-stumbled his way to the window. Down on the assembly floor, a dozen men and women in cammies were examining the *Corvus* and the *Kickstart* jet.

"I'm sure you were convincing," he said. "But I can't do what you're asking."

"What if I call you back to active duty and give you a direct order?"

"Then you'll have to lock me up for dereliction and failure to obey."

"You want to help us," said General Byrd. "I can tell."

"I *do* want to help you," said Paul. "Help you stop the Russians. Destroy the weapon. End the threat. I'm just not willing to kill my child to get there."

"She's not a child. She's got nearly as many combat citations as you do."

"I'd help you if I could," said Paul. "I swear I would."

The general got to his feet. "This has to be done. We'll do it with you or without you, but we're going to do it."

Paul kept his eyes on the *Corvus*. "Then it'll have to be without me."

"That's your final answer?"

"It's my only answer," said Paul.

TEN

President's Park South
Washington, DC
(Expiration of Deadline: 52 Hours / 46 Minutes)

The size of the crowd was not the problem.

Between plain clothes spotters on the ground and a pair of tethered CyPhy reconnaissance drones hovering overhead, the Secret Service was estimating 50,000 demonstrators in the Ellipse and the surrounding areas. Given the size of the park, that worked out to a little over 1,000 people per acre—roughly the population density of a max capacity day at Disneyland. Only about ten percent of the 2017 Women's March on Washington and tiny in comparison to the massive Viet Nam War Era rallies and the Black Lives Matter protests.

The Secret Service and the DC Metropolitan Police Department had dealt with much larger gatherings in the past, so the number of demonstrators wasn't the issue. The problem was a lack of homogeneity. This wasn't a gathering of like-minded activists with a common social agenda. It was two rival mobs with diametrically opposing goals who happened to be occupying the same piece of ground at the same time.

One faction carried placards and banners calling for capitulation and immediate nuclear disarmament. To their way of thinking, the Russian ultimatum was a gift to humankind and the planet. An opportunity to lay down the tools of Armageddon and build a civilization not predicated upon the threat of utter annihilation.

The opposing faction had signs and banners of its own, demanding swift and overwhelming military action against Russia.

Fuck surrender! Crush the bastards *now*, and never knuckle under to the demands of foreign dictators.

The interaction between the opposing assemblies had (so far) been limited to chanted slogans, bellowed insults, and rude gestures. But it would only take one shove—one carelessly thrown fist—to turn the rival protests into an uncontrollable brawl.

DC Metro had riot response teams standing by and the Secret Service had erected steel mesh security barriers and quietly tripled their perimeter defenses, but neither organization was prepared to cope with 50,000 rioters within a few yards of the south White House fence. Human beings are prone to do irrational things when they're frightened or angry, and these people were both.

If things got out of hand and a thousand (or ten thousand) of the rioters got crazy enough to go over the barrier and fence, teargas and other nonlethal crowd control deterrents might not be enough to turn them back. The Secret Service would either have to allow the mob to overrun the White House, or start gunning down large numbers of American citizens on the back lawn of 1600 Pennsylvania Avenue.

The scenario was unlikely, but it wasn't impossible, and the President's Protection Detail had not built its reputation by trusting to luck. So there were agents stationed with automatic weapons in concealed positions, while everyone from the Secret Service Command Post staff, to the White House roof snipers, to the DC Metro street cops, held their collective breath and hoped that nobody was stupid enough to rush the fence.

About 4,861 miles away, a not dissimilar drama was playing out in Moscow's *Krásnaya plóshchad'* (Red Square) under the light of a setting sun.

Although the square was covered by numerous surveillance cameras, the Russian Presidential Security Service (SBP) had nothing analogous to the automated head-counting software of the U.S. Secret Service. The SBP Tactical Staff in the Kremlin estimated the crowd at 60,000 people, but that number might have been low or high by as much as twenty percent.

Like the protest in Washington, this was a standoff between factions with wildly conflicting ideologies.

Opponents of Polichev's scheme were calling their president a madman; accusing him of courting nuclear genocide; yelling for his resignation and for immediate reparations to the victims in America. Supporters of Polichev's plan were equally fervent. Here, at last, was a chance to disarm the other nuclear powers of the world; to elevate Russia to her rightful position at the top of the pyramid. To effectively end war by ensuring that only Russia held the ability to wage it.

Also like the demonstration in Washington, the rival factions in Red Square were one aggressive act from erupting into a riot. But, unlike those of the White House, the Kremlin's defenders were not concealed from the public eye.

Four hundred soldiers from the Kremlin Regiment's 2nd, 4th, 7th, and 9th Companies lined the crenelated tops of the wall facing the square, their Kovrov A545 assault rifles held at the ready.

More than twice that number were stationed inside the walls of the fortified enclosure.

If the protesters rioted, they rioted. They might beat, stab, or shoot one another. They might smash the plate glass shop windows along the northeastern side of the square. They might overturn or burn vehicles on the adjoining streets. If they did those things, they'd have to contend with the police officers of the Moscow City Militia.

The demonstrators would *not* rush the walls of the Kremlin. If they tried, their bloodied corpses would litter the paving stones of Krásnaya plóshchad'.

The Russian Federation had freedom of a sort and its citizens enjoyed their own peculiar version of democracy. But such things had limits, and the people of Russia were generally prudent enough to respect the boundaries.

Those who forgot the limits of public protest were sometimes reminded that life is hard, and its ending can be brutal and abrupt.

While Russian and American citizens marched and protested in their respective capitals, the International Space Station passed silently over the Western United States.

For anyone who knew where to look (and what to look for) the station was visible from the ground: a pale dot of light streaking across the blue morning sky. Easily mistaken for a high-altitude jet moving at multi-Mach speed, the passage of the ISS went unobserved and unremarked.

Probably, the majority of sighted people on Earth had seen the station at least once—either by night or by day—without awareness of what they were witnessing. In a world that had become inured to the miracles of flight and space travel, the sight of an unknown object traversing the heavens was no longer worthy of attention.

Similarly unwatched by its cosmonaut operators at this particular moment, the tactical display in the Nauka Module continued updating itself in real-time. Targeting reticles spawned automatically in response to the terrain scrolling below, accompanied by blocks of Cyrillic tracking data for every city and sizable town within the footprint of the EMP weapon.

Portland. Seattle. Sacramento. San Francisco. Fresno. Los Angeles. San Diego. Spokane. Reno. Las Vegas. All sliding smoothly through the footprint of a weapon that could render them uninhabitable in mere seconds.

The inhabitants of those cities went about their lives, unaware that the sword of doom was passing unnoticed over their heads.

ELEVEN

Green River Gardens
California City, California
(Expiration of Deadline: 52 Hours / 21 Minutes)

Watching the playback on the screen of her MacBook, Amy Spicer was (once again) amazed by the persuasiveness of the illusion.

All the pieces came together so seamlessly. The video running in the "Composite" window of the Cinemagix software was—as far as she could tell—indistinguishable from what you'd expect to see on a major cable news show.

On the screen, an attractive and smartly dressed female news anchor was seated at a curving desk of frosted glass with the studio backdrop and network livery behind her, while a cutaway window showed an animated lightning bolt superimposed over stock footage of the International Space Station. At the bottom of the display, in the usual news ticker position, was the obligatory digital clock counting down to the expiration of the Russian ultimatum.

The ISS footage dissolved into a stylized logo with the letters "S" and "R" intertwined, as the news anchor segued into her wrap-up. "I'm Amy Spicer, and you've been watching the Spice Report. Don't forget to click 'Like' and 'Subscribe,' and let us know what you think in the comments below."

The clip ended and Amy sat back in her chair. Not bad. Pretty damned good, in fact.

She would watch the piece a couple of more times before uploading it to YouTube, but the latest edition of the 'Spice Report' seemed to be about ready to go.

Judging from the comments her channel had accumulated so far, her subscribers (all 4,206 of them) apparently regarded the Spice Report as a legitimate online news venue. As a female human posting video to the web, she got the usual pervy remarks from basement-dwelling creepazoids who only wanted to talk about the size of her boobs, complain about the lack of visible cleavage, or speculate about Amy's sexual orientation. But the ratio of lucid conversation to sleazy bullshit was about what she saw on the channels of more successful internet news providers, so she must be doing something right.

The illusion was working. She was evidently managing to convince her viewers that Amy Spicer was the real deal.

She wondered how quickly her subscribers would evaporate if they could see the reality behind the facade.

Her state-of-the-art news studio was an unused walk-in storage closet in her grandfather's house. Her video camera was a secondhand Nikon D3500. She'd gotten it cheap because the former owner had broken the casing. The duct tape that held the thing together was starting to peel up at the corners. She'd have to replace the tape again pretty soon, because she sure as hell couldn't afford to replace the camera.

The ergonomic glass news desk was the top from a coffee table that she'd picked up at a yard sale. She'd unscrewed the legs and laid the thing across a pair of old sawhorses that remained carefully out of frame thanks to some strategic camera alignment.

The video editing software that she used to knit everything together was a five-year-old copy of Cinemagix II. She couldn't upgrade to a newer version of the software because her ancient MacBook Air didn't have the horsepower to run it.

She shot the Spice Report in front of a green piece of felt stapled to the closet wall, and then used the Cinemagix chroma-keying feature to layer in whatever backdrops she wanted.

Her professional-looking studio background was a single frame digital image, rendered in some—probably pirated—CGI engine by a graphic design student in Romania for thirty bucks. The clever "SR" logo had come from the same guy, and possibly from the same pirated software. Another thirty bucks.

The stylish blouse she was wearing had the (still attached) price tag tucked out of sight in the left sleeve. She'd be returning the blouse for a refund in a couple of days, along with three other tops that she had "bought" for the same purpose.

If she changed stores every week or so and was careful to never damage the clothes or detach the price tags, she could keep her on-screen wardrobe in a constant state of rotation without spending any money. Or at least not permanently.

Her wardrobe problem was cut in half by the fact that ensembles only had to cover her from the waist up. Below the desk, out of the camera's field of view, she wore comfy old running shorts and bare feet.

The trickery didn't end there. Amy herself was part of it. She was—all modesty aside—one of those rare people who are naturally photogenic. For whatever reason, cameras loved her. They imbued her with beauty and charisma that she simply could not replicate in real life.

Guys who went gaga over her Instagram pics always ended up trying to hide their disappointment when they met her face-to-face. She wasn't ugly or anything. Not even plain. She was—in her own (admittedly biased) judgment—sort of cute.

Not *really* cute. Just sort of. And definitely not the kind of knockout that she looked like on screen. Whatever genuine attractiveness she had, it came nowhere close to the false radiance conjured up by camera lenses.

Somehow, all the shabbiness and fakery seemed to vanish when an episode came together. The piece became real, or as real as anything on the web ever got.

Amy wanted her news coverage to be real. She'd been a second-year journalism major at Cal State Northridge when the COVID pandemic had thrown a monkey wrench into her plans. She'd decided to take a gap year while everyone was waiting for an effective vaccine.

Between logistics issues with the vaccines and mutations of the virus, one year had turned into two years. And then, Mom's second heart attack had left Amy on her own.

Well, *mostly* on her own.

There was still her grandfather, Papa Nick. He could sort of take care of himself. He just needed a little help with dressing, especially when his arthritis was flaring up. Of course, he couldn't drive, and it wasn't really safe for him to cook his own meals.

If things had gone differently, he might have ended up in an assisted living facility. But after the way the Coronavirus had burned through nursing homes across the country, Amy couldn't stop thinking of those places as death traps for the elderly.

Most of the nursing facilities hadn't done anything wrong. Many (if not most) of those deaths had likely been the logical consequence of gathering sizable populations of high-risk people in fairly close proximity.

The chances of another pandemic hitting the nursing homes within the next couple of decades might be vanishingly small. Amy wasn't willing to take that risk.

The sweet old guy would stay right here with her, in his wonderfully ramshackle house. There might come a day when she couldn't meet his care needs anymore, but she'd put that off as long as possible.

Until then—between Papa Nick's Air Force pension, his Social Security, and what Amy brought in from waiting tables at the Flying Steer—they could pay the property taxes, keep the utilities turned on, and put food on the table.

Maybe the Spice Report would eventually build up a strong enough base of YouTube subscribers to pay the bills. All it would take was one really good story going viral.

But arranging for a video to go viral was like arranging for a movie to win an Oscar. All you could do was create the best content you could figure out how to make, shove it out into the world, and hope for the best.

She pulled out her phone to check the time. Almost an hour

before she had to get ready for the lunch shift. Enough time to screen the new episode again, heat up some soup for Papa Nick, and slip into her work clothes. She'd taken care of her hair and makeup before shooting the episode.

And… she had a text from Randy Fleming. Lovely. Just lovely.

Randy was one of the gamer nerd/wannabe party boys from the house next door. This looked to be another of his cryptic messages promising a killer idea for a news story.

So far, Randy's killer ideas had ranged from lame non-stories, to obscure conspiracy theories, to outright nonsense. On the rare occasion when he hit on an angle that might be workable, it was always something requiring A-List press credentials, a massive production budget, or something else that put the story out of Amy's reach.

She half regretted giving him her number. But she needed somebody to look in on Papa Nick when she worked double shifts, and Randy was a fifteen-second walk away from the house. Also, he was a subscriber of the Spice Report, and Amy didn't have enough of those to go chasing any away. Besides, other than a general lack of social skills, Randy wasn't all that bad.

The only real downside was that he insisted on revealing his killer ideas in person, as if every lead he came up with was so hot or so controversial that he couldn't trust it to the web.

Maybe he truly *did* think his ideas were that good. More likely, he just wanted excuses to meet with Amy face-to-face.

He wanted to get in her pants, that much was clear. But he didn't have the self-confidence to come within light-years of the subject. He seemed to be hoping that Amy might somehow forget that they weren't having sex and invite him back to her room for a quick smash.

She sighed and replied to his text. "Getting ready for work. Talk tonight, after my shift."

With that out of the way, she turned back to her MacBook and hit the Play icon to rescreen the new episode.

TWELVE

White House
Washington, DC
(Expiration of Deadline: 50 Hours / 55 Minutes)

National Security Advisor Michael Lazlow was already talking when he followed the Secretary of Defense into the Oval Office. "Article Five, Mr. President. It's our get out of jail free card."

President Roth stood near an armchair in the grouping of furniture at the southern end of the room. He settled into the chair and gestured for his two visitors to find seats on one of the sofas. "I've just asked the Securities Exchange Commission to suspend trading until the Russia situation is sorted out."

Secretary of Defense Ernesto Ortiz took the sofa to the president's left. "*If* the Russia situation gets sorted out."

"It will," said the president, "or else our friend, Leonid Igorevich Polichev, will cook our bacon for us. In which case, a crashing stock market will be the least of our worries."

The National Security Advisor had chosen the sofa on the president's other side. "We need to be looking at the North Atlantic Treaty," he said. "An attack against any member nation is an attack against NATO itself. You invoke Article Five, Mr. President, and Russia has to fight us *all*."

83

Secretary Ortiz shook his head. "Any military alliance is dead before it starts. That damned EMP device can take out every command and control center in the U.S. and Europe in a single orbit. One flyover to disarm us, *and* our allies."

"We call for an emergency meeting of the UN Security Council," said Lazlow. "Rally every country that stands to lose under an all-powerful Russian hegemony. France. Japan. Australia. South Korea. India. Fucking Tahiti. *Everybody*. The Russians can't stand against the whole planet."

"They won't have to," said Secretary Ortiz. "We're the only remaining superpower. If we get hammered into the Bronze Age, nobody else is going to be stupid enough to risk the same treatment."

"You're saying we've already lost?"

"I'm saying the EMP thing is a game-changer. We can't resolve this by rounding up military allies. Circling the wagons gets us nowhere."

"We should ask for a special session of the UN General Assembly," said the president.

"With all due respect, I don't see where that gets us," said Lazlow. "The General Assembly will dither until the ultimatum expires and then pass a sternly-worded resolution that the Russians will promptly use for toilet paper."

"We're not supposed to abandon diplomacy when things get difficult," said President Roth. "Maybe having to stare down 192 other countries will give Polichev something to think about. Remind him that maintaining a stranglehold on seven and a half billion angry people is not going to be a walk in the park."

"You think that will make a difference?" asked Lazlow.

"I'd be surprised if it did," said the president. "But it costs us nothing to try, and it's what our country agreed to do when we ratified the United Nations Charter."

Lazlow nodded. "Understood, sir. As long as we're not relying on the UN to pull us out of this mess."

"Fair enough," said the president. "What about that indie spaceplane? The *Corvus*. How soon before it's ready to launch?"

"I believe they're doing the prep work now," said the National

Security Advisor. "I'll see if we can get a time estimate."

"Fine. What's our Plan B?"

When no answers were forthcoming, the president lifted an eyebrow. "Come now, Gentlemen. One untested spacecraft? That's all we've got? That's the entirety of our options?"

"We could open a back channel to Polichev," said Secretary Ortiz.

"And what would our message be?"

"We try to find out if there's middle ground."

The president nodded. "Keep talking...."

"Maybe we don't have to surrender our entire arsenal. What if we agree to eliminate certain classes of missiles and warheads, and—in return—they let us hang on to the rest? Dismantle say sixty percent of our stockpile, starting with the most obsolete weapons platforms. Stuff we were already planning to phase out. Russia gets to declare a win, and we're still a serious nuclear player."

Lazlow shook his head. "Even if Polichev would go for it—and he *won't*—Russia already has more than half the nukes on the planet. We cut 3,000 warheads, and we're handing them absolute military dominance. They become the only grownup at the table, and they don't have to threaten nuclear attacks to keep us little kids in line. Just wave that EMP weapon, and we all sit up straight and eat our vegetables."

The Secretary of Defense crossed his arms. "You have another suggestion?"

"I can't believe I'm saying this..." said the National Security Advisor, "...but maybe we should hit them *now*, while we've still got the capability. Preemptive nuclear strike. Take out Moscow and every major military target in Russia."

No one responded, so he continued into the incredulous silence. "We can do it. There's a forty-two-minute period in every orbit where the ISS doesn't have line of sight to the U.S. mainland. Every ICBM in our inventory can hit Russia in thirty minutes or less. We can time the launch windows so the EMP weapon never gets a shot at our missiles in flight."

"No!" said the president.

"But sir. We've got to—"

"I said, '*no!*' We can't protect civilization by starting the apocalypse."

"The Russians started it," said Lazlow. "They've already fired the first shots."

"No," said the president for the third time. "There have to be better options, Gentlemen. I refuse to believe that our only choices are global tyranny and thermonuclear war."

National Reconnaissance Office Headquarters
Chantilly, VA

It didn't look at all like the heart of America's ultra-secret surveillance satellite program.

The Ops Floor was a labyrinth of technology, like a cross between NASA Houston's Mission Control, a call center for telemarketing scams, and the server room of any good-sized company. Racks of IT equipment were laid out in patterns that made sense to engineers (but to no one else). Conduit and trays of fiberoptic cables spanned the ceiling and wiring bundles ran down the walls. There were rows of operator stations, each with a technician handling multiple screens and keyboards.

At one of these stations somewhere near the center of the maze sat Maya Chandra, the operator assigned to CALI (Collision Avoidance Logistics and Integration). Her job—and the job of the CALI software—was to keep U.S. spy satellites from colliding with other satellites, space junk, and anything else large enough to provide a measurable radar return from orbit.

As a second-generation American raised in Eastern Maryland, Maya spoke in what a sociolinguist would classify as a "coastal accent," similar to a Boston patois but less flamboyant. By contrast, the English of her parents was colored by their former lives in Haryana, before they immigrated from India.

When she spoke to the satellites (as she usually did) Maya tended to mimic the voices of her parents, exaggerating the musicality of their speech almost to the level of parody.

She punched up the Keyhole satellite designated as K56 and examined its vital statistics on her screen. She ignored the central display, which contained a graphic depiction of the satellite's orbital track, intersected at several points by the paths of other objects circling in Low Earth Orbit.

The visual cueing system was indexed by color for easy interpretation. Green curves were safe, no projected collision opportunities for at least the next three orbits. Yellow curves signaled caution conditions, relative geometries building toward a flyby within three orbits at a range that violated the minimum safe perimeters established for NRO satellites. Orange and red curves were for increasing probabilities of collision.

Maya paid attention to the graphics only in passing. The real meat of the CALI software was in the callout boxes around the edges of the display. Not as flashy, but they provided a grasp of traffic patterns and relative motion that went far beyond green-is-good and red-is-bad.

Speaking softly in her faux Indian accent, she nodded to the screen. "Ah, Mr. K56, you are doing nicely today. Using your turn signals. Obeying the speed limit. Safe Driver Discount for you!"

She cleared K56 from her display and queried CALI for the next satellite in the queue.

Maya had been heavily involved in the development of the CALI software, and she had pushed for the acronym that gave the program its name. (She had secretly wanted to call the software KALI, after the Hindu goddess of death, time, and destruction. Maya had no interest in any religion, but the notion of referencing a Hindu deity in an American surveillance operation appealed to the more perverse side of her humor. Unfortunately, she'd never been able to come up with a good "K" word for the first letter of the acronym, so she'd been forced to settle for a homophone instead of a homonym.)

The next candidate on her screen was K61. She examined the satellite's particulars and nodded again. "And Mr. K61. I see that you are keeping to your own lane and watching your mirrors. Safe Driver Discount for you as well."

She tabbed to another candidate, K23. The satellite's orbital arc was yellow, and one of the crossing curves was orange, for reasons that were immediately clear when she read the data in the callout boxes.

"Oh, my goodness, Mr. K23, you are *not* being careful of other vehicles. No Safe Driver Discount for you!"

Maya opened a message window on one of her side screens and typed, "K23 close intercept with Starlink-1028. Non-Polar, PER 549, ECC 1.45E-04, INCL 53.00, PER 95.6. Recommend DAM +16V."

She pulled the microphone boom for her headset closer to her mouth and pressed the 'Talk' button. When she spoke, she dropped the parody of her parents and lapsed into her natural Boston-lite dialect. "Steve, this is Maya. I'm flagging Keyhole 23 for a Debris Avoidance Maneuver. It's about to get frisky with one of the Starlink birds. We're going to have to do a burn."

There was a brief delay as her supervisor called up the endangered satellite on his end and studied the data. "Looks like K23's been up there since dinosaurs roamed the Earth," Steve said. "Doesn't have a lot of delta-v left for maneuvers."

"I see that," said Maya, "But we can adjust K23's orbit, or we can bring it down. Otherwise, it's going to punch a hole through Elon Musk's broadband internet constellation. And then..."

She stopped talking as an idea went off in her brain like a firecracker.

Then, she was tabbing through the entire lineup of NRO and DoD satellites, scanning the position, altitude, direction of motion, and fuel reserves for each bird as she went.

"And then, *what?*" asked Steve.

Maya reached K108 and paused in her search. She shifted to a side screen and began tapping out some quick calculations.

"And then, *what?*" asked Steve again.

"I've just had an idea," Maya said.

Steve's sigh was audible over the headset. "You've never had an idea in your life that didn't cost half a billion dollars."

Still pecking away at the keyboard, Maya smiled. "This one is going to cost more like two billion. And we will *not* be saving fifteen percent on car insurance."

White House Situation Room
Washington, DC

Looking over the shoulder of the Sit Room Duty Officer, General Christopher studied loops of satellite video on one of the wall-sized geographic displays. A large number of armored vehicles and troop transports near the outskirts of a sizable metropolitan area, clearly driving toward the heart of the city. "Where is this?"

"Kharkiv, sir. City of about one and a half million in eastern Ukraine. Those are mechanized units and infantry from the Russian 42nd Guards Motor Rifle Division and 6th Tank Brigade, supported by the 31st Air Assault Brigade. This is not a reconnaissance-in-force and it doesn't have the right composition to be a defensive deployment. The Russians are moving in to set up shop."

"Any diplomatic traffic from Moscow?"

The Duty Officer shook his head. "Negative, sir. Usually, they try to soften up the international community with accusations of Ukrainian violence against Russian citizens. Subversion of border security measures. Something like that. This time, they're not saying a word."

General Christopher continued to watch the satellite imagery. "They're invading a city the size of San Diego and not even trying to justify it?"

"Mr. Polichev no longer feels obliged to play by the rules. Guess he figures Russia can take whatever it wants, whenever it wants.

"Well they can't," said the general. "Not yet anyway."

THIRTEEN

Stockdale Estates
Bakersfield, California
(Expiration of Deadline: 47 Hours / 51 Minutes)

The pork chop hit the skillet and began to sizzle. Paul Keene turned the burner down a notch and shifted the chop with a fork to keep it from sticking to the hot cast iron.

Neither action was conscious. He was operating from somewhere just above the autonomic level. Not thinking. Not even hungry. Stumbling through the motions of life because he didn't know what else to do.

They were going to kill Sarah.

That thought looped endlessly in his head.

With or without his help, it was going to happen. They were going to do it. They were going to kill Sarah.

From somewhere outside came a jingling noise, muted by distance and by the double panes of the closed kitchen window.

Even with his mental processes running in circles, Paul's pilot training registered the sound and identified the source. The Francher kid from three houses down. Orson, or Carson, or Bryson, or whatever god-awful name the boy's parents had foisted on him. Riding his two-wheeler up and down the sidewalk, plinking away at the little bell clamped to his handlebars.

Ring-ring.

It was the kid's first bike. Still had the training wheels on.

Ring-ring.

Paul prodded absently at the pork chop in the skillet, remembering a different bicycle.

A different evening.

A different place.

Ring-ring.

Warrington, Florida, back when Paul had flown *Tomcats* out of Naval Air Station Pensacola. That hideous pea-green stucco ranch house on Sherman Avenue. Gwen leaning against the peeling paint of a front porch column, trying to hide a smile as Paul unbolted the training wheels from Sarah's pink Barbie bike...

Sarah, five years old, hops from one foot to the other with her usual mixture of excitement and impatience.

Paul removes the second training wheel and drops it on the withered grass next to its partner. "You sure about this, Sprite? We could leave 'em on another couple of weeks..."

Without hesitation, Sarah clambers onto the pink bicycle seat. The toes of her tennis shoes barely reach the ground.

Keene puts one hand on his daughter's shoulder and the other on the back of her seat. "Are you ready?"

Sarah thumbs the bell.

Ring-ring.

Stealing a glance toward her mom, she starts to pedal. Moving down the sunbaked stretch of grass next to the road where a nicer neighborhood would have a sidewalk.

Jingling the bell as she rides.

Ring-ring.

Paul trots alongside, keeping her steady.

"Okay Daddy," Sarah says—not completely certain, but gaining confidence. "I've got it. You can let go, now..."

Paul continues to run with her, still holding on.

"Daddy, let go!"

Paul stays with her for another five or six steps before he releases his grip.

Sarah peddles away, with an occasional wobble but getting steadier as she finds her balance.

Paul looks around to share a quick smile with Gwen.

She starts to say something, but her voice is drowned out by a high-pitched squeal that sounds nothing at all like Sarah's bell.

A visible haze hung in the air.

The pork chop was burning, and the kitchen smoke alarm was screaming like a banshee.

Fumbling the pan off the burner, Paul opened the kitchen window and grabbed a dishtowel to fan the smoke toward the opening.

He caught a lung full of smoke and started to cough.

Out on the sidewalk, the Francher kid was peddling in the other direction. Back toward his house.

Ring-ring.

FOURTEEN

U.S. Air Force Lieutenant Colonel Floyd Garrett was passing 95,000 feet—the sky turning black in the forward cockpit windows—when things started to get away from him.

The *Corvus* was climbing faster than anything he'd ever piloted, each of its three linear aerospike rocket engines cranking out more than a quarter of a million pounds of thrust, sending the tiny spaceplane toward the firmament of the gods on a roaring pillar of silver-white fire.

Strapped into each of the twin seats at the rear of the cramped cockpit were nine U.S. M2 twenty-pound assault demolitions. The Marines had only needed one of those mothers to flatten a building during the Second Battle of Fallujah, so having eighteen of them wedged into the space behind his shoulder blades should have been terrifying.

That idea was scary enough, but he was only dimly aware of his volatile cargo. Pressed hard into his seat by acceleration—the sound of his breath magnified in the confines of his helmet—with his whole body vibrating at the frequency of combusting rocket fuel, his full attention was on maintaining control of this crazy fucking machine.

For all the advanced materials and brainy engineering, the *Corvus* was a prototype. A proof-of-concept demonstrator, built on a shoestring.

Luxuries like computer-assisted flight controls were planned for later generations of the spacecraft, after a successful orbital launch had attracted funding for additional development. But Garrett wasn't piloting some future version of what the *Corvus* might one day become. He was flying *this* version: a strictly seat-of-the-pants job with a margin of error so narrow that it scared the living shit out of him.

A small LCD screen displayed the curve of his climb, and he was too shallow. Not by much. Just a hair....

He pulled back on the pistol grip control stick, bringing the nose up a tad. And knew instantly that he had over adjusted, passing the critical angle of attack where the airflow separated from the upper surface of the wings and lift disappeared with the suddenness of a magic trick.

The *Corvus* stalled and began to lose altitude.

In another type of plane, recovery would have been simple enough. Drop the nose to increase airspeed, restore airflow over the wings and reestablish lift. Garrett had done it so many times that the correct reactions were coded into his muscle memory. But this was nothing like an F-35, even on afterburner. This was a marginally stable lozenge of plasticized carbon fiber, moving at better than Mach four atop a river of exploding monomethylhydrazine and dinitrogen tetroxide.

He felt like a butterfly riding the torrent from a fire hose.

The situation was complicated by a few degrees of yaw to starboard, which caused one wing to stall a fraction of a second before the other. That was all it took.

Garrett was slammed sideways by rotational force, thrown against the restraint webbing as the *Corvus* rolled over and began a spiral toward the ground. The darkening sky in the windows was replaced by the madly spinning browns and greens of the desert floor rushing up to swat him.

He let go of the stick and shouted into his helmet mic. "Abort! Abort! Shut down and reset!"

After the usual two-second lag, the flight was at an end.

The sound effects chopped off with an abruptness that left his ears ringing. The thunder of rocket engines replaced by the chirps and squeals of high-speed electric motors as the three-axis motion simulator rotated the "cockpit" back to a level position.

The scenery depicted in the windows gave way to the blue start screen of the operating software, the words "GAME OVER" flashing in large capital letters. The "O" in "OVER" transmogrified itself into a grinning cartoon skull that may have been cribbed from an 80s era video game.

That last touch had to be the work of the guy they called Handsome Dan. The man had a perpetual gleam of mischief in his beady little eyes.

Garrett took a moment to regulate his breathing and bring his heart rate down to normal.

"All right," he said into the mic. "Let's try it again."

In the observation room, General Byrd looked up from the repeater screens into the elaborately innocent expression on the face of Handsome Dan Conway. The man wasn't smirking on the outside, but he was mentally grinning his ass off. Byrd knew the look.

"Can Keene really fly that thing?" Byrd asked.

Conway nodded. "Absolutely. He started out like your man—crashing and burning every time. But he can do it in his sleep now."

Byrd sighed. "How long did it take him to learn?"

"Six weeks, give or take," said a voice from the far end of the room.

Byrd turned to see Paul Keene leaning against the frame of the open door.

Keene gestured toward the repeater screens of the simulator. "Your pilot has good instincts. Quick reflexes and a knack for the stick. He'll probably get it figured out in half that time."

"He's not my pilot," grumbled Byrd. "I had to borrow him from the Air Force. And we don't *have* three weeks."

The general softened his tone. "We don't even have three days."

"Then you're gonna need a pilot who already knows how to fly the *Corvus*," said Keene.

"Does that mean you've decided to help us?"

"I'm not going to help you destroy the ISS," said Keene. "But I have an idea for a way to take back the station without destroying it."

General Byrd shook his head. "Can't be done. Impossible."

"Maybe not," said Keene. "Ever hear of something called fentanyl?"

FIFTEEN

#3 Sutton Place
Manhattan, New York
(Expiration of Deadline: 44 Hours / 39 Minutes)

In diplomatic circles, his family name was a word to conjure with.

Rolf Hammarskjöld, Secretary-General of the United Nations, was a son of Swedish nobility. He was also a grandnephew of the legendary Dag Hammarskjöld, who had been the second person appointed to Rolf's current office.

Like his famous granduncle, Rolf had trained and practiced as an economist before turning his life's focus to the field of diplomacy. Unlike his late relative, Rolf was unlikely to win the Nobel Peace Prize, or to have buildings, plazas, and scholarships dedicated in his honor. Hell, the UN's highest medal for peacekeeping was named after his uncle. How could anyone compete with that?

An op-ed in *Göteborgs-Posten* had once compared Rolf to America's President John Quincy Adams, a man who had followed poorly in the footsteps of his more successful father.

Rolf could hardly argue with the jab. John F. Kennedy had repeatedly identified Dag as the greatest statesman of the twentieth century. There was no one of JFK's caliber left to proclaim Rolf's excellence to the world, even assuming that he accomplished some diplomatic miracle worthy of the accolade.

If Rolf brought about global peace, cured cancer, and liberalized the offside rule in European football, he'd still be what J.R.R. Tolkien had called a "lesser son of great sires."

He sat on the balcony of the neo-Georgian townhouse that was the official residence of the Secretary-General and sipped from a glass of lingonberry saft.

In Sweden, the sweet and fruity juice concentrate was traditionally a drink for children, but Rolf sometimes reverted to it if he was feeling nostalgic or inadequate. The comforting flavor of the saft brought back memories of a pleasant and unthreatening time in his life, when the world had seemed far more rational and predictable than he now knew it to be.

He took another sip of his boyhood and looked out over the enclosed garden that his townhouse shared with the sixteen other townhouses that surrounded it. It was a private bastion of green magnificence, walled away from the eyes and access of the public.

In many ways, this residence was the antithesis of everything he had tried to accomplish with his life. Most of the world's problems seemed to stem from hoarding wealth and resources, or from squandering them. This mansion—and (with its five stories and its 14,000 square feet) there was no point in pretending that it was anything else—was both a concentration of wealth and an unnecessary expenditure of materials and physical space.

But the mansion went with the position. If he chose to live in more frugal accommodations, his critics would inevitably interpret the move as virtue signaling: a pampered top echelon diplomat from a wealthy family pretending to be a common citizen. His departure from the established traditions of his office would become a footnote to every action Rolf undertook.

With a small pivot of his wrist, he rotated the glass in his hand, watching the saft swirl around the circular barrier of its enclosure. Perhaps the age of political footnotes was passing. Short of some astounding reversal of fortune, or a coup that exchanged Leonid Polichev for a less megalomaniacal leader, the United States had something less than two days remaining as a major world power.

The Americans would be forced to surrender their strategic arsenal or suffer the eradication of their technological infrastructure. Whichever choice they made, their tenure as a global superpower was coming to an end.

With the Americans removed from the table, the other countries would topple like the dominoes of Cold War metaphor. Which meant that the days of the United Nations were also numbered.

Polichev might decide to keep the UN around as an exercise in vanity, or as an organ of propaganda for his coming world-state, but Rolf Hammarskjöld would no longer be its titular head. If Polichev did not remove him from office, Rolf would have to resign. He was not willing to participate in a charade to simulate credibility for a regime that would be oppressive by its very nature.

Rolf was tempted to fly home before the deadline expired. To be with his family and friends in Uppsala when the world began its descent into tyranny.

But his Granduncle Dag had died flying *into* danger, not away from it. Dag had been on the way to negotiate a cease-fire in the Congo when his plane went down in what had then been called Northern Rhodesia. The cause of the crash was still officially undetermined, but there was a growing consensus in the international intelligence community that the aircraft had been shot down by the KGB, to protect the Soviet Union's uranium mining concessions in the region.

Regardless of whether the rumors of Russian involvement were true, Dag had certainly understood that he might be flying toward his own end. He'd accepted the possibility (or perhaps the likelihood) of his death as a fair cost in the pursuit of peace.

Lesser son though he might be, Rolf's instincts for self-preservation were outweighed by his desire to remain worthy of his office, and true to the example set by his more famous relative.

Tomorrow, at the request of the American Ambassador to the UN, Rolf would preside over a session of the General Assembly.

Privately, he saw not even the slimmest prospects for a useful outcome. Speeches would be made, invectives would be flung, fists would be pounded upon tabletops, and pleas would fall on deaf

Russian ears.

Humanity's great international organization for peace, security, and hope would deliver none of the things that it had been founded to protect.

SIXTEEN

Green River Gardens
California City, California
(Expiration of Deadline: 42 Hours / 36 Minutes)

Randy was waiting under the streetlight at the corner of the fence when Amy turned her crappy little Hyundai into the driveway.

Lovely.

She'd forgotten about agreeing to meet him tonight. The idea had seemed harmless enough before her shift, but now she was exhausted, and her feet were killing her. She wanted to have a quick bite with Papa Nick, then watch an old movie with him until she fell asleep on the sofa.

But if she went inside, Randy would want to follow, and he would interpret entrance to the house as a social call. It would take half the night to get him back out the door.

If she planned to rendezvous with the sofa anytime soon, Randy's latest *news-story-of-the-century-revelation* would have to take place out here in the yard.

Amy put on her best fake smile: the one she reserved for diners who wanted fourteen substitutions with every order, then low-balled her on the tip.

She got out of the car and slid around to sit on the rear fender.

The cool metal felt good through the denim of her jeans, and sitting would keep the weight off her feet while Randy unveiled his latest brainstorm.

Her mistake became evident as soon as Randy ambled to within easy conversation range. She could actually see his struggle to maintain eye contact.

Crap.

She was still in Boobzilla Mode.

The top three buttons of her black work shirt were undone, and she was wearing a padded push-up bra that enhanced her cleavage and added dimension to her boobs.

Not a sufficient change to attract attention from across the room. Nothing ridiculous. Just turning the heat up a couple of degrees. Enough for someone to notice if they were inclined to take interest in female secondary sex characteristics.

Most of the creeps in the comments section of her YouTube channel would spot the difference in a heartbeat.

The Boobzilla thing was research for an upcoming episode of the Spice Report. An experiment to determine how much impact—if any—that her (apparent) breast size would have on the tips she received for waiting tables.

She had done her best to employ a methodical approach to her data gathering.

Phase 1 had been to establish baseline conditions by working ten consecutive shifts with a regular bra and only her top button open. (Normal Mode.)

Phase 2 was to work ten shifts with the Wonder Bra and three buttons undone. (Boobzilla Mode.)

Phase 3 would be ten shifts in which she alternated between modes: a night in Normal Mode, a night in Boobzilla Mode, then back to normal again.

Tonight had been the final night of Phase 2. Amy had come straight home from the restaurant without changing, so she was still showing enhanced boobage, a fact that registered clearly in Randy's ongoing battle to keep his eyes north of her collarbone.

In a perfect world, her cleavage should make no difference for any job that didn't specifically require physical attractiveness. She wasn't a fashion model or a movie star. She waited tables in a steakhouse. The tips she took in should reflect the quality of the service she provided, and nothing else.

Only her appearance *did* make a difference. The data collection wasn't complete yet, but the outcome was already a foregone conclusion. Even the relatively minor changes of a padded push-up and a few open buttons were enough to increase her nightly tips by an average of forty dollars.

As news stories went, it was not exactly a bolt from the blue. Amy's informal study was—at best—a reconfirmation of sociosexual biases that had long ago been mapped out by studies far more rigorous than her small experiment.

But this was something she could do herself. An easy way to create original content for the Spice Report that didn't glom on to stories already being covered by mainstream journalists. And the experiment wasn't just inexpensive; it was profitable, to the tune of forty or so bucks a night.

Her manager didn't care one way or the other, as long as Amy wore the basic Flying Steer uniform—black jeans and a black long-sleeved shirt—and she didn't flash enough skin to look like a stripper.

Now that Phase 2 was complete, she was having second thoughts. She would basically be doing a story where the through-line was, "Breaking News! Men like boobs!"

Anyway, how would she present it? How could she angle the content and delivery to make it seem like legitimate news, instead of a self-obsessed YouTube wannabe trying to pass off armchair psychology as journalism?

She was fighting to be taken seriously. A story that spotlighted her sexuality was probably the last thing she needed.

Or maybe the *next* to the last thing. She wished she'd taken the time to button up before coming within range of Randy's girl radar. She couldn't do it now without calling attention to his adolescent fixation on her mammaries.

So, she maintained her put-on smile and decided to get this over with as quickly as possible.

"Let's hear it," she said. "What's this amazing story idea that you can't wait to tell me about?"

"It's a good one! I think it's… I think maybe it could be a good one! Probably…"

"Don't keep me in suspense."

Randy was practically dancing with suppressed excitement. "You know I work for Sentinel-Pro, right? Private security company. I man the guard shack at an aerospace startup out on Route 58. Apogee Launch Systems. The two top guys in the company used to be astronauts."

"I remember," said Amy. And she did sort of remember. Not that she paid much attention to whatever was going on in Randy's life, but the part about working for ex-astronauts sounded familiar. The kind of nerd stuff that Randy liked to brag about.

"So, I'm in the guard shack this morning," said Randy. "Business as usual. Not a thing going on. Playing with my phone and trying to stay awake, when this whole fucking fleet of dark blue SUVs rolls right up to the gate and soldiers start jumping out. At least forty or fifty of 'em. Camo uniforms, with guns and fucking everything. And some general right in the middle of it. I thought he was Air Force, but it turns out that he's Space Force."

The yawn that had been creeping up on Amy suddenly subsided. This didn't sound like Randy's usual worthless BS.

"They took the place over," said Randy. "All of it. The whole damned place."

He grinned. "Sent me home. I got the week off with full pay. I'm supposed to call in on Monday, to see if they want me back. If they don't need me, I get next week off with pay too."

"What do you think is going on?"

"Damned if I know," said Randy. "But *something* is happening. The U.S. military just grabbed control of a civilian aerospace facility, and there's just *got* to be a news angle in that. Maybe Apogee has been stealing government secrets, or like they invented warp drive, or something else that the government wants to classify the shit out of. The best part is that nobody's picked up on the story. Not a thing about it on TV, or radio, or the web, and I've been checking."

Amy felt her bogus smile morph into the real thing. This had all the signs of an actual news story. And—if Randy was right—Amy might have it all to herself.

She slid down off the fender of the car, suppressing a wince as her sore feet landed on the driveway. "I need to go inside and heat up some dinner for me and Papa Nick. Are you hungry?"

Randy's grin got even wider. "I sure am."

SEVENTEEN

Stone Malone's was dead tonight, even for a Tuesday.

There was a lighted marquee out by the nightclub's entrance: 'Live Music by **Angel Feat** – No Cover Charge.'

It wasn't exactly reeling in the customers.

On the minuscule stage, Gil Lawson ran his fingers up the neck of his 1999 reissue Fender Jaguar; sliding into the lead guitar solo of *Batteries Not Included*.

Gil closed his eyes and concentrated on his finger work, shutting out the empty tables, the lone couple on the dance floor, and the people sitting at the bar with their backs to the stage.

He'd borrowed big stretches of the solo from *Phantom Limb* by Alice in Chains, but no one ever called him out for plagiarism. Either his rework of the riffs was enough to disguise their origins, or he sounded so little like Jerry Cantrell that nobody made the connection.

To Gil's ear, the band seemed to suck less than usual tonight. All the members of Angel Feat had day jobs at Johnson Space Center, and they didn't get in much time for practice. So, any reduction in the overall suck factor was progress. Sort of.

Gil vibratoed his way through the end of the solo. Sheila started a low buzz roll on the snare, and—miracle of miracles—Teddy's bass kicked in perfectly on the downbeat.

Everything was right on cue except for the soldiers.

Gil opened his eyes and there they were. Two men in camouflage, standing right at the edge of the stage. Staring directly at him.

The one on the left raised his voice to be heard above the music. "Gilbert Lawson?"

Gil tried to keep his head in the song. Soldiers? What could they possibly want with him?

The one on the right spoke. "Mr. Lawson, we need you to come with us, please."

Gil's playing stuttered to a halt. "What?"

The interruption caused Teddy's bass to falter, but Sheila held the beat and Teddy found his way back into the song.

"We need you to come with us," said the soldier again.

"I don't understand," said Gil. "Am I under arrest or something?"

Soldier #1 pulled a phone from somewhere and held it out toward Gil. "They want you at Mission Control. Somebody named Director Harper says you can call to verify."

Gil eyed the phone without reaching for it. Harper? NASA's Director of Flight Operations? Gil was frankly astonished that someone of her paygrade was aware of his existence.

"Time is critical, sir," said Soldier #2.

Gil unplugged from his amp and let the cable fall to the floor.

The strap of the Jaguar still slung around his neck, he stepped down from the stage and followed the soldiers toward the exit, leaving his bandmates to muddle along without a guitarist.

As Gil walked out the door—mind abuzz with unanswered questions—he heard a parting call from the bartender.

"Come on, guys... He wasn't *that* bad."

EIGHTEEN

Everything about the breakfast reinforced Sarah's status as a prisoner.

The reconstituted scrambled eggs and pouch of coffee weren't much above room temperature. (Not nearly hot enough to scald if thrown into someone's face.)

Her only utensil was a spoon made of some rubbery material that she could probably tie into a knot. Undoubtedly brought aboard by Volkov's thugs for this very purpose. Zero potential for jabbing or slashing, and Sarah couldn't imagine any way to modify the thing into a shiv.

She guided a spoonful of tepid eggs into her mouth and tried not to let Dmitri catch her watching the Russians out of the corner of her eye. Volkov, Syomin, and Levkin were doing something in the Columbus Laboratory Module. She could see them through the open hatchway.

Sarah had no idea what they were up to in there, other than conversing softly in Russian, but two things about the situation struck her as interesting.

First, the newcomers were all in one place.

Second, the module was a cul-de-sac. The only exit was the hatch that Sarah was carefully pretending not to watch.

She looked around for Rutger. His orientation was inverted compared to hers.

He poked at his own lukewarm eggs with another of the bendy non-weaponizable spoons. Showing no enthusiasm for actually putting the yellow lumps into his mouth.

Dmitri hovered several meters away, well outside the reach of both prisoners; right hand conspicuously close to the Taser on his belt.

According to Anya, those things were overamped. Lethal on the max setting, for taking down a prisoner without risking hull penetration. Assuming that Anya hadn't been talking shit.

Rutger shoved his spoon into his pouch of eggs. "*Lunnaya Pesnya?* What sick bastard decided that *Moon Song* was a good name for a doomsday weapon?"

"Not doomsday," said Dmitri. "We're ending the threat of nuclear aggression."

The cosmonaut's attention seemed to be on Rutger for the moment.

Sarah used the opportunity to make a visual survey of her immediate surroundings.

"Yeah," said Rutger. "Right. You honestly think the Americans will give in to armed extortion? Has your country learned nothing from history?"

Sarah's eyes lit on a nylon strap hanging from the quilted door of a sleeping module.

The plan—such as it was—came together instantly in her head. It might actually work if Rutger could keep Dmitri talking.

"History has many hard lessons to teach," said Dmitri. "Perhaps we are no longer willing to repeat our past mistakes."

A gentle push off the bulkhead sent Sarah drifting toward the sleeping cubicle. She spooned more eggs into her mouth as she floated, feigning interest in the unimpressive breakfast in case Dmitri happened to look her way.

"You should have called it *Lopast' Damaklova*," said Rutger. "The Sword of Damocles."

As she passed the sleeping cubicle, Sarah lifted the nylon strap from the door, thankful not to hear the trademark *skretch* of releasing Velcro. A subtle shove with one foot put her on a slow glide toward the hatch of the Columbus Module.

Rutger was maintaining eye contact with Dmitri, but Sarah was definitely within the Dutch astronaut's field of vision. She hoped he was aware of her slow-motion antics and could hold Dmitri's attention for a few more seconds.

"The Russian phrase is *Damoklov Mech*," said Dmitri. "And it would have hardly been wise to telegraph our intentions."

Sarah arrived at the hatch to the Columbus Module. She pushed the door quietly shut and began inching the dogging lever toward the sealed position.

Rutger's laugh was humorless. "If you think what you're doing is *wise*, you've never seen Dr. Strangelove. Half the Americans lose their minds at the thought of sensible gun control laws. You try to take away their nukes, and they'll go straight into Apocalypse Mode."

Sarah had the dogging lever cinched as tight as she thought she could manage without making noise. She tucked one end of the strap through a hatch handle, looped the other end over the dogging lever, and silently prayed that the thin strip of nylon would be strong enough.

The temptation to sneak a final look at Dmitri was almost overwhelming, but there was no time for that. Even if Dmitri was already flying toward her, she was in position to execute her plan.

Left hand clamped around the strap, she opened the protective cover for the Cabin Depress switch and brought her right palm down on the emergency switch.

The Columbus Module was equipped with a pair of large electrically operated valves designed to rapidly depressurize the laboratory in the event of fire. With the switch engaged, the valves slammed open and the air started screaming out of the isolated module, venting the atmosphere into the vacuum of space.

The depressurization alarm kicked in with a howl that could be heard throughout the station and the dogging lever began jerking as one or more of the Russians in the Columbus Lab fought to unseal the hatch.

There was a scuffle behind Sarah. Thrashing sounds and cursing in Dutch and Russian as Rutger evidently struggled to keep Dmitri off Sarah's back.

The strap yanked and bucked in Sarah's hand, nearly wresting itself from her grip—the movements of the dogging lever becoming ever more frantic.

Just a few more seconds...

The pressure in the laboratory module would be approaching zero now. It wouldn't take long for Volkov and his goons to lose consciousness. Then they would die.

It was working! She just needed a few more seconds... Just another...

Her body went into a crippling convulsion as 50,000 volts of DC electricity ripped through her central nervous system.

The Taser...

Dmitri's goddamned Taser...

The nylon strap slipped away from Sarah's twitching fingers and the world went black.

NINETEEN

President Roth stood at the railing of the Truman Balcony, gazing into the night sky. Somewhere up there—hidden amongst the stars—was the International Space Station and the weapon poised to destroy America.

A Secret Service Agent stood in the shadows with his back to the wall. Others of the agent's calling were stationed on the roof, throughout the White House, and in places of concealment around the grounds. Each of them was sworn, trained, and dedicated to safeguarding the president, but no force on Earth could defend him (or the American people) from what was coming.

National Security Advisor Michael Lazlow opened the French doors and walked out onto the balcony. He joined the president at the railing. "Looking for the ISS?"

The president shook his head. "With a little help, I might be able to spot the Big Dipper."

Lazlow smiled. "Pretty sure you weren't elected for your astronomy skills, Mr. President."

"I've been thinking about Patrick Henry's speech to the Second

Virginia Convention," said the president. "What he said about having to choose between life and freedom. Not the famous '*give me liberty or give me death*' quote that kids learn in Civics class. I mean the question leading up to that bit. And Patrick Henry's own answer to it."

"Can you refresh my memory, sir?"

Eyes still on the stars, President Roth quoted the lines. "Is life so dear, or peace so sweet, as to be purchased at the price of chains and slavery? Forbid it, Almighty God!"

"He must have been quite the orator," said Lazlow.

"Thomas Marshall was sitting next to Washington and Jefferson when that speech was delivered. He called it, 'one of the boldest, vehement, and animated pieces of eloquence that had ever been delivered.' But it's the question I'm thinking about. Not the loftiness of the rhetoric."

"Sir?"

"Henry decided that freedom was more precious than life. His actions during the revolution proved he wasn't speaking figuratively. He promised to risk his life to throw off the yoke of rule by a foreign power, and he backed up his words with action."

"I still don't see what you're getting at, Mr. President."

"However courageous Patrick Henry might have been, he was only choosing for himself," said the president. "I'm being asked to make that same choice for every person in the United States. And for billions of others around the world. Is freedom more important than survival? How am I supposed to make that decision for all humanity?"

"Maybe you won't have to, sir."

The president turned to face his National Security Advisor.

"You told us you wanted another option," said Lazlow. "We may have found one."

"I'm listening."

"I just had a meeting with the Director of the National Reconnaissance Office. NRO has a Keyhole satellite in a good position to ram the ISS."

The president said nothing.

"I had the same reaction at first, Mr. President. But we're not talking about a fender bender. A KH-14 series satellite has a mass of nearly fifteen tons, and NRO estimates relative velocity at about 9 miles per second. The impact would be like a city bus plowing through a house trailer at twenty times the speed of a rifle bullet. If that thing hits the station, we're talking total destruction."

"*If* it hits the station?"

Lazlow nodded. "Yes, sir. *If.* NRO estimates the odds of a hit at eighty percent plus, but nobody's ever tried this before. They can't guarantee success."

"What happens if we miss?"

"The satellite will be on a downward trajectory. It hits the upper edges of the atmosphere and burns up during reentry. The Russians will never even know."

"NRO is pretty confident this can work?"

"Confident enough to destroy a two-billion-dollar satellite, sir."

The president's gaze returned to the night sky. "Do it. But we keep moving forward with the *Corvus*. I'm not putting all my eggs in one basket."

"Of course, sir."

"And let's keep the satellite thing on close-hold. You, me, and whoever's already in the loop at the NRO. Nobody else knows about this."

"Sir?"

"We don't need any help from DoD or NASA to make this happen, and I don't want to distract them from the *Corvus* angle."

"In case this doesn't work out?"

"Exactly."

"I… think I understand, sir."

"Eighty percent isn't too bad," said the president.

"No, Mr. President, it's not bad at all."

TWENTY

Johnson Space Center
Houston, Texas
(Expiration of Deadline: 38 Hours / 45 Minutes)

Rotors turning languidly, a Space Force HH-60G Pave Hawk helicopter squatted under the sodium vapor lights of the Johnson Space Center Heliport.

Gil Lawson restrained an almost overwhelming desire to involve himself in the logistics operation on the landing pad. He stood with his hands in his pockets—an unwilling spectator as four people in cammies wrestled the Oxygen Generation System rack from the bed of a truck and carried it toward the open side door of the helicopter.

It was his equipment they were manhandling. He wanted to be in there, hands-on, guiding, and giving direction. But the soldier in charge had made it politely clear that Gil's help was not welcome, and (if Gil tried to insist) would not be tolerated.

Military types had that passive-aggressive thing down pat; the ability to couch absolute inflexibility in the most respectful language. In the absence of superior military authority, they were going to do things their way and civilian engineers could go screw themselves.

Politely, of course.

115

The rack was the size of a small refrigerator, although nowhere near as heavy. Built for the ISS, the unit—like all equipment intended for use in space—was engineered to minimize mass and conserve fuel during the boost up from Earth.

With the tanks empty, the rack was surprisingly light. But it was delicate and awkward to handle: characteristics that increased the likelihood of damage during transport.

Oh well. If they broke the thing, no one could blame Gil.

His hand came across something at the bottom of his jeans pocket. Triangular. Flexible. Plastic.

He wrapped his fingers around it. A Fender Thin guitar pick.

The interrupted gig at Stone Malone's already seemed like a lifetime ago.

Sheila was probably burning up her cell phone, trying to find out where Gil had been dragged off to. Teddy—a man of predictable habits and incurious mind—would be eating Cheetos and getting his ass stomped by a gang of pre-teen console warriors in Grand Theft Auto.

One of the soldiers stalked over to Gil. "You sure this is everything you need?"

Gil nodded. "Yeah. I mean, *pretty* sure…"

The soldier stared at Gil without speaking.

Fingers still toying with the guitar pick, Gil took the hint. He visualized the ISS Life Support System and compared his mental image to the equipment rack, components, and connectors gathered in the cargo area of the helicopter.

"Yeah," he said again. "We've got everything."

The soldier gave his shoulder a gentle shove in the direction of the open aircraft door. "Okay then, let's get you aboard."

Five or six minutes later—strapped into one of the rear seats with sound-muffling intercom headphones clamped over his ears—Gil felt his stomach flutter as the lights of the heliport fell away and the Pave Hawk lifted him into the night.

The chorus of *Batteries Not Included* ran through his mind.

Gropin' in the darkness.
Can't see a path ahead.
No more light to see by.
All batteries are dead.

The lyrics had carried no special significance when Gil had written them. Just gnomic phrases strung together in a way that he'd hoped might remind people of Layne Staley or Jerry Cantrell.

Against the staccato thunder of the helicopter's rotors and climbing into the darkened sky, the words seemed to create the meaning they had always lacked.

No more light to see by.
All batteries are dead.

TWENTY-ONE

International Space Station
(Expiration of Deadline: 38 Hours / 29 Minutes)

It wasn't quite a dream and wasn't quite a memory.

Sarah's mind wavered in that nameless and borderless country that lies between sleep and wakefulness. Replaying (or reframing) half-forgotten experiences in a realm where the boundaries of conscious and subconscious thought were indistinguishable.

Sarah is nine years old—carrying a breakfast tray up to Mom's room.

A small bowl of oatmeal; two lightly scrambled eggs; half a slice of dry white toast; a few spoonfuls of applesauce. All covered by inverted saucers.

It's hard to know what sights or smells will send Mom into a bout of nausea. Sometimes, even the mention of food can be a trigger. It's getting tougher to make sure she gets enough calories.

At the top of the stairs, Sarah turns the knob slowly, balancing the tray with one hand as she shoulders through the door with the soundless expertise of too much practice.

She's learned that trying to tiptoe doesn't make her steps any quieter. She relies on the carpet to mute the sounds of her bare feet.

Doesn't matter this morning anyway. Mom is awake. She smiles and flicks her eyes sideways toward the chair where Dad is snoring.

Sarah nods and keeps her movements quiet as she folds out the legs of the breakfast tray.

When she leans in close to get the tray settled, Mom gives her a kiss on the cheek. Lips too warm and too dry against Sarah's skin.

"How's my favorite doctor this morning?" Voice more like a croak than a whisper.

Sarah straightens up, puts on a smile that she isn't feeling, and answers in hushed tones. "Fine, Mom. You get any sleep?"

"Some. More than enough for what's on my schedule."

"How about Mr. Droolyface over there?" Sarah asks. "How long has he been out?"

This brings a sigh from Mom. "Couple of hours. When I'm awake, he tries to keep me company."

Sarah glances at her sleeping father. Pale skin; dark bags under his eyes. He doesn't look much better than Mom, but—underneath the worry and the exhaustion—he's strong. Healthy. His body is not a battleground between chemo and cancer.

Sarah feels around in her pocket for the morning pill case. The AM regimen includes Tamoxifen, which tends to bring on Mom's nausea.

Sarah's probably the only kid in fourth grade who knows the word Tamoxifen. Or Abraxane. Or metastatic. Not the kind of words that show up on spelling tests.

"How's your tummy?" she asks. "Think you can eat something?"

Mom tries to hide a shiver of disgust. "I'll try. Maybe some sliced banana?"

Sarah shakes her head. "Got some applesauce. But I can scoot down to the kitchen."

"Applesauce will be fine."

Sarah reaches for the saucer that covers the applesauce.

Mom says something, but another person's voice comes out of her mouth. Male. Muffled, and speaking a different language.

Russian...

Sarah opened her eyes into near darkness and pain.

She had a throbbing headache, but the pounding in her temples couldn't override her instincts as a pilot. Her brain went straight to work orienting itself. Determining her location. Taking stock of the circumstances around her.

Establishing situational awareness.

She was in the Cupola Module and the lights were out.

The only illumination came from the Earth, pale blue light filtering in through the module's round array of windows.

Any other time, Sarah might have taken a second to drink in the magnificent view of the blue-green planet rotating below her. But she wasn't alone in the module and the muffled Russian voice was still talking.

Rutger Braam hovered a few feet away from Sarah, his face battered; one eye swollen almost completely shut. He held a finger to his bruised lips.

"Volkov," he whispered. "Pissed off because Dmitri didn't kill you. Didn't kill us both."

Another muted Russian voice came through the closed hatch. Softer. Farther away.

"Dmitri," whispered Rutger. "He says corpses make lousy hostages."

Volkov said something again—his speech no more than a murmur now.

"Didn't catch that," said Rutger, no longer bothering to whisper. "Something about an airlock."

"Probably wants to shove our asses out the nearest one."

"Could be," said Rutger. "I'm kind of amazed they haven't done that already."

Sarah tried the dogging lever for the hatch. It wouldn't budge—not even when she braced herself against the bulkhead and put some muscle into it. "We're locked in."

Rutger's automatic grin was distorted by the pain it triggered in his damaged face. "I know. It seems they've interpreted your attempt to kill them as an indication that you and I are not altogether trustworthy."

"We're officially off their Christmas card list then?"

"So it would appear," said Rutger. Mention of the holiday brought a quality of unruffled acceptance to his words.

He, like Sarah, had internalized the unspoken truth.

Neither of them would ever see another Christmas.

TWENTY-TWO

White House Situation Room
Washington, DC

(Expiration of Deadline: 36 Hours / 1 Minute)

President Roth walked through the door of the Sit Room, trailed by his Secretary of Defense and National Security Advisor.

The president took his chair at the head of the table and glanced up at a clock with the local time. "In about forty seconds, we'll be halfway to the Russian deadline. What I need you to show me right now is the sneakiest goddamned plan since Hannibal crossed the Alps.

General Christopher pointed a remote at a wall-sized display screen. "I'm not sure we can rise to that level, Mr. President, but we'll give it our best shot."

He thumbed a button and the presidential seal on screen was displaced by an animated diagram. A rendered image of the International Space Station followed an orbit (marked by a circular white line) around a representation of the Earth.

The general nodded toward the display. "A typical Soyuz rendezvous with the ISS takes two days from launch to docking."

On screen, a conical spacecraft arced up from the planet and assumed a lower orbit (marked by a circular red line).

"The vehicle completes thirty-four orbits at lower altitude before executing a Hohmann transfer to match orbits with the Space Station."

On screen, the ISS and spacecraft both circled the globe several times before the Soyuz increased altitude to converge with the station symbol.

"NASA used a similar flight profile back when the shuttle was in service, but the SpaceX Crew Dragons and Boeing Starliners have cut the transit down to about nineteen hours. Significantly shorter, but still allowing time for crew acclimation, vehicle maintenance, and broad safety margins. This has become the established U.S. method for manned missions, and that's why we're not going to follow it."

The spacecraft symbol vanished from the screen and the animation restarted.

"The *Corvus* will utilize a two-orbit approach that's reserved for unmanned supply missions."

On screen, a delta-winged icon rose and circled the Earth only twice before climbing to intercept the ISS."

"Four hours from launch to rendezvous," said the general. "Nobody's ever done that with a manned vehicle. We don't think the Russians will be expecting it."

President Roth raised a finger. "Isn't that kind of ambitious for an untested spacecraft?

"Yes, sir," said the general. "But shorter time of flight means a lower probability of detection. Less time for the Russians to spot the *Corvus* and figure out what we're up to."

The president did not appear to be convinced, but he gestured for the briefing to continue. "All right. Then what?"

"The *Corvus* takes up a parking orbit about ten meters from the ISS and the insertion team makes an EVA crossing to the Quest Airlock."

The display zoomed in on the station. Much enlarged, the spacecraft came to a stop a short distance away. Three space-suited figures appeared and floated across to the airlock.

"That seems like an unnecessary complication," said National

Security Advisor Michael Lazlow. "Why not just dock with the station?"

"The *Corvus* is a proof-of-concept vehicle," said Secretary of Defense Ortiz. "Not equipped for docking."

The general paused for further comments or questions. When none were forthcoming, he continued. "The team infiltrates through the airlock. Once they're inside, Lieutenant Colonel Garrett taps into the Environmental Control and Life-Support System, overrides the atmospheric contamination sensors, and floods the ventilation ducts with a fentanyl-derivative gas. Anyone not wearing a spacesuit or a respirator will experience muscle paralysis within twenty seconds and unconsciousness in under a minute."

Lazlow nodded. "And then?"

"Our team destroys the weapon, at which point the primary objective is complete. Then, they shift to the secondary objective, using the two docked Soyuz spacecraft to return themselves and the hostages to Earth."

"Why not the *Corvus*?" asked the president.

"The *Corvus* can't take five passengers, sir. And it doesn't have enough fuel reserve for the return flight."

"Now for the million-dollar question," said Lazlow. "Is it gonna work?"

"No reason it shouldn't," said the general. "Lieutenant Colonel Garrett and both of our astronauts aboard the ISS are qualified to pilot the Soyuz."

"I'm not talking about the evacuation flight," said Lazlow. "I mean the overall mission concept. Will it work?"

The general was slow to respond. "NASA thinks it's technically feasible..."

President Roth spoke up. "We're not asking NASA. We're asking for your assessment."

General Christopher seemed to choose his words with care. "Given our situational constraints, I think it's our best chance of success. But I'm frankly not comfortable doing anything without a backup plan, Mr. President."

"Neither am I," said the president. He turned toward his Secretary of Defense. "Do we have an aircraft carrier anywhere close to the

Barents Sea?"

Secretary Ortiz nodded. "Yes, sir. The *Abraham Lincoln* Strike Group is steaming off the coast of Norway. They just wrapped up that NATO exercise, Trident Blue."

"Good. If we get them moving right now, how long will it take them to get into the Barents Sea?"

"I'll have to check, sir. If you want a rough guess, I'd say somewhere between six and ten hours."

"Give the order," said the president. "Put the *Lincoln* in the Barents and take us to DEFCON 2."

Secretary Ortiz looked doubtful. "Sir? The Russians are going to see that as a provocation."

"Which is just what we want," said the president. "If it looks like we're sitting on our hands, Polichev is going to get suspicious as hell. So, we do a bit of saber rattling. Give Moscow a little diversion while our guys make a grab for the ISS."

"What if Polichev overreacts?" asked Ortiz. "He might decide to start frying our strategic command and control."

The president looked toward his National Security Advisor. "Then we fall back on Michael's plan. Launch every nuke we've got, while we still can."

TWENTY-THREE

Apogee Launch Systems
Mojave, California
(Expiration of Deadline: 33 Hours / 4 Minutes)

Gil Lawson downed a swig of espresso and stifled his tenth yawn of the morning. Or maybe his twentieth.

Under Gil's droopy-eyed gaze, Lieutenant Colonel Garrett was working elbow-deep in the Oxygen Generation System rack. The guy wasn't bad for an Air Force wonk. Reasonably smart, not a stuffed shirt, and not entirely hopeless around unfamiliar equipment. He also didn't seem to have a problem accepting guidance from someone well below his rank, which also earned him a few points.

Gil watched as Garrett attached jumper wires to the Carbon Dioxide Removal Assembly, the Secondary Particulate Sensor, the Photoionization Detector, the Solid-phase Microextraction Sampler, and a few other strategic points within the rack. The guy almost had the right sequence this time. Not quite there yet, but nearly.

Garrett made a final connection, then pulled back to survey his work. Satisfied with his preparations, he used a hose with quick-release fittings to connect a hexagonal gas canister to a manifold on the air scrubber.

He opened the valve and there was a hiss of flowing gas, almost immediately followed by an alarm siren and flashing tattletales on the rack's status panel.

Garrett dropped his hands. "Shit."

Gil used his coffee cup to motion toward the collection of jumper wires. "Take a close look and tell me what you missed."

Garrett traced the wires with his eyes. "I forgot to bypass the Major Constituent Analyzer?"

Gil yawned as he spoke. "Yep. If you don't cut out the MCA, your gas trips the contamination sensors, announcing to everybody on the station that somebody's dicking with their oxygen supply. About eight seconds after that, you've got pissed-off Russians climbing all over you."

Garrett rubbed the back of his neck. "Right... Let's reset and try it again..."

Gil started disconnecting jumper wires. "Don't worry. You're picking this up fast. Two or three more practice runs and you're gonna have it down pat."

From the observation room, General Byrd watched the training simulator tilting and pitching in its articulated cradle. A repeater screen showed the interior of the *Corvus* simulator cockpit. Paul Keene and Handsome Dan Conway in spacesuits, with a weighted mannequin in the spot where Garrett would ride during the actual flight.

In the rear of the cockpit, three hexagonal gas canisters were strapped into the tight recess between Conway's engineer seat and Garrett's passenger seat.

Unlike the less-than-stellar attempts with Garrett at the controls, the practice flight was going smoothly. Keene really did know how to fly his weird little craft.

Conway's voice came over the speakers. "Burn rate's still a little high. Ease off on the gas pedal there, Mario."

"If you wanna fly this thing, I'll be happy to swap seats with you," said Keene.

"Be nice to arrive with a couple of gallons in the tank," said Conway. He looked over his readouts. "Okay... That's a little better. Whatever you did just now, keep doing it."

"When we do this for real," said Keene, "I'm leaving you at home."

TWENTY-FOUR

Johnson Space Center
Houston, Texas
(Expiration of Deadline: 32 Hours / 23 Minutes)

Director of Flight Operations Irene Harper sat at her desk, leafing through data printouts from the Magnetospheric Multiscale Observation satellites. A spreadsheet nerd in the Office of the Chief Engineer had tweaked the MMO database to isolate emanations from the ISS. Whenever the satellites passed within line-of-sight of the station, the database spat out three and a half reams of electromagnetic observations.

This was the latest batch.

The idea was to search for a precursor power spike or some other signal that the EMP weapon was winding up to fire. To (hopefully) identify an early warning mechanism for purposes of what the military called "enhanced tactical awareness."

Harper wasn't sure how much difference a few seconds—or even a few minutes—of advance warning would make. But it couldn't hurt to develop a better understanding of the technologies the Russians were using. Maybe the MMO data would turn up a weakness in the weapon that could be exploited. Certainly worth checking.

In a bookcase against the far wall, a television was playing with the sound down low. Harper was mostly ignoring it, but every ten or fifteen minutes she'd pick up the remote and do a quick surf through the major news channels.

For now, she was trying to keep her head at least partly in the data.

She had no illusions that she'd be the one to spot an anomaly or whatever. If there was anything useful buried in the columns of figures, it would be ferreted out by one of the math wizards, or by some data analysis tool that ate spreadsheets and plopped out pellets of technical wisdom.

Harper was only bothering with the printouts because Eleanor Moseley was damned well going to ask about them. When that happened, Harper wanted to look the acting Deputy Administrator in the eye and honestly say that she had reviewed the data.

Also—if the United States somehow came through this crisis intact—there would be congressional investigations. When the subpoenas started flying, Harper would likely be asked under oath if she had carefully examined the MMO data.

So, she was forcing herself to go through every page of the printouts, uncomfortably aware that the only useful outcome would be keeping her ass covered against the barbs of bureaucrats and politicians.

She kept at the task until her brain refused to cooperate. When her eyes began wandering off the page, she decided it was time for another break.

Marking her place in the stack of printouts, she picked up the TV remote and started flipping through the news stations.

MSNBC was covering a standing-room-only throng in Saint Peter's Square: thousands of Catholics gathered in Vatican City to hold a prayer vigil for peace. Inspiring, but not particularly informative.

On CBS, FEMA trucks were rolling into the Florida disaster zone carrying food, water, medical teams, and emergency generators. Their progress was clearly being slowed by dead vehicles on the roads leading into the area hit by the EMP.

The top story on ABC was a national wave of panic buying.

Families across America rushing to stock up on food, water, first aid supplies, and—for the segment of the population that was so inclined—ammunition. The commentary of the news anchor ran over B-roll footage of emptying supermarket shelves: frightened shoppers scuffling to grab as many of the dwindling canned goods as possible.

CNN was following a special session of the United Nations General Assembly. The French Ambassador to the UN was on her feet, gesticulating dramatically, demanding guarantees of peaceful intent from her Russian counterpart.

The camera cut to the Russian UN Ambassador, whose facial expression and body language made it clear that he wasn't remotely concerned with anything the General Assembly might do or say. He was a man going through the motions of a ritual that had lost all significance.

Harper had seen that expression before, but never in public, and only on the faces of politicians who had you backed into a corner and wanted you to know it.

After centuries of false starts and failed attempts at empire-building, Russia was about to have dominion over the entire planet. Their ambassador to the United Nations didn't give a rat's ass about the impotent posturing of his colleagues.

The recognition of this simple fact was more chilling to Irene Harper than anything that had happened yet. For the first time, she wondered whether she might be looking at the last days of America.

At the bottom of her television screen—wedged between the ticker and the CNN logo—the network's clever animated doomsday clock continued to count backward toward zero.

TWENTY-FIVE

Common Defense – Firearms & Accessories
Sunbury, Nevada
(Expiration of Deadline: 30 Hours / 27 Minutes)

They were lined up outside the store. More customers than Jeff Tucker had ever seen. Seemed like fifty of them out there, down the sidewalk and milling around the parking lot, waiting their turns to come inside.

He thought about bending his "four on the floor" rule that limited the store to four customers at a time. Some of the folks out there would get tired of waiting and leave. Jeff hated to lose potential customers, but four was about as many as he and Charlie could keep an eye on at one time.

Usually, most of his patrons were people he knew, by sight if not by name. But not a single face in this crowd looked familiar. A whole bunch of strangers, all trying to get their hands on guns and ammo in a big goddamned hurry.

Jeff wondered how many of these yahoos knew how to shoot, or—for that matter—how many could load and unload without blowing their toes off. He also wondered how many of them were from California. Idiots coming across the state line to grab some guns because Nevada didn't have a ridiculous ten-day waiting period.

He couldn't sell to anybody without Nevada ID, so the Californiacs were shit out of luck. And it was their own damned fault. That was what they got for voting Democrat, paying taxes in a state that didn't respect the constitutional right to bear arms.

If the Russkies really were going to zap the living shit out of America day after tomorrow, even a three-day waiting period would be too long to do the Californiacs any good. That was assuming there was any truth behind that countdown-to-doomsday crap on the TV.

But a lot of these boys (and Jeff didn't see any girls out there) had Nevada IDs because the cash register was hopping, and the shelves were starting to empty out. If things kept going like this, the store would run out of stock before closing time.

The thought of bare shelves brought him up short.

What if this Russian thing wasn't just another hoax by the liberal media, like global warming or that made-up virus? What if the lights *were* going to go out in just a little over thirty hours?

This latest scare was probably just another tempest in a teapot, but what if it wasn't? Could he afford to take that chance?

If the news was telling the truth for once, then all the money he was taking in right now would become worthless paper by about bedtime tomorrow night. The only real currency would be things of actual value, like canned food and water. Or guns and ammunition.

The idea took root in his mind and grew so quickly that it shoved everything else out of the way.

All four customers were browsing the cases right now, so no one was at the counter. Jeff leaned over toward Charlie and whispered, "Go lock the door."

Charlie looked around in surprise. "What?"

"Keep your voice down," said Jeff. "Go lock the door and turn the sign around. We're closing up shop."

Obviously puzzled by the order, Charlie nodded toward the people lined up outside the barred windows of the store. "What do we tell those folks?"

"We tell 'em the computer is down and we can't run background checks."

"They're gonna believe that?"

Jeff groped under the counter, found the power cord for the computer monitor, and jerked it from the outlet. The screen went dark. "*There*. It's down."

"What the hell are you doing?" whispered Charlie.

"I'll explain it to you later," Jeff said softly.

He raised his voice so that the four shoppers could hear him. "Can I have your attention, folks? Sorry, but the computer just died on us. We can't run background checks, so we can't sell you anything."

He didn't expect them to be happy with the announcement, and they weren't. They all started to complain at once, but he held up one hand and raised his voice even further.

"We're just as disappointed as you are. I'm not a man who likes turning away business. But the law is the law, and we can't sell weapons or ammunition when the computer is down. We're closing up, now. I need you to make your way to the door."

Charlie was doing a lousy job of hiding his confusion. "You really wanna do this, Boss?"

Jeff didn't answer.

He didn't know why the Russian space ray suddenly seemed like a real possibility to him.

But he was picturing what life might be like in two days, when electric lights didn't come on with the flip of a switch and clean water didn't flow freely when you twisted a tap handle.

An existence without phones, cars, airplanes, or even trains. Where sheriff's deputies didn't come barreling up in their hot rod Dodge Chargers to arrest looters or keep the peace. A country where ninety percent of the population wouldn't know how to feed itself after the grocery stores ran out of sliced ham and Twinkies.

How long would it take for civil order to break down completely? How long before your neighbors would be ready to cut your throat for a can of Del Monte peaches?

A man would have to be ready to defend home and family. To protect what was his. And the stock on the shelves in his little shop would be worth more than all the gold in Fort Knox.

TWENTY-SIX

National Reconnaissance Office Headquarters
(Expiration of Deadline: 30 Hours / 2 Minutes)

This was not how Maya had pictured things.

The scenario had gamed out two different ways in her imagination. Either the muckety-mucks would shut down her idea (the most likely possibility), or they'd give her the go-ahead; she'd issue the requisite maneuver commands and then monitor the intercept event from the privacy of her operator station.

In hindsight, she should have realized that using a two-billion-dollar satellite for a kamikaze attack was bound to get political. She'd been so focused on the basic craziness of the idea that she hadn't factored politics into her thinking.

As a rule, the higher-ups tended to maintain a safe distance from risky projects, right up until the instant of success. (After which, the orphaned plan—whatever it happened to be—would suddenly have thirty parents, all of whom had been nurturing it from the moment of inception.)

So, Maya had expected to be left in relative isolation until the outcome was known, at which point the people above her would either rush in to claim a share of victory or put still more distance between themselves and defeat.

She'd never imagined any scenario that involved her supervisor hovering over one shoulder, the Director of the NRO hanging over the other shoulder, and the President of the United States and his National Security Advisor piped to a side display by encrypted video link.

Maya kept her attention on the readouts for Keyhole satellite K108 as it continued its charge toward the International Space Station.

"How's it looking?" asked the president from the screen.

Before Maya could respond, the NRO Director spoke up. "On track, Mr. President. K108's trajectory is nominal."

Yeah. Like Mr. Harvard-Necktie had the foggiest idea of how to read the satellite's motion in relation to the ISS.

Probably, the guy was watching CALI's graphic display, crossing his toes that the red track lines and '*COLLISION WARNING!*' alerts were omens of impending success.

Maybe they were.

K108 was right on the dime, as tight to the predicted profile as anything Maya had ever seen.

When the bump came, it was going to be epic. Spectacular. In addition to the devastating mechanical damage, the force of the impact would generate several hundred (or several thousand) megajoules of raw heat. Like a miniature sun.

Too bad the intercept would occur over Eastern Europe. People on the ground were going to get a hell of a show.

"When this baby hits eighty-eight miles per hour," said Maya under her breath, "you're gonna see some serious shit."

The NRO Director leaned forward. "What was that?"

Maya kept her eyes on the callouts. "Impact in five seconds, sir."

Low Earth Orbit

K108 shot forward at many times the speed of a bullet. With a 3.4-meter primary mirror and image processing capabilities so specialized that even the name of the technology was classified, the satellite had been engineered as an all-seeing eye in the sky. An electro-optical crystal ball for the American intelligence community, revealing secrets that adversaries of the United States went to extreme lengths to conceal.

Its designers had never considered the possibility that their multibillion-dollar masterpiece of surveillance hardware would be employed as a hypervelocity battering ram.

In the far distance, the ISS appeared as a speck of light, getting brighter and larger with almost unimaginable speed. Converging on the same physical location that K108 was about to occupy.

If K108's miraculous optics had been functioning, the satellite would have seen the weird Rube Goldberg contraption of the International Space Station expand from the size of a toy to an enormous piece of infrastructure in an interval of time shorter than the blink of a human eye.

Satellite and station came together, arriving at the same spatial coordinates simultaneously. If K108 had been a foot closer to the main structural truss, the hoped-for cataclysm would have occurred right on schedule.

The satellite threaded the needle between the solar arrays of the P3 and S3 Trusses. For a fraction of a second, K108 was surrounded on three sides by components of the station, coming within inches, but never quite touching any of them. Its massive form shot through the opening like an oversize football going through the uprights of a goalpost.

Then, K108 was past, continuing its plunge into the gravity well of Earth.

National Reconnaissance Office

On Maya's CALI screen, the icons for K108 and the ISS diverged, each following its own path, their curved orbit lines flicking from red to green.

Maya studied the callout boxes in disbelief. "We missed!"

The Director of the NRO repeated her words, changing the statement to a question, and altering the pronoun that threatened to associate him with the failure. "It missed?"

On the teleconference screen, President Roth lowered his head and breathed a sigh heavy with disappointment.

Low Earth Orbit

K108 fell into the thickening atmosphere of the planet below.

The satellite had no heat shield and no thermal ablative coatings. It lacked the conical shape and weight distribution to support the blunt-body gas flow that might have carried away the scorching heat of reentry.

The heat load spiraled to twice the melting temperature of steel. Outer fixtures and skin peeled away in fiery showers of molten metal as the disintegrating machine burned across the night skies of Eastern Europe.

Moscow

From his guard post atop the crenelated wall of the Kremlin, Corporal Rykov shifted the strap of his rifle into a more comfortable position on his shoulder.

Down in Red Square, behind crowd control barriers, protesters waved signs and chanted slogans. Some of them shouted for peace, others for world domination. As long as they stayed on the proper side of the barriers, those *svolochi* could protest until their asses fell off.

A streak of light appeared in the sky. Rykov had no way of knowing that he was witnessing the destruction of an American spy satellite.

He nudged his buddy and jabbed a finger toward the sky. "Aleksei! It's a falling star! Make a wish!"

Aleksei scratched his neck and didn't look up. "I wish... for this shit to be over."

TWENTY-SEVEN

International Space Station
(Expiration of Deadline: 29 Hours / 14 Minutes)

Rutger was sleeping. His body lolled like a jellyfish in the darkened air of the Cupola Module, his posture formless in a way that was only possible in microgravity. Even in the feeble earthlight coming through the windows, the swellings and contusions of the astronaut's recent beating were visible on his face.

Sarah was putting that dim light source to use—examining the module one inch at a time. Going over every cable run, pipe, junction box, and fastener. Searching for any device or feature that she and Rutger might use to escape or to gain an advantage. She didn't expect to turn up anything useful, but she had to check.

Her back was to the hatch when the dogging wedges retracted with a dull clang. She turned to see the hatch swing open.

Anya Malikova floated in the hatchway, backlit by the lighted node behind her.

Acclimated to the dark now, Sarah had to squint and blink to look toward the light.

Anya held one of the overamped Tasers at the ready, her once-friendly eyes hardened with mistrust. For a moment, she looked like a stranger—the soldier of some conquering army. Then, she took in

Rutger's ravaged features, and her expression softened a little. "He's okay?"

"A little bruised," Sarah said, "but he'll be all right."

Anya nodded and started to shut the hatch.

Sarah reached out and stopped it from swinging closed. Gently. Not wrestling for control, just signaling a request to leave it open for a few seconds more.

"I told you about flying with my dad, right?"

Anya's voice was tinged with suspicion, but not overtly hostile. "More rudder, less stick..."

Sarah let the corners of her lips come up in the barest suggestion of a smile. "At least a thousand times. More rudder, less stick. Even after I could fly that old trainer as well as he could. And I always gave him the same response. 'Dad, I know what I'm doing.'"

The Taser in Anya's hand remained steady. "Your point *is*?"

"He kept telling me what to do, long after I quit listening to his instincts and started paying attention to my own."

Anya's answering smile was slow in coming, even more understated than Sarah's. "If you stop following your father's advice, no one shoots you for treason."

"True," said Sarah, "but there's more than one kind of treason."

Anya was starting to close the hatch when she noticed a small dark object tumbling slowly toward her. She stopped with the hatch partway open when she recognized the shape.

She plucked it out of the air. It was a chess piece. The black queen.

"You gave her to me," Rutger muttered, voice still logy with sleep.

Anya looked past Sarah to the newly awakened Dutchman. "What?"

"You left your queen undefended," Rutger said. "Didn't even make an effort to protect her."

"I didn't see your bishop..." said Anya.

"You saw it all right," said Rutger. "I don't think you wanted to win."

The Russian cosmonaut was about to respond when the illumination in the module behind her dimmed.

"Son of a bitch!" said Sarah. "They just fired that thing again, didn't they?"

Anya flicked the black queen back into the cupola and closed the hatch. The dogs slammed into place, leaving Sarah and Rutger in darkness.

TWENTY-EIGHT

USS Abraham Lincoln
Barents Sea
(Expiration of Deadline: 29 Hours / 1 Minute)

Following the lighted wands of a yellow-shirted flight deck crew member, Lieutenant Rob Monkman (call sign Monk) taxied his F/A-18E *Super Hornet* into position on the carrier's number two catapult. His stomach heaved uneasily with every pitch and roll of the ship beneath him.

The seas were a rollercoaster tonight, and the near gale force winds peppered his canopy with sleet. He was quietly grateful that he couldn't see the massive waves swelling and subsiding out beyond the throw of the amber deck lights.

A green shirt ran forward with the holdback assembly—disappearing below the rim of Monk's canopy to slot the launch bar of the warplane's nose gear into the catapult shuttle and lock the holdback into place.

Monk felt sorry for the flight deck personnel, working out there in the freezing chaos that passed for weather in this part of the world. He tried to keep his thoughts on the choreographic precision of their efforts. Every step executed with the expertise of long practice.

It was intentional self-distraction, and he'd relied on the technique more than once to keep his mind from focusing on his fear.

Night carrier landings were legendarily terrifying. A surprisingly large number of otherwise excellent pilots couldn't wrap their heads around trying to hit the minuscule sweet spot of a rolling steel deck in the dark. Even pilots who'd done it a hundred times were not immune to the knowledge that the *next* night landing could kill them.

Night landings were scary as hell, but—for Monk—a night launch in heavy seas was worse.

Up forward, in his recessed blister between the two bow cats, the "Shooter" would be watching the waves. Trying to time his signal for a moment when the deck was facing downward into a trough, so the bow would be on the rise when Monk reached the end of the catapult stroke and shot into the air.

If the Shooter timed it right, Monk's angle of launch would take him upward, away from the rolling dark mass of the sea. Into the sky, where he could depend on his reflexes and skills to keep himself alive.

If the Shooter's timing was bad, Monk's landing gear could clip the crest of an enormous riser. His *Hornet* would become 55,000 pounds of disintegrating junk, scattering itself over the wave tops.

Good luck ejecting out of that shit.

Task complete, the green shirt reemerged from beneath the nose of Monk's aircraft and retreated behind the red and white striped "shot" line on the deck.

The yellow shirt gave a final visual inspection, looking up and down the length of the catapult track. Then, he or she (between the cranial helmet, ear protection, goggles, and the darkness, Monk couldn't tell which) gave the "take-tension" signal, left hand and wand pointing upward, right hand and wand pointing toward the bow of the ship.

In response, Monk pushed his throttle to "military power." The roar of his engines increased in pitch and his *Hornet* strained forward against the holdback.

With his right hand, he cycled the stick, moving all control surfaces on the plane through their full ranges of motion. A final check that his aircraft was flight-ready.

He was seconds from launch now. The deferred fear exerted itself—rushing over him like a tsunami in a desperate attempt to prevent him from doing something insanely dangerous (like hurtling down the pitching deck of an aircraft carrier into the frozen night).

As always, Monk fought down that familiar swell of terror. Left hand still on the throttle, he wrapped his pinky around the switch that would toggle the plane's exterior lights.

It was too dark in the cockpit for the deck personnel to see Monk's hand salute, so the nighttime equivalent of the ready-to-launch signal would be his lights flicking on.

He squeezed the switch, but his exterior lights didn't flash to life.

Instead, everything went dark.

The green glows of the HUD and his instrument lamps went black. Outside his aircraft, the deck edge lights winked off, along with the sodium vapor stadium lights mounted on the carrier's island, the ship's running lights, and every other source of manmade illumination within visual range.

It all went black at the same time. Like someone had pulled the plug on his plane, the ship, and everything else.

The *Hornet's* twin F414-GE-400 turbofans continued to spin, the compression/combustion cycle self-sustaining without the need for electronics, drawing JP5 from the fuel tanks by a capillary feed system with no electrical components.

Like many military aircraft, the F/A-18E had mechanical backups for all flight controls. Cables, pulleys, and linkages to operate the throttles, manipulate the control surfaces, and keep the plane flying in the event of catastrophic electrical failure. Deprived of its electronic gizmos, the *Hornet* would not fall out of the sky like most civilian aircraft.

But there was no way to get Monk's plane into the air now. The *Lincoln's* catapult system was actuated by a series of electrical solenoid valves. If main electrical power was down throughout the ship—as it appeared to be—the catapult would be dead.

Even if the cat was still functional, and the Shooter gave Monk the signal, and Monk could somehow see that gesture in the darkness, he'd be launching blind.

No radio. No radar. No instruments. Not so much as a glow-in-the-dark compass to navigate by.

He throttled down his engines. He wasn't going anywhere anytime soon.

It would be several hours before he understood how accurate that passing thought had been.

White House Situation Room
Washington, DC

General Christopher was leafing through a force readiness report when it happened. A brief burst of static, then all radio chatter from the *Abraham Lincoln* Strike Group chopped off in mid-word. The aircraft carrier, her jets, helos, escort ships, and drones all ceased communicating at the exact same instant.

One of the wall-sized video screens was dedicated to a geographic display of the Barents Sea, overlaid with color-coded tactical symbols representing the ships, aircraft, and sensors of the strike group. Every symbol in the area blipped out and was replaced by a last-known-position marker.

The continuous background babble of the warship formation gave way to a silence so abrupt that it was jarring.

Christopher looked up from his report folder. "Did we just trip a circuit breaker or something?"

A Sit Room technician scrambled to check her equipment. After a quick half-minute of diagnostics, she shook her head. "Negative, sir. It's not our gear. The problem's on the other end."

An Air Force lieutenant tapped a flurry of commands into a satellite operator console. "Sir, ELINT is reporting loss of all electronic emissions from the *Lincoln* Strike Group. Every shipboard and airborne radar in the formation stopped transmitting about forty seconds ago."

Christopher was digesting the news when the Signals Office

reported an incoming call from the NASA Director of Flight Operations.

The general accepted the phone. "I already know what she's gonna tell me," he said. "The Russians have fired their goddamned weapon again."

USS Abraham Lincoln

The origin of the term "SCRAM" is a matter of debate.

According to historian Tom Wellock of the Nuclear Regulatory Commission, the most likely source is the English slang word for departing quickly and urgently. Other researchers into the history of nuclear power insist that SCRAM is an acronym for "Safety Control Rods Activation Mechanism" or "Safety Control Rod Actuator Mechanism," but the etymological evidence for both alternatives is slim.

Modern folklore attributes SCRAM to Enrico Fermi, who supposedly coined it when the world's first nuclear reactor was built under the west viewing stands at the University of Chicago's Stagg Field. Legend suggests that a graphite control rod dangled above that first reactor at the end of a rope, with a "Safety Control Rod Axe Man" stationed nearby to chop through the rope if the nuclear core went out of control.

Regardless of the term's origin, both of USS *Abraham Lincoln's* nuclear reactors SCRAMed automatically. When electrical current was cut off by the EMP surge, a cluster of neutron-absorbing control rods slammed down into the core of each reactor, terminating the fission reaction, and shutting the reactors down.

As an emergency safety precaution, the SCRAM mechanism performed flawlessly. There were no meltdowns, no explosions, and no release of lethal radiation.

Nor was there any power. The ship's electrical systems were dead, and—with the reactors down—there was no steam to drive the turbine engines.

Without electricity, the aircraft carrier had become a warren of unlit compartments and passageways, as black as the depths of any mineshaft. Stygian darkness relieved only by the feeble glow of luminescent markings on damage control stations, First Aid boxes, and selected safety gear.

Like all U.S. Navy vessels, USS *Abraham Lincoln* was equipped with hundreds of relay-operated battle lanterns—powered by batteries and built to activate when the electricity failed. But the relay circuits in each lantern contained electronic components that had been destroyed by the pulse.

The ship's emergency diesel generators were out of action for the same reason. Mechanical components were unharmed, but the control circuits were fried.

Every other vessel in the aircraft carrier's defensive screen formation was just as dark and just as powerless. The once-fearsome warships could not fight, maneuver, or even send out a distress call.

In less than a millisecond, one of the most powerful military forces on the planet had been reduced to a collection of metal cans wallowing helplessly on the waves.

TWENTY-NINE

Apogee Launch Systems
Mojave, California
(Expiration of Deadline: 22 Hours / 57 Minutes)

Elbow-deep in the Oxygen Generation System rack, Floyd Garrett attached a jumper lead between the Low Voltage Power Supply and the Mass Spectrometer Assembly of the Major Constituent Analyzer.

Slumped in a chair next to the rack, Gil Lawson was snoring loudly and beginning to drool.

Garrett went back over his work, tracing the various jumpers by eye. When he was sure that he'd carried out all the required steps, he connected a hose from a hexagonal gas canister to the piping manifold on the air scrubber.

He turned the valve on the top of the canister. "Here goes nothing..."

There was a whisper of gas flowing from the canister into the system, followed by... nothing.

Silence.

No alarms.

No flashing lights.

Garrett reached out with one foot and nudged Gil's ankle.

The young engineer emitted an explosive snort and came awake with a jerk that nearly landed him on the floor. "Hurrrr... What? *What?*"

Without speaking, Garrett pointed to the equipment rack.

Gil lurched out of the chair and tried to focus his eyes and his brain. He studied the hoses and wiring with growing approval.

When his inspection was complete, he fist-bumped Garrett on the shoulder—nearly missing. "And they told me you Air Force types couldn't be trained!"

He rubbed his eyes and continued evaluating the rig. "One canister should give you adequate concentration and dispersal of your agent..."

He yawned. "...but you might want to carry an extra, just in case."

"Mission parameters call for *two* backup canisters," said Garrett.

"Two is overkill. You don't want to waste delta-v hauling unnecessary mass. I can have a word with your mission planners..."

Garrett started disconnecting hoses and wires, preparing for another run-through. "Thanks. I'll pass your advice up the chain."

Gil paused for a second—clearly not ready to let the matter drop. Then, he shrugged. "Okay... I guess we do it again."

THIRTY

**White House
Washington, DC**
(Expiration of Deadline: 22 Hours / 15 Minutes)

The door opened and a deputy from the National Security Council ushered the Chinese Ambassador into the Oval Office.

The deputy stopped a respectful distance from the president and made her announcement. "Mr. President, may I present Ambassador Shaozu Tian, minister plenipotentiary of the People's Republic of China?"

President Roth smiled and stepped forward to shake the ambassador's hand. "Good evening, Ambassador, and welcome. It's a pleasure to have you in the White House again."

The ambassador returned the handshake and the smile. "Good evening to you, Mr. President. I bring good wishes and messages of solidarity on behalf of the People's Republic of China."

He released the president's grip and turned to shake hands with the White House Chief of Staff. "Mr. Forrester, I understand I have you to thank for helping me circumvent the usual State Department channels."

Clayton Forrester nodded. "Your Deputy Chief of Mission informs me that your business is urgent."

"And so it is," said the ambassador. "So it is."

The president walked to the rectangle of sofas and chairs opposite his desk. He settled into a chair and motioned for Forrester and Shaozu to take seats. "Then, let's not waste time," he said. "What can we do for you, Ambassador?"

"It is I who can do something for you, sir. Or rather, my country can."

"I'm listening," said the president.

Shaozu looked at the famous Seymour grandfather clock standing to the right of the fireplace. "Your deadline with the Russians expires in just over twenty-two hours." He lowered his voice. "Are you considering a preemptive nuclear strike?"

The president's answer was not immediate. "We are... studying a number of alternatives."

"Of course. But my government has trouble accepting that the United States will surrender its most powerful strategic weapons to a hostile foreign power without a fight."

"I have to admit; it's not an attractive option," said the president.

This brought a nod from the ambassador. "My country finds the idea equally unappealing. If you decide on a preemptive strike—"

The president cut him off. "We're not prepared to discuss that."

"I understand your reluctance," said the ambassador. "Our countries have not been traditional military allies and there are issues of trust between your government and mine. However, if I may borrow an aphorism from Hippocrates, 'extreme diseases often require extreme remedies.'"

President Roth showed the faintest ghost of a smile. "In America, we say that desperate times call for desperate measures."

The ambassador nodded. "These are most assuredly desperate times. I've been instructed to assure you that the People's Republic will stand with the United States in the unhappy event that a preemptive nuclear attack cannot be avoided."

There were several seconds of silence, which Forrester finally broke. "You're proposing a counter-ultimatum? Russia backs down, or both of our countries hit them with *everything*?"

The Chinese Ambassador shook his head. "Polichev will not back down. And it would be a mistake to broadcast our intentions. If we take joint action, it should be a decapitating nuclear strike. No diplomacy. No negotiations. No warning."

"Now, just a second," said Forrester. "We're not going to—"

The president motioned for silence. "Let's not take any options off the table."

He made eye contact with the ambassador. "If I agree to this, how much time do you need?"

Shaozu didn't seem to understand the question.

The president continued. "Many of your long-range missiles are truck-mounted. They have to be moved into firing positions and fueled. How long will it take you to prepare for launch?"

A tiny crease appeared on the ambassador's forehead. "I'm not at liberty to disclose technical details of my country's strategic assets."

"This is no time to be coy," said the president. "You can't expect me to coordinate a strike if I don't know how much time you need to prepare."

The ambassador considered this and then nodded. "Two hours. Our quick-reaction assets can be ready in a few minutes, but—as you say—some of our high-yield missiles will need to be fueled and positioned."

"All right then," said the president. "If I decide to launch against Russia, you'll get two hours of notice."

Forrester stared at his president. "Sir, I can't believe we're even *talking* about this."

"I share your distaste for the subject," Ambassador Shaozu said. "But this Russian device is not just a weapon, Mr. Forrester. It's the off switch for civilization. And a nuclear strike—as terrible as that prospect seems—may turn out to be the least dark of our possible futures."

THIRTY-ONE

Apogee Launch Systems
Mojave, California
(Expiration of Deadline: 21 Hours / 29 Minutes)

"Please tell me you know where my hotel is," yawned Gil Lawson, "because I've got no earthly idea." The last part came out so heavy with fatigue that it was barely recognizable as speech.

The sergeant (Whidbey by the name tape on his cammies) held up a phone and pointed to the screen. "Says here you're booked at the Best Western Desert Winds. A little short of five stars, but probably as good as you're going to find around here."

Gil nodded blearily. "I don't care if it's a Motel 6. If I don't lie down pretty soon, I'm going to fall down."

Whidbey used a key fob to unlock the doors of a dark blue Chevy Suburban. "Well, good news for you, Cinderella. Your coach has arrived."

He climbed into the driver seat.

Gil poured his enervated form into the passenger's side and groped for the lever to recline the seat. He was lying as close to horizontal as the seat would allow when the SUV rolled out of Apogee's front gate.

Looking up through the windows into the late afternoon sky, he

154

caught sight of a dark bird silhouetted against the clouds. He would have paid the creature no attention, but it came to a stop and hovered in place. Not a mode of flight you expected to see from your average bird.

Gil groped again for the seat lever, bringing himself back to an upright position. "Stop the car!"

Whidbey glanced sideways at him. "What? You forget something?"

Gil was fully awake now. "Stop the car! Right here!"

Sergeant Whidbey did as ordered, braking the Suburban to a halt in the right-hand lane of State Route 58.

Gil fumbled for the door handle and stumbled out into the street.

"What's wrong?" asked Whidbey.

There it was, cruising above the Apogee hangar building. Not a bird. A drone. Gil thought he could hear the faint insectile buzz of its rotors.

Some type of quadcopter, by the looks of it. Whatever kind it was, the thing had a camera.

Gil fished for his iPhone and flicked through to the camera icon. He swung the phone up, sweeping and searching until he had the drone on his screen.

There was something meta about that: using a digital recording device to record the actions of another digital recording device.

Whidbey leaned over in his seat and called through the open door. "Mind telling me what we're doing?"

Gil concentrated on keeping the drone on his camera screen. "Either Apogee has got nosy neighbors, or we're being surveilled. Get on the phone and call whoever it is you report to."

Two seconds later, he hustled back into the SUV and slammed the door shut. "It's leaving! Forget the call; follow the drone!"

Whidbey shifted into Drive but kept his foot on the brake. "What drone?"

"Never mind," said Gil. "Just drive where I tell you!"

The Suburban started rolling. "Say the word..."

Gil hit the power window button and stuck his head out of the vehicle, craning his neck to look behind the Suburban. "Make a U-turn. Do it now!"

After a quick mirror check, Whidbey hauled the steering wheel hard to the left. The tight turning radius brought a squeal from the tires. "If I get a ticket for this—"

"Don't worry about tickets," said Gil, his head swiveling around as the SUV changed directions. "Slow down a little."

The Space Force man did as instructed.

"Okay," Gil said, "left lane."

"You've been awake like thirty-six hours. Are you sure you're not imagining...?"

"Left lane!" yelled Gil.

Whidbey swerved into the left lane.

Gil banged the side of his fist on the door. "Goddamn it! I lost it!"

He climbed farther out the window, tugging against the seatbelt that held him in place. "Where is it?"

Except for clouds and contrails from a high-flying airliner, the sky was empty.

Gil kept looking, moving his head around so violently that he nearly injured his neck.

He was starting to wonder if the drone really *had* been a hallucination, when he spotted it again. "Okay! Yeah! Get ready to turn left."

"That's a parking lot," said Whidbey.

"Now! Left turn!"

Whidbey veered off the highway into a large parking lot. Mostly empty now, toward the end of the workday.

"Straight," said Gil.

"I can't! There's like curbs..."

"Straight!" shouted Gil.

The front wheels hit the ten-inch-high concrete parking divider at about twenty miles an hour. Gil and Whidbey bounced hard in their seats, then the heavy front end of the Suburban took a nosedive on its suspension as the rear wheels bumped over the barrier.

"I'm not paying for this," said Whidbey.

"Just drive!"

"Here comes another one!"

They jackrabbited over a second concrete divider, and only the seatbelt kept Gil from being catapulted out the window.

"Go right!"

Whidbey yanked the wheel around. An ominous scraping sound came from under the left fender well.

"Excellent," said Gil. "Drive right up to the fence. Hurry!"

The Suburban leaped forward, and Whidbey braked just short of the tall chain-link fence, stopping with the front bumper just inches from a fencepole.

Gil was out of the vehicle almost before it stopped moving. Scrambling up onto the hood, where it took him a couple of seconds to stagger to his feet.

He could see the drone coming down near a side street about eighty feet away. The guy operating the controller was easy to spot because he was wearing VR goggles. Seeing the world through the camera lens of the drone.

There was a woman too, both people standing near a silver beat-to-shit Hyundai. Ten years old or more and showing its age.

Gil zoomed in on the pair and their car, then panned to the rear license plate. Got it! He had the number, easily readable in the iPhone recording.

The woman had spotted him. She was tapping the drone operator on the shoulder, pointing toward Gil and the Suburban.

Within thirty seconds the drone had been tossed into the backseat, and the Hyundai was doing its best to roar away on its shitty little underpowered engine.

Let them go. That was fine. Gil had what he needed.

He hopped down to the ground, tweaking his right ankle when his exhausted body didn't adjust to the impact well.

He limped to the open passenger door and pulled himself painfully into his seat. "Back to Apogee."

"What about your hotel?"

Gil sighed. He would have given a week's pay for two hours of uninterrupted sleep. "Apogee," he said reluctantly. "The hotel will have to wait."

Five minutes later, Gil was standing before the desk that General Byrd had commandeered.

The general looked up from a stack of papers. "Mr. Lawson? I'd have bet ten dollars that you'd be comatose by now."

"I wish," said Gil. "I've been clinically dead for the last hour and a half, but that's not the big problem."

"You have something bigger than Darth Polichev's Death Star hovering overhead?"

"Same general ballpark," said Gil. "We're going to need one of your Military Police, or maybe some kind of federal agent. Somebody with access to the California DMV database and the power to make arrests."

The general shoved the paperwork aside. "Arrests? What in God's name are you talking about?"

Gil leaned on the desk for support. He was getting dangerously close to falling down. "We just got overflown by a drone. Somebody is shooting video of this place."

"Surveillance?"

"That, or something like it," said Gil.

General Byrd's features clouded. "The Russians are on to us."

"I don't think so," Gil said. "Looked like locals to me."

"And you want to arrest them?"

"I'm hoping we won't have to. But we need to know who they are and what they're trying to do. We may have to lock them up for a few days, until the *Corvus* mission is over. Maybe it won't come to that, but we've got to be ready."

Byrd pulled out a phone and selected a number from his speed dialer. "Billy, this is Hiram. I need to borrow one of your DCIS agents. Somebody who can get out to Mojave pretty damned quick."

"By the way..." said Gil softly. "I think I trashed the suspension on one of your SUVs."

The general pulled the phone away from his ear. "What was that?"

"Nothing," said Gil. "I'll tell you later."

THIRTY-TWO

Imperial County Medical Center
El Centro, California
(Expiration of Deadline: 20 Hours / 31 Minutes)

Six-thirty on a Wednesday evening and the Emergency Department waiting room was still overflowing. All fourteen chairs were filled, and sixteen people were standing along the walls or sitting on the floor.

Seated behind the Plexiglas sneeze guard of the Admissions desk, Shanice Tillman scrolled down the list of symptoms in her triage queue.

Chest pains. Chest pains. Nausea. Heart palpitations. Diarrhea and nausea. Shortness of breath. Chest pains. Blunt force trauma to humerus with possible fracture. Nausea. Second-degree burn. Dizziness. Chest pains. Migraine. Heart palpitations. Shortness of breath.

A few of the non-injury ailments would turn out to have actual medical etiologies, but a lot of them were going to be psychosomatic. The human body had many ways of physically expressing anxiety, and a surprising number of the symptoms could resemble indicators for a heart attack.

The hard part wasn't identifying the real cardiac victims. Doctors could separate the sheep from the goats with ECGs and lab tests for troponin I, troponin T, and creatine kinase (the cardiac enzymes). The tricky part was convincing the hypochondria cases that they weren't on the verge of myocardial infarction, or a massive stroke, or Dragon Pox, or something equally dire.

It wasn't fair to think of them as hypochondriacs. Most of these people didn't spend their lives in repeating cycles of self-diagnosis for imaginary medical conditions. These were not chronic snifflers, who compulsively scoured the web for lists of symptoms that they could match with their illusory disorders.

These people were just afraid, and their terrors were manifesting as pain and physical ailments.

Shanice had been a nurse trainee at El Centro Regional ten or twelve years back, when the big earthquake had hit. There'd been almost no physical injuries, but the Emergency Department had been swamped for three days. A hospital that usually saw a hundred emergency cases in a twenty-four-hour period had evaluated and treated more than four hundred patients in less than twelve hours.

Shanice had been on that shift. Nearly all the incoming cases had been anxiety attacks presenting as chest pains, shortness of breath, and all the same things that were showing up in her triage queue right now.

You couldn't blame people for being afraid. Shanice was about as scared as she had ever been in her life.

And the current situation was nothing like the earthquake. This wasn't a single traumatic event that would disappear into memory with the passage of time. If the doomsayers on the news weren't talking out of their sphincters, technological civilization itself could disappear before this time tomorrow evening. Not from the world, perhaps, but certainly from the United States. (America *was* the world as far as most of these people were concerned.)

CNN kept replaying the quote from that scientist on the Senate EMP Task Force, or whatever it was called. The one about how ten percent of the U.S. population could be expected to survive the first year without electrical power.

People had every reason to be afraid. Terrified even. If the Russians carried through with their threat, something like three hundred million Americans were going to die over the next twelve months.

A country with a third of a billion people couldn't feed itself without mechanized agriculture, high-speed transportation, and communication. If that wasn't cause for panic, Shanice didn't know what was.

As she looked up from her triage screen, a new patient—young, early-twenties by the look of him—made his way to the Admissions desk. He moved with the cautious shuffle of a man three or four times his age. Like every step took something out of him.

"How can I help you?" Shanice asked.

"I'm having like... chest pains," said the man.

Yeah, thought Shanice. *Aren't we all?*

THIRTY-THREE

Green River Gardens
California City, California
(Expiration of Deadline: 19 Hours / 40 Minutes)

The door opened and Papa Nick stood in the entrance to Amy's closet studio. His careworn face was as kindly as ever, but there was an unfamiliar concern in his eyes.

"Don't like to interrupt you when you're working on the show," he said, "but there are two federal agents at the front door, and they're asking for you."

The drone footage from Apogee Launch Systems was on the screen of Amy's MacBook. She'd been marking shots for her next episode, so she had a fairly good idea of why somebody might be taking an interest in her.

But feds? That was kind of overkill, wasn't it?

She felt the expected swell of fear, even though she hadn't done anything illegal, as far as she knew. Maybe trespassing in the airspace of a private business? Was that against the law?

Before her mind could run too far down that rabbit hole, one word of her grandfather's announcement rose to prominence in her thoughts.

"You said they're *asking*?"

"Well," said Papa Nick, "they phrased it politely. But I've got a hunch that things could get less polite pretty quick."

Amy closed the lid of the MacBook and stood up. "You're probably right about that."

As she squeezed past Papa Nick at the door of the closet, he spoke softly. "Listen... If you've done something—I don't care if it's peddling heroin to Baptist choirboys—I'm in your corner. You're my girl, and I've got your back. Understand?"

She kissed him on the cheek. "Love you too. It's nothing like that. I promise."

"We gonna need a lawyer?"

"I don't know yet," said Amy. "Let's go find out."

The agents were waiting outside the front door. That was a good sign. If this were really serious, they would have surrounded the house and barged their way inside. Or maybe that was just how things worked on TV.

Amy went to the door and opened it wider. When she spoke, she was surprised and pleased to hear the steadiness in her voice. "Come in, Gentlemen."

When she got a look at the two men under the living room lights, they were a study in contrasts. One was in his mid-fifties, decked out in an immaculate slate gray suit, and looking very much like a fed. The other guy was maybe half that age, unshaven, and dressed in badly wrinkled street clothes. He looked like he hadn't slept in a week.

"I guess you fellows heard about the meth lab in the basement," Amy said. She held out her wrists in front of her. "Go ahead. Slap the cuffs on me."

The younger guy yawned. "You have a meth lab? Cool! I've never seen one."

"We don't even have a basement," said Papa Nick.

The older man unfolded a black leather wallet thing to reveal a badge and a photo credential with a federal seal. "Special Agent Donovan, Defense Criminal Investigative Service. Are you Louise Amelia Spicer?"

"Amy. Don't call me Louise or I'm going to ask for a lawyer."

Donovan didn't react to the joke, half-assed as it was. So much for getting things off on a friendly footing.

Out of the corner of her eye, Amy saw the younger guy crack a smile. Not a complete strikeout, then.

Amy looked in his direction. "Where's *your* badge?"

The man held up empty hands. "Gil Lawson. I'm an engineer with NASA."

"Curiouser and curiouser," said Amy. "What exactly have I done to attract the attention of NASA and the Department of Defense?"

Lawson lowered his hands. "That drone video you shot of Apogee... You're planning to use it in the Spice Report, right?"

Amy didn't answer.

"I love your channel," said Lawson. "I've only seen the first five videos, plus your newest one, but it's good stuff. I'm subscriber number 4,209."

"You've been cyberstalking me?"

Lawson smiled again. "Just a little. Enough to make sure that you're a YouTube news presenter and not an agent of a hostile foreign power. Unless the Spice Report thing is your cover, and you really *are* a foreign operative. In which case, well done! You've got us all fooled!"

Amy didn't quite laugh. This was nothing like any picture she'd ever had of a federal interrogation.

She turned to Special Agent Donovan. "You're awfully quiet over there. Isn't it about time you started in with the bad cop routine?"

"Not my job," said the fed. "Mr. Lawson is asking the questions. I'm just here to make the arrest if things go down that way."

Amy's brain latched on to one word. "Arrest?"

"Well, technically not an arrest, since you won't be charged with a crime. More of a precautionary detention in the interest of national security. Temporary, of course."

"*How* temporary?"

"No more than forty-eight hours without approval from a federal judge," said Donovan. He looked at his watch. "But the Russians are scheduled to zap us before this time tomorrow evening. If that happens, we'll probably release you right after they fry the grid. You'll be out just in time to enjoy the collapse of civilization."

Amy turned back to Lawson. "He's kidding, right?"

"We'd rather keep this friendly if we can," Lawson said.

"That's enough with the threats," said Papa Nick. "We're calling an attorney."

"Give me two minutes to explain," said Lawson. "Then, if you want a lawyer, have at it."

Papa Nick looked at Amy.

She nodded.

"First, let's talk about your story angle," said Lawson. "Somebody clued you into the Space Force presence at Apogee. A bunch of military personnel suddenly crawling all over a tiny civilian aerospace company. And—given the timing—you figure there just *has* to be a link to what's happening with the International Space Station. So, your plan is to ring the alarm bell and start a national dialogue about covert military space stuff in the California desert. Maybe you'll get lucky and the major networks pick up on your story. Then, everybody will be running clips from the Spice Report on primetime. Is there more, or does that about sum things up?"

Amy gave a reluctant nod. "Close enough."

A yawn went through Lawson's body, so powerful that he nearly shuddered. When it was over, he rubbed at his eyes. "You don't have a story. What you've got is a *piece* of a story, and you're hoping it's enough to get the ball rolling."

Amy nodded again.

"Well, there *is* a story," said Lawson. "I can't offer any details, but I can tell you that it's fucking massive. The kind of thing that Pulitzers are made of."

"And?"

"And we're willing to give you an exclusive if you'll keep it in your pocket for a few days."

"Won't everything be over by then?"

"Yeah," said Lawson. "The crisis will be past if we're lucky. And every news anchor on the planet will be trying to reconstruct what just happened. But only Amy Spicer will have the inside story. Facts. Video footage. Interviews. Content that will have the major media peeing all over itself."

"And all I have to do is sit on the story?"

"Yep."

"For how long?"

Lawson shrugged. "A couple of days. Three days tops."

"You think we'll all still be around in three days?" Amy asked.

"We're working on that," said Lawson. "Which is why we need you to keep a lid on things."

"I don't understand why you're offering me a deal," said Amy. "Why not just lock me up? You've apparently got the power to do it."

"I've managed to convince my superiors that putting the snatch on you could accelerate the release of the story," said Lawson. "You might have given your files to somebody on a thumb drive or a cloud folder that we haven't tracked down yet. If you disappear, that might spur some web-friend of yours to blast the story all over TikTok, Twitch, Reddit, Instagram, and half the Discord servers in North America. Not to mention whatever social media apps the cool kids are using these days."

Amy tried not to let her facial expression change. The only copies of the files were on her Mac. If these guys dragged her away in handcuffs, there would be no hue and cry on the web. She would vanish quietly, with no one to broadcast her story to the world.

Lawson paused for another yawn. "Taking you into custody would be our last resort. Apart from the obvious risks, you haven't done anything wrong. You just happen to be in a position to cause us some problems."

"What kind of problems?"

"I'm sorry; I can't tell you that."

"What *can* you tell me?"

Lawson exchanged a glance with Donovan. "I can tell you that going live with your story now will get good people killed."

"People you know?"

"Some of them. People who are hanging their asses over the edge, trying to save civilization."

"One more question," said Amy. "Whose idea was it to bribe me with an exclusive?"

"That was me," said Lawson. "I had to convince the big dogs to go along. But everybody agrees that it's better than locking up innocent people."

Amy held out her hand. "How do we make this official? Do we shake on it?"

Lawson accepted her hand and shook it.

"Are you really a subscriber?" Amy asked.

"Absolutely," said Lawson. "Your newest fan."

THIRTY-FOUR

Apogee Launch Systems
Mojave, California
(Expiration of Deadline: 13 Hours / 27 Minutes)

Seated behind his desk in a form-fitting blue spacesuit (minus helmet), Paul Keene held a framed photo of his daughter at age seven or eight. Sarah grinned out at him from the image with gapped teeth, her lopsided Lego *Tomcat* clutched like a precious relic.

Paul tried to brush a lock of hair from Sarah's forehead, but his gloved fingers slid over the glass of the picture frame. "Hang in there, Sprite. Daddy's on his way."

Unnoticed by Paul, Handsome Dan stood in the doorway with his pressure helmet tucked in the crook of one arm. His suit was also blue and form-fitting, but the form in question had considerably more paunch around the waistline than Paul Keene was carrying.

Dan waited for several seconds before knocking quietly on the doorjamb. "Heads-up, Boss. Time to go do that astronaut thing."

Paul set down the photo and reached for his helmet.

Canaveral, FL

About 2,200 miles to the southeast, Emergency Camp #3 was a small town of tents, portable toilets, and water trucks. The generators hauled in by FEMA were up and running now, but they mostly powered the big lights around the camp perimeter. Inside the hastily strung fence, most of the illumination came from propane camping lanterns.

The camp could have been a refugee center in any undeveloped country, or any American city hit by natural disaster. But this was not a disadvantaged country, and the catastrophe had been entirely of man's own making.

In one of the hundreds of identical tents, Terry Watts lay awake on a surplus U.S. Army cot.

Mom was asleep in the cot next to his. Terry couldn't see her face in the darkness, but he didn't need to. Every line of her features was carved into his memory. The kind/tired eyes of a single mother who works too hard for too little pay, but never lets herself give up. Worn to the point of exhaustion but still doing her best, even when the world itself was breaking down around them.

Terry peeled back the blanket and rolled out of his cot. Wiggled his sockless feet into his sneakers and slipped out into the starlight beyond the canvas flaps that served as a door.

In the distance, the city was dark. Unlighted shapes of houses and other buildings black under the quarter moon.

Under the perimeter lights, National Guard soldiers kept watch at the fence, protecting the camp against the looters who have taken over the blacked-out city.

Terry looked up to the stars, burning in the night sky without need for electrical power.

Face tilted skyward, his mind made a random connection, and he heard himself whisper the opening call to action from his Singularity War game. "All pilots to your planes!"

Apogee Launch Systems
Mojave, CA

Paul Keene, Dan Conway, and Floyd Garrett (in his own blue spacesuit) strode across the floodlit runway apron toward the *Corvus*. The engines of the *Kickstart* jet were already spooling up.

As they walked, Handsome Dan began a loud atonal humming that sounded like a moose trying to breathe through a snorkel, but which was probably intended to be musical.

Paul slapped his friend on the shoulder. "What's that you're serenading us with, Pal?"

"I'm guessing it's a Wookie mating call," said Garrett.

Dan snorted. "Neither one of you has got an ounce of culture. That's *Fanfare for the Common Man*. Aaron Copland. It's like the theme song for the astronaut walk."

Paul knew what Dan was talking about, but he recognized his responsibility to play the straight man. "What's the astronaut walk?"

Dan threw his arms wide to take in the runway, the *Corvus* and the *Kickstart* jet, the stars, and all of creation. "*This* is the astronaut walk. What we're doing right now. Like in the movies. *Apollo 13. The Right Stuff*. Intrepid astronauts, swaggering toward destiny."

"I don't feel all that intrepid," said Paul.

"And I've never really been comfortable with my swagger," said Garrett.

Their voices rose in volume as they walked into the rising wail of the *Kickstart's* turbines.

"Can we skip the Apollo 13 part?" asked Paul in a near-shout. "I'd rather not blow up half my ship and limp home without accomplishing the mission."

"No sense of grandeur," shouted Handsome Dan. "None at all."

They reached the foot of a rollaway ladder held against the paired jet and spaceplane by two Apogee ground personnel.

The boarding order was determined by cockpit seating position. Garrett went up first, followed by Handsome Dan, and then Paul.

When Paul reached the head of the ladder, he stood at the threshold of the cockpit and turned toward the Apogee hangar.

General Byrd and his Space Force contingent were standing at attention outside the hangar door. Byrd raised his right hand in salute.

Paul returned the salute. Then, he ducked into the hatch of the *Corvus* and disappeared from sight.

NASA Mission Control
Houston, TX

The Communications and Tracking Officer surveyed the settings on his console, eyes darting over various readouts. "Looks like the duct tape and paperclips are holding."

He tapped an icon and several callout boxes on his screen changed in size and content. "Voice and telemetry are up. We're piggybacking on commercial satellite television feed. Sports Channel, 'cause they have enough excess bandwidth to handle it."

Director Harper leaned over the CATO's shoulder. "Are we gonna get sued for this?"

The CATO cycled up another set of readouts. "Probably."

Most of the display stations in Mission Control were shut down. Unlike official vehicles of the space program, NASA didn't have control or visibility of every function on this unfamiliar civilian craft. They were limited to reading fuel levels, engine state, and positional information.

But the wall-sized master screen was active and prepared to track the spaceplane throughout its flight.

The Guidance, Navigation, and Controls Flight Controller looked over her GNC console. "*Corvus*... I've been meaning to Google that. The only reference I can think of is that freaky goth kid from the *Fantastic Beasts* movies, and that doesn't seem right. So, what is Corvus supposed to mean?"

Director Harper started back toward her seat. "Greek mythology. Corvus was a trickster figure. A raven who ignored the commands of the Sun God, Apollo. Basically, made the big guy look like an incompetent asshole."

"The Apollo program was NASA's crowning achievement," said

the GNC controller. "You think Paul Keene is giving us the middle finger?"

Harper settled into her chair and smiled. "As punishment, Apollo hurled Corvus into the sky, where he became a constellation. If you ask me, it's Keene's way of saying he'll make it to the stars, if he has to defy all the gods to get there."

Apogee Launch Systems
Mojave, CA

As the *Kickstart* taxied the *Corvus* to the head of the runway, Paul Keene and Handsome Dan ran through their pre-launch checklist—Keene reading items from his screen and Dan tabbing through the corresponding icons and indicators on his engineering display.

"Primary power bus..."

"Go."

"Secondary power bus..."

"Go."

"Cabin pressure..."

"Go."

"Seal integrity check..."

"Go."

"Gyro sync..."

"Go."

"Fuel pressure..."

"Go."

"Payload check..."

"Stand by."

Dan examined the tie-down straps on the gear stowed between the seats: oxygen bottles, external cooling units for the suits, and the three hexagonal canisters of knockout gas. There was a dab of yellow paint among the caution labels on one of the gas canisters, but he wasn't looking for variations in the markings and his eyes slid past without notice.

The payload was properly secured, so he gave an affirmative report. "Go."

"Weapons check..."

Each of the three men looked over the dart pistol and pouch of tranquilizer cartridges strapped to his suit—a precaution that General Byrd had insisted upon, in case their entry to the ISS turned out to be less covert than the plan called for.

Inspections complete, each man in turn gave the "Go" response.

"It's not on the preflight," said Handsome Dan, "but I also checked the turn signals and topped off the windshield wiper fluid."

Paul keyed the intercom. "*Kickstart*, my board is green."

"Roger that," said the *Kickstart* pilot in his trademark molasses drawl. "And just a friendly thought for you fellas... Only *my* half of this contraption has been certified as airworthy."

"That's a fair point," said Handsome Dan. "Hey Paul, is it too late to get a couple of parachutes?"

"Only a couple?"

"Well, Garrett's an Air Force type. If anything goes wrong, I figure he can fly home on the wings of eagles."

Paul switched his mic from intercom to the encrypted satellite lash-up. "Houston, we are *go* for launch."

The voice of the NASA Capsule Communicator (CAPCOM) came over the speaker. "Roger, *Corvus*. Good luck and Godspeed!"

With the *Corvus* riding its back, the *Kickstart* jet began accelerating down the desert runway.

"Exactly how fast *is* Godspeed?" asked Handsome Dan.

"I think we're about to find out," said Garrett.

The landing gear of the *Kickstart* lifted from the runway and the conjoined planes turned their paired noses toward the night sky.

THIRTY-FIVE

Corvus and Kickstart
(Expiration of Deadline: 12 Hours / 48 Minutes)

The vibration was hardly noticeable at first. Just one more frequency of tremor amid a cacophony of noises and oscillations. But it gained intensity as the *Kickstart* and *Corvus* approached the speed of sound.

Passing 500 knots, the vibration gave way to a rattle and the rattle turned into a buffeting that had never shown up in the computer models, nor in the numerous simulator runs.

Handsome Dan flipped his mic to the intercom. "Hey, Boss... You drop a decimal place in your calculations?"

"Better hope not," said Paul.

He spoke in the deadpan calm that military pilots spend their careers perfecting. The one that's used to casually announce engine fires, catastrophic damage, and unrecoverable spins as though they're minor inconveniences that are scarcely worthy of mention.

And just when it seemed that the *Corvus* would shake herself apart, all noise and vibration were gone.

Sudden quiet.

Even the roar of the engines had vanished—all sound left behind in the slipstream of the (now) supersonic planes.

The *Kickstart* pilot's twang came over the intercom. "Mach One. And I officially owe Handsome Dan a bottle of Sailor Jerry."

"Two bottles if we survive Mach Two," said Dan.

Between the helmet and safety straps, Paul couldn't turn far enough in his seat to stare at his partner, but he tried. "You're taking bets on whether or not we'll die?"

"Best deal ever. If we bite it, I don't have to pay up."

"Mach One-point-five," announced the *Kickstart* pilot.

"Don't forget the pineapple," said Handsome Dan.

The smile was audible in the *Kickstart* pilot's voice. "Mach Two. And that's two bottles of Sailor Jerry and a pineapple."

"Fresh," said Dan. "None of that canned crap."

Paul checked his instruments. "Coming up on 52,000 feet."

"Flight profile is nominal," said the *Kickstart* pilot. "Prepare for sep."

Paul tapped a soft key on his display and was rewarded with a green indicator. "Roger. Mounting pawl retracted. Auto-separation enabled."

"Stand by," said the *Kickstart* pilot. "Mechanical separation in three... two... one... mark!

With a metallic *thunk*, the latching mechanism detached.

Freed of its burden, the *Kickstart* jet dropped away and nosed into a dive, leaving the *Corvus* to glide without motive power.

There was a frozen second in which it seemed as if the spaceplane might surrender to gravity and fall back to Earth.

Then the Aerospike rocket engines erupted with columns of fire and drove the streamlined spacecraft up and out of the atmosphere—toward the star-flecked blackness of space.

"This is right about the point where the simulator usually kills me," said Garrett.

Paul worked the controls with a feather touch, keeping the *Corvus* on the planned trajectory as much by instinct and muscle memory as by deliberate intent. "Well, let's see if we can bypass that part," he said.

White House Master Bedroom
Washington, DC

James Roth lay beneath high thread count Egyptian cotton sheets, pretending that sleep might actually be a possibility.

He was trying not to think of himself as President Roth at the moment. Just letting himself be James for a while. Or maybe even Jimbo: the nickname he'd gone by in his first year at Tulane.

Jimbo would be snoring like a lumberjack—dreaming about parties that he wouldn't get invited to, or cars that he couldn't afford, or strategies for buying a keg without proper ID.

Jimbo would not be staring up at a shadowed ceiling, attempting to hypnotize himself to sleep by tracing the swoops and flourishes of the crown molding with his eyes.

Jimbo wouldn't be trying to avoid a mental rehash of OPLAN 8010-12, *Strategic Deterrence and Force Employment.*

And Jimbo would most definitely not be wondering if he'd be forced to start a global thermonuclear war sometime before lunch the following day.

Of course, Jimbo's hypothetical ability to doze through the eve of the apocalypse was of no significance. James Everett Roth was President of the United States. Any attempts to make believe otherwise were as ludicrous as they were futile.

Still, he owed it to his country (and the world) to at least try to get a little rest. The Commander-in-Chief of the U.S. military should not face his nation's moment of greatest peril in a state of sleep deprivation.

The problem was that he couldn't shut off his brain. He couldn't stop running through every scenario that the coming day might bring, and none of the imagined outcomes were good.

Any confidence he might have felt in the *Corvus* plan had given way to the deepening suspicion that the United States was living out its last night as a free nation.

Wildcat astronauts and untested spacecraft? What in the name of God had he been thinking? What brand of damned-fool optimism had persuaded him to hang the safety of millions on so slender a thread?

Not that he'd been overburdened with choices. From the moment of the Russian ultimatum, he'd only ever had two options (aside from this silly *Corvus* business). He could knuckle under to Moscow or come out with guns blazing.

He turned his head on the pillow and regarded Lily's sleeping form. Nearly invisible under more layers of comforter than any human could reasonably need, her presence was reassuring. Listening to the gentle sibilance of her breathing, it was almost possible to believe that there was some kind of future ahead.

He thought about waking her up and trying to talk through all the stuff in his head. Better to let her sleep while she could. This might be—quite literally—the final night of peace.

NASA Mission Control
Houston, TX

The GNC regarded the shifting data curves on her console. "Flight, we're seeing a high burn rate."

Director Harper—sitting in as Duty Flight Director for the launch—turned away from the master screen. "Talk to me."

The uppermost curve on the Guidance, Navigation, and Controls display was shading from green toward amber. The GNC Flight Controller called up a supporting readout. "Consumption is about seven percent over projection for this phase of the flight. They're burning through a lot of fuel."

Director Harper shifted her attention to the Controller at the Flight Dynamics Officer station. "FIDO, what have you got?"

The FIDO checked his own readings. "Trajectory is nominal. He's keeping it in the groove."

Harper left her seat and crossed to the GNC's station. Over the controller's shoulder, she watched the amber fuel consumption curve darkening toward orange. "How bad is that seven percent going to hurt us?"

No one bothered to ask why the burn rate was high. They knew so little about the *Corvus* and had such limited visibility into its operating characteristics, that no one at NASA could be expected to understand what was causing the lack of efficiency.

The GNC tapped at her keyboard and cranked out some quick calculations. "There wasn't a whole lot of fuel margin to begin with. But—if it doesn't get any worse—they should still be able to make rendezvous with the station."

She looked over the numbers again. "I *think*."

"You're not overwhelming me with confidence," said Harper.

The GNC didn't look up from her console. "Sorry about that. Best I can do."

Corvus
In Flight

Handsome Dan thumped the back of Paul's seat. "Whoa there, Major Tom! Throttle it back a little! Your burn rate is redlining."

"I'm flying the profile," said Paul. "Either your engines aren't properly tuned, or they suck more fuel than your computer models projected."

"Didn't anybody ever tell you that a good pilot doesn't blame the plane?"

"We can discuss my shortcomings later. For now, I need you to count on your fingers and toes—or whatever it is that you do—and tell me if we've got enough fuel to complete this mission."

Dan tabbed through several menus on his engineering screen. "If you get your foot out of the gas tank, we should be okay. Speaking of which... Main engine shutdown coming up in five... four... three... two..."

When the count reached one, Paul flipped off three parallel paddle switches.

The rocket engines fell silent.

Having reached orbital insertion speed, the *Corvus* coasted through the starlit darkness of space. Below them, the curved Earth glittered like an impossibly large jewel.

Paul lifted his hand from the stick. "My foot is out of the tank."

"Good boy," said Handsome Dan. "Now, try not to touch anything important, okay?"

White House Situation Room
Washington, DC

Everyone in the Sit Room came to attention when President Roth shambled through the door.

It took an effort not to wobble as he walked. Neither he, nor just-plain-James, nor Jimbo had managed three minutes of sleep.

He took his seat and motioned for his officers and advisors to do likewise. He decided to start with something that might have a positive resolution. "Where are we with the *Lincoln* Strike Group?"

General Christopher consulted a briefing folder. "We're not making a lot of progress, sir. Fleet Forces Command is rounding up emergency generators and supplies to be flown out to the ships by helo. That should keep the crews from freezing to death while we try to put together the resources to tow an entire carrier strike group."

He closed the briefing folder. "Our nearest ocean-going tugs are coming out of Norfolk. At top speed, it'll take them nearly two weeks to reach the Barents. And then there's the long haul back to a friendly port, through some of the nastiest seas on the planet."

"What about allies? Can we borrow tugs from friendly countries in the region?"

"We're trying," said the general. "The Swedish and Norwegian navies have the assets for a large-scale towing operation, but they're politely ducking our requests for assistance. They're nervous about providing us with aid while we're square in Russia's crosshairs."

The president nodded. "You think some pressure from the State Department would help?"

"Frankly, I doubt it, sir." The general looked up at the master clock. "As far as our friends in Europe are concerned, the United States is going to surrender its superpower card in a little under twelve hours. Either that, or we'll get the same treatment the Russians gave to the *Abraham Lincoln* Strike Group. In other words, our allies don't think we're going to be in a position to exert diplomatic leverage."

The president turned his attention to the big tactical display, which was currently slaved to the main screen from Mission Control in Houston. An icon representing the *Corvus* was orbiting at a lower altitude than an icon depicting the ISS. "What about *that*? Is it going to work?"

"With a bit of luck, sir."

"I stopped believing in luck fifty-nine hours ago," said the president. "Talk to me about this backup plan of yours."

THIRTY-SIX

Sarah Keene is nine years old—kneeling on the grass of her backyard—writing a message in purple marker on a slip of notepaper that she's cut into the shape of a heart. Between the tears in her eyes and the trembling of her hands, it's hard to make out the words she's already written. But she forces herself to finish.

At the bottom of the paper, she writes 'Love you forever!' Then, she signs her name and draws three hearts in purple ink. A final repetition of the message, in case some of her words are too wobbly to read.

She rolls up the paper like a little scroll and tries to tie it to the ribbon of a powder blue helium balloon that her dad is holding. Her shaking fingers are too clumsy to make the knot, so Dad takes over.

When the message is securely tied, he puts the ribbon carefully back into her unsteady grasp.

Sarah holds on to the ribbon much longer than she intends. Trying to think of something—the right thing—to say.

But if there are words for times like this, she can't find them. Can't even imagine what they might be.

Swallowing past a lump so large that it's painful, she releases the ribbon.

Eyes following the balloon, she takes her father's hand as the message floats toward heaven. "You really think it'll get to her?"

Dad gives Sarah's hand a gentle squeeze. "I don't know, Sprite. I sure hope so."

She watches the blue of the rising balloon merge into the blue of the sky. "Yeah. Me too..."

Sarah floated near the Cupola Module's circular array of windows; eyes not quite focused. Seeing (but not seeing) the dusky blue curve of horizon that was the Earth. The planet seemed almost the same shade as the balloon in her memory.

In high school physics, Sarah had learned about what happens to helium balloons released into the atmosphere. An ordinary party balloon might reach the upper half of the troposphere, roughly the altitude of a commercial airliner, before the latex expanded to the failure point and popped, leaving the shredded remains to fall out of the sky.

That knowledge was deliberately sequestered in her mind. She knew full well that the physical laws of the universe do not make exceptions for grieving children. Nevertheless, she chose to believe that *one* balloon had miraculously evaded destruction and continued rising to its impossible destination.

It was magical thinking; Sarah recognized that, and she was okay with the knowledge. As an astronaut and a fighter pilot, her life was built around understanding and embracing the realities of physics. But she was allowed an unfounded fantasy or two, in the privacy of her mind.

Rutger drifted over to join her at the windows. "You've got the thousand-mile-stare," he said. "If you're devising a brilliant plan to turn the tables on our cosmonaut-captors, please tell me it doesn't involve a tunnel."

Sarah blinked and then rubbed her eyes. "No brilliant plan and definitely no tunnels."

"Good. Because I hate getting dirty and I seem to have lost track of my spoon."

Sarah was thinking up a reply when an odd look came over Rutger's face.

"You hear that?"

Sarah stopped and listened. She *did* hear it. A rumbling sound that started near the bottom end of her hearing threshold and gained in strength.

"Yeah," she said. "I think we're boosting."

And they were.

NASA Mission Control
Houston, TX

The FIDO saw the numbers on his display start to change. He watched just long enough to be sure of what was happening, then he pressed his mic button. "Flight, be advised... The ISS is conducting an unscheduled re-boost."

Warning chimes began sounding on various consoles, and the GNC made her own report. "Flight, GNC concurs. We're seeing an unscheduled translational burn. Unknown duration."

Director Harper keyed her mic. "Understood. Keep me advised."

On the master display, the line representing the orbit of the ISS began to flash and sprout the dashed lines of additional curves.

Harper didn't allow herself to sigh. What was that line from T. S. Eliot? *Not with a bang but a whimper?*

A short while later, she was sequestered in a private conference room, delivering the news to the president and the White House Situation Room staff over a secure video teleconference link. As expected, her announcement caused a lull in the usual background babble of the Sit Room.

General Christopher was the first to respond. "You think the Russians are on to us?"

"Not necessarily," said Harper. "The ISS loses approximately one mile of altitude every month. The corrective maneuver is called a re-boost, or a translational burn. Basically, they fire the engines and push the station up to a higher orbit."

President Roth crossed his hands on the table in front of himself. "You're saying this might be a routine orbit correction?"

The word that came to Harper's mind as she studied his image on the telecon screen was *haggard*. Not a term she'd ever used in conversation, but the president appeared to be languishing in some energy depletion zone on the far side of exhaustion.

"Probably not, Mr. President," she said. "This is a longer burn than usual."

The president gestured for her to continue.

"A typical re-boost is fifteen minutes or less," said Harper. "Call it two meters per second of delta-v. The ISS is past that already and still climbing. We think they're going for max altitude. About 280 miles."

"They've detected the *Corvus*," said General Christopher.

"That's one possibility," said Harper. "It's also possible that this is an arbitrary preemptive measure, to complicate any attempt to target the ISS."

She intended to elaborate, but her next words were interrupted by a knock at the door.

Lloyd Etheridge opened the door partway and held up a data tablet for her to see.

Harper crooked a finger, beckoning him into the room.

Lloyd crossed to the table quickly, studiously keeping his eyes averted from the teleconference screen. He handed the tablet to Harper and then retreated from the conference room without a word.

It took Harper a minute or so to page through the information on the device. Her hopes for the mission—already dwindling—sank even lower as she studied the data.

She dropped the tablet on the table. "Not what we were hoping for, Mr. President. The *Corvus* has enough fuel to climb to the max altitude of the ISS, but they'll be running on fumes when they get up there. No reserve for breaking maneuvers. No possibility that they can rendezvous with the station."

This pronouncement brought another period of silence as Harper and everyone in the Sit Room processed the idea that the mission had failed.

A civilian advisor cleared his throat.

Harper still couldn't remember the man's name, but it was the same Wile E. Coyote super-genius who'd fired off one impractical idea after another during the planning meeting. The kind of guy who's constitutionally incapable of recognizing situations in which he is out of his depth.

"So, we skip the rendezvous," said Super-Genius. "Forget braking maneuvers. If they can reach the higher orbit, they can ram the station. Use the *Corvus* as a kinetic kill vehicle."

Harper admitted to herself that the suggestion was not entirely idiotic. "Might work..." she said reluctantly. "That kind of impact could do major damage. Maybe destroy the ISS completely. At the very least, it'll perturb the station's orbit and knock out some—if not all—of the infrastructure supporting the EMP device."

"Then let's do it!" exclaimed Super-Genius.

General Christopher shook his head. "Keene will never go for that. Not with his daughter up there. He's shown more than once that he's willing to lay down his life if the tactical situation demands it. But he's not gonna sacrifice Sarah. And I frankly can't say that I blame him."

There was a shade of outrage in Super-Genius's voice. "You can't *blame* him? The United States is about to go down in flames, and you can't blame him for refusing to stop it?"

The general turned a withering glare in Super-Genius's direction. "Your boy's at Georgetown, right? Pre-Law?"

No response from the advisor.

"Suppose you could end this situation right now?" asked the general. "Destroy the EMP weapon and send the Russians packing. All you have to do is toss one grenade into your son's political science class. America comes out on top, and everybody's safe and happy. But you've got to turn your son—and a couple of his classmates—into hamburger to get there."

Super-Genius started to respond, but General Christopher wasn't through yet.

"I mean do it *yourself*," growled the general. "Not give an order that somebody else has got to carry out. You've got to do the dirty work with your own two hands. Pull the pin and throw the grenade. Murder your own boy to guarantee the future of your country."

The general turned away from the advisor. "If you can do that, you're a hell of a lot tougher than I am."

To Super-Genius's credit, he didn't actually sputter. "It doesn't *have* to be Keene."

Every eye turned toward the advisor.

"Order Garrett to do it," said Super-Genius. "Unless he's got kids up there, too."

The general's glare swung back around to focus on the clueless advisor. "Keene won't give up control without a fight, and Conway will have his back. Now you've got Garrett outnumbered two-to-one in a cockpit that's not much bigger than the front seat of a Volkswagen Beetle. If Garrett gets his ass kicked, we lose. If he comes out on top, he doesn't know how to fly the damned thing and we *still* lose."

Super-Genius started to respond, but the president leaned forward in his seat. "I've heard enough. The mission is aborted. Let's get 'em down."

"Just a second, sir..." said Super Genius. "We can..."

President Roth stood up. "Enough! Send out the order. This operation is canceled."

Director Harper nodded. "Yes, Mr. President."

THIRTY-SEVEN

Corvus
(Expiration of Deadline: 10 Hours / 29 Minutes)

Paul Keene keyed his microphone. "Say again, Houston?"

The CAPCOM's voice was oddly metallic over the satellite lash-up. "Don't shoot the messenger, *Corvus*. The mission is scrubbed. You are ordered to use your remaining fuel to de-orbit and return to base."

Paul didn't respond to the command.

Ordered?

He switched his comm set to the intercom. "Hey, Dan... You remember being called back to Active Duty?"

Handsome Dan's eyes didn't leave his screen. He was setting up a trial projection for a two-engine burn at minimal impulse. "Active Duty? Not unless they swore us in when I was catching some Zs."

"Ordered, my *ass*..." said Paul to himself.

Checking over his variables and assumptions, Dan touched the 'Execute' icon. The answer that came up on his display was not to his liking.

The maneuver would conserve *some* fuel, but not nearly enough.

He zeroed out his inputs and started again. What about a series of short single-engine burns?

He started to tap in the new variables.

As he typed, the *Corvus* crossed the terminator, passing above the half of the globe that lay in sunlight. The moon slid out of sight behind the rim of the Earth.

"I keep meaning to ask you," said Garrett. "Why does everyone call you Handsome Dan?"

"Not quite *everyone*," said Handsome Dan without looking up from his console. "My ex-wife calls me Shithead."

"Fine," said Garrett. "Everyone except your ex-wife."

"Well, that should be obvious," said the distracted engineer. "My first name is Daniel."

Cupola Module
International Space Station

Sarah brought her mouth close to Rutger's ear. Her words were only slightly louder than a breath. "I have to get into the Z1 Truss Dome."

Rutger's response was just as quiet. "Why are we whispering? I don't think there are any surveillance devices on the station."

"Maybe. But there weren't any weapons on the station until Volkov's crew showed up."

Rutger nodded. "Fair point. So, what about the Z1 Dome?"

"I need three minutes in there," whispered Sarah. "Four minutes, tops. I'm going to rotate the Solar Arrays away from the sun, and then short out the Beta Gimbals."

"That's your master plan?"

"Yeah. It'll take those bastards weeks of EVA work to free up the arrays. They might not be able to restore main power at all."

"That'll take the weapon out of action?"

"I don't see why not. Every time they fire that thing, it browns-out the lights. It's pulling way more power than they can get from the batteries."

"I like it," said Rutger. He nodded toward the locked hatch. "Any ideas on how we get out of here?"

"I've taken charge of sabotage," whispered Sarah. "Escape is *your* department."

Corvus
In Flight

Handsome Dan's engineering display showed yet another unsuccessful trial solution. He wiped the disappointing projection from his screen. "No good, Boss. No matter how I figure the approach, we don't have enough go-juice to match orbits."

"Like a firetruck with no brakes," said Paul. "We can barrel ass to the scene of the fire, but we can't stop when we get there. All we can do is smile and wave as we blow past at 60 miles an hour."

"Yeah," said Handsome Dan. "We..."

He stopped.

When it was clear that Dan wasn't going to continue with the thought, Paul prodded him. "Major Tom to Ground Control. You dropped signal."

"Say that again," said Handsome Dan.

"What? The Major Tom thing?"

"No. *Before* that."

"I don't know. Something about waving as we blow past?"

Dan started entering variables into his console. "Yeah... Maybe we can do a little more than that."

NASA Mission Control
Houston, TX

Readouts on the GNC's console began to change rapidly. She thumbed the mic button. "Flight, the *Corvus* is firing main engines."

"Confirmed," said the FIDO. "*Corvus* is maneuvering."

Director Harper swirled the last bit of cold coffee around the bottom of her cup and decided not to drink it. "Acknowledged. That'll be the start of their de-orbit burn."

The FIDO's response came over the net. "Uh... that's a negative, Flight. *Corvus* is increasing altitude. Climbing toward a higher orbit."

Harper looked up at the main screen. Sure enough, the *Corvus* was climbing. She keyed her mic. "CAPCOM?"

The Capsule Communicator was already moving into action. "On it..." He switched his headset to the satellite lash-up. "Corvus—Houston. We're tracking an increase in altitude. Explain, please."

There was no response.

CAPCOM repeated the call. "Corvus—Houston. We're tracking an increase in altitude. Explain, please."

Again, there was no response.

"Corvus—Houston. Comm check. Do you read?"

The CATO ran through a quick series of keystrokes on her console. Status menus flitted by until she settled on the one she was hunting for. "Satellite link is still good, and telemetry's coming through fine."

Director Harper raised an eyebrow. "They're ignoring us?"

The CATO shrugged. "No opinion on that. I'm just telling you what the equipment says."

Harper's eyes were still on the main screen. The change in orbit was becoming pronounced now. The *Corvus* was clearly trying to match altitudes with the ISS, and the spacecraft just as clearly didn't have the necessary fuel for the maneuver.

"Talk to me, Keene," Harper said under her breath. "What are you doing up there?"

THIRTY-EIGHT

Green River Gardens
California City, California
(Expiration of Deadline: 9 Hours / 28 Minutes)

Amy Spicer lay on her side, burrowed under the covers, trying to decide whether or not to call out sick.

She felt fine. As well as anyone could expect to be feeling with the scheduled destruction of her country less than ten hours away.

The work thing just did not seem important. If civilization were going to crumble this afternoon, she'd rather be at home when it happened. And—if things didn't go to shit—there would be the Spice Report episode to get ready. The big one. The one that would (fingers and toes crossed!) finally put her YouTube channel on the map.

One way or another, today was going to transform the life of Louise Amelia Spicer. She could not picture herself waiting tables and fetching steak sauce on this of all days.

That settled one thing. She was going to burn a sick day. Who would be going to a restaurant today anyway?

She'd go stock up on canned goods and bottled water (just in case) and then spend the rest of the day working on her channel. The Spice Report needed a punchier intro anyway, and this was a good time to put one together.

Thinking about the channel was a Pavlovian trigger. Her hand emerged from under the pile of covers and groped the nightstand until it located her phone.

Still curled up beneath the blankets, she brought up her YouTube account and checked her subscriber list. She was up to 4,212. Three new subscribers last night. Not a big jump, but progress was progress.

Near the bottom of the list was subscriber number 4,209, with a user handle of *AngelFeat*. If the Lawson guy had been telling the truth last night, that should be him.

The hyperlink led to the channel of an alternative rock band called Angel Feat, based out of the Houston area.

Amy sent her questing hand back out into the world to explore the top of the nightstand. A few seconds later, it returned with her earbuds.

When they were comfortably seated in her ears, she tapped the first video in the queue. The band on stage in some rinky-dink nightclub, playing old school grunge. Sounding like a watered-down version of Screaming Trees. Like somebody learned all the wrong lessons from Stone Temple Pilots and taught them to less talented musicians.

They weren't any worse than a lot of bar bands. Not really bad. Just not particularly good.

There was Lawson, front and center, a guitar strapped around his neck and mumbling out the vocals.

Stumblin' through the shadows.
Darkness up ahead.
No more light to see by.
All batteries are dead.

Passable voice. Not memorable, but okay to listen to. He made her think of Mark Lanegan with a shot of novocaine.

Amy scrolled down to the details block and read promo notes about the band and the song.

As far as she knew, grunge wasn't making any kind of comeback, and—if it was—Gil Lawson was not shaping up to be the next Kurt Cobain.

But the man had a nice smile, and he did good things for a pair of jeans.

She flipped forward to the next song and hit *Play*.

THIRTY-NINE

White House
Washington, DC
(Expiration of Deadline: 9 Hours / 12 Minutes)

President Roth slumped into his chair behind the *Resolute* desk.

America needed him to be on his A-Game today, and he was anything but. His brain was muddy with fatigue toxins and mere exhaustion felt like a distant and happy memory.

He thought about calling his doctor for a shot of something to clear his head and maybe give him some energy. But he couldn't make himself do that. Whatever happened over the next few hours, he wasn't going to see it through the prism of any drug more mind-altering than caffeine.

If he couldn't replace lost sleep, restore stamina, or clear his mind, at least he could face the day's challenges without the cognitive distortions of amphetamine.

He sat up straighter in his seat and nodded to his chief of staff. "All right, let them in."

Clayton Forrester crossed to the door and admitted Secretary of Defense Ernesto Ortiz and National Security Advisor Michael Lazlow into the Oval Office.

"Somebody needs to give me some good news," said the

194

president.

"Well," said Lazlow, "the *Corvus* crew is off the leash."

"They're what?"

"They appear to be ignoring the recall order, Mr. President. Refusing to abort the mission."

The president felt a microscopic stirring of hope. "You think they've figured out a way to rendezvous with the ISS?"

"Not likely, sir. NASA has analyzed the new trajectory. The best the *Corvus* can manage is a fly-by. Paul Keene's supposed to be some kind of hotshot pilot, but the laws of orbital mechanics bend for no one."

"What use is a fly-by?" asked Secretary Ortiz.

"None at all," said Lazlow. "As far as we can tell."

The president tried to keep the exasperation out of his voice. "Have we tried *asking* them what the hell they're doing?"

"The *Corvus* has stopped communicating, sir," said Lazlow. "Not a word since we issued the recall order."

"Let's skip ahead to the part where this is good news," said the chief of staff.

Lazlow lifted a shoulder in a half-shrug. "It's *interesting* news. And that's about the best I can manage right now."

President Roth settled back into his chair. "Forget good news. I'll settle for brilliant ideas."

No one spoke.

"Fine," said the president. "I'll open up the floor to not-so-brilliant ideas. Any course of action that doesn't involve surrendering to Russian global domination or jumpstarting World War III."

Again, no one spoke.

"If anyone has got something to say, now is the time. Because I'm about five seconds from ordering preparations for a nuclear strike."

The National Security Advisor, Secretary of Defense, and White House Chief of Staff all exchanged looks, but none of them spoke.

The president nodded slowly. "I guess that settles it. Ernesto, take us to DEFCON 1. Clayton, tell Ambassador Shaozu to wake up his Minister of Defense. It's time for our Chinese friends to join the party."

Kremlin Senate Palace
Moscow

Seated in his private dining room on the third floor of the Senate Palace, President Leonid Igorevich Polichev felt none of the dread or uncertainty that plagued his American counterpart. The Russian president was a man very much at ease—serenely enjoying the trappings of his office and the promise offered by the ripening international situation.

The room in which Polichev dined was a reflection of the future he intended to build for his country. Extraordinarily opulent, it had—on his orders—been restored to something approaching the grandeur it had held during the reign of Catherine the Great. With its gilded baroque wall panels, domed bas-relief ceiling, and inlaid parquet floor, the room was a visual reminder of Mother Russia's lost magnificence, as well as a token of the greater heights to which the country could (and would) ascend, thanks to its faithful son, Leonid.

The dining table and its twelve matched chairs were cultural artifacts. Polichev had personally selected them, along with a number of other items, from the Romanov Collection in the Kremlin Museum—over the strident objections of the senior curator. Each piece had been handcrafted for Tsarina Aleksandra Feodorovna by the master nineteenth-century artisan, N. F. Svirsky, and they were all quite beautiful.

Even so, the museum vaults contained furnishings that were more splendid, more valuable, and of greater historical significance. But these particular items were important to Polichev because they had belonged to the last ruling generation of the Russian royal family.

Tsar Nicholas II had sat in these chairs and supped at this table, accompanied by Tsarina Aleksandra and their children: Olga, Tatiana, Maria, the famous Anastasia, and Alexei—who would have been heir to the throne if Russia had not taken her seven-decade detour through communism and cronyism into socioeconomic collapse.

For Polichev, the reconstituted room and its royal amenities represented signposts on his country's road back to greatness.

The stone-faced Federal Security Service Agent standing guard by the door would not recognize the symbolism of the room. Nor would the white-jacketed serving attendant hovering near the sideboard. To these underlings—and to most Russian citizens—the storied antiques and the grand surroundings probably seemed like fuel for their president's vanity.

He could live with that. Even the dimmest of his countrymen would understand soon, when Russia was the dominant world power.

Polichev folded a blini into a triangle and used a tiny silver spoon to garnish the crepe with a small dollop of caviar. As the delightful confection went into his mouth, the door opened, and Ivan Gusev waddled into the room.

The plump little aide went immediately to Polichev's side and leaned close to speak in low tones. "Apologies for the interruption, Mr. President, but the Defense Center is requesting your presence. It's urgent."

Gusev was slightly out of breath. He'd run up the stairs again rather than waiting for the lift. That was the man's way of demonstrating self-sacrifice and dedication to his position.

Unhurried, Polichev chewed slowly and took a sip of black tea afterward. "The Defense Center thinks *everything* is urgent," he said. He began spooning more caviar onto the blini.

Gusev leaned in closer and lowered his voice still further. "Sir, the Americans are dispersing their strategic bomber wings, and we have satellite footage of the Chinese fueling long-range ballistic missiles!"

Polichev set down the little caviar spoon. "It's the growling of caged tigers. They snarl and show us their teeth so that we'll back away. But the Americans don't have the stomach for nuclear war, and the Chinese are not strong enough to attack us alone."

Gusev nodded, but he didn't look convinced.

Polichev dabbed at his lips with a napkin. "Relax, Vanya. The Defense Center will request an escalation of our nuclear readiness level, which I will approve. Not because the threat is serious, but because our friends in Defense cannot yet understand that we have passed an inflection point. The dynamics of military force have been irrevocably altered."

Gusev repeated his nod without any real sign of comprehension.

"The Americans and the Chinese are playing at Cold War brinksmanship," said Polichev. "But their posturing will come to nothing because we have the weapon that guarantees victory."

He gestured to the attendant. "Bring a cup of tea for my nervous friend."

The attendant hastened to obey.

Polichev's stone-faced bodyguard took in everything but said nothing.

FORTY

Seiders Kidney Health Center
Haster Cove, Maine
(Expiration of Deadline: 8 Hours / 13 Minutes)

Lionel Penobscot chose a well-thumbed issue of the *Northwoods Sporting Journal* from the communal table and eased his seventy-six-year-old bones into a waiting room chair.

It wasn't his kind of magazine. Lionel was not a hunter, a fisherman, or an outdoorsman of any sort. He was more of a wear cardigans, drink tea, read novels, and paint watercolor landscapes type of man. Only, he'd left his current book at home on the coffee table, and he needed something to occupy himself while Phyllis went through her Thursday treatment.

He wanted to be in the back, talking to Phyllis. Holding her hand. Just being close to her.

The clinic allowed husbands or wives to visit with patients during dialysis sessions. The prohibition against his presence came from his wife, not the staff. She didn't like the idea of having Lionel in the room when she was connected to the machine.

Medicare would have covered in-home dialysis as well, or eighty percent of the cost, which was all they paid for clinic sessions. But she'd vetoed that idea for the same reason. Not out of modesty. She was still trying to protect him from the realities of her condition.

Her heart condition (another thing she was trying to protect him from) made her ineligible for a kidney transplant. Not that Phyllis would have been high on the list of recipients at age seventy-three.

So, Lionel read novels in waiting rooms during her dialysis treatments, and during visits to her cardiologist, and during appointments with the cadre of other doctors who managed her growing catalog of chronic health issues. Except when he forgot his book at home, and then he made do with whatever magazines happened to be lying around.

He wouldn't have been able to concentrate on *Bleak House* today anyway, even if he'd remembered to bring the dratted book along. And he was having no luck losing himself among the pages of *Northwoods Sporting Journal*.

His eyes kept straying from the magazine to his wristwatch. A little over eight hours 'til the Russian deadline.

Then what would happen? He could not imagine President Roth surrendering America's weapons. That would be an abject betrayal of the man's oath of office, and his duties as Commander-in-Chief.

What alternatives did that leave?

An all-out attack? Try to obliterate Russia before the clock ran out? Sit tight, and hope the Russians were too cowardly to follow through with their threats?

Lionel didn't pay much attention to politics, but he knew in his heart that the Russians were not bluffing. When the United States failed to bend a knee, that weapon in space would strip the country of all electronic technology.

Whether the president started launching ICBMs or the Russians started in with their space ray, the human race was moving into its end game.

Unless something miraculous happened, today was almost certainly the last dialysis treatment Phyllis would receive. She and Lionel had avoided talking about that, but it was true.

There would be no more visits to the Seiders clinic, or the cardiologist, or any of the other medical facilities involved in her ongoing care. No more high-tech sorcery to fan the ember of life within her beloved (but failing) body.

When the electricity went off, how long would her medications in the refrigerator last? How long before her arms and legs began to swell with retained fluids? How many days before the buildup of toxic wastes in her system exceeded some critical tolerance, and she fell into a coma and died?

Of greater importance to Lionel, how painful would her final deterioration be without continual treatment? Without the oxygen concentrator that helped her breathe on bad days? Without doctors and ambulances on speed dial?

He'd never thought about these things before. He hadn't needed to. Access to medical technology (and technology in general) had always been a given in his plans for the future. He'd never been forced to consider what Phyllis's life might be like without the countless things that depended on a reliable supply of electrical power. Or, come to think of it, what his own existence might look like under such circumstances.

When bank computers were erased, and pension checks stopped coming, and grocery stores were no longer taking in daily shipments of supplies, the pantry wouldn't take long to empty itself.

Hollywood loved to produce movies about that kind of future. Earth in the aftermath of civil collapse. After a nuclear war, or zombies, or a plague, or an alien invasion. Lionel had seen two or three of those films, before his interest in commercial cinema had begun to wane. Depressing post-apocalyptic blockbusters starring Mel Gibson, Kevin Costner, or Jean-Claude What's-his-name.

There would be different and younger actors now, but the movie industry was still turning out those films. Leather-clad scavengers battling over the dregs of civilization in a contaminated wasteland. Scabrous maniacs to whom a can of beans was wealth undreamt of, but who somehow never ran out of bullets, pyrotechnic explosives, or gasoline for their armored hotrods.

Lionel idly turned a page of the *Northwoods Sporting Journal*. A half-page painting showed a black bear on the bank of a stream, muzzle pointed down toward the water as if the animal were preparing to drink, or perhaps watching for a fish.

The colors were more vibrant than you could usually achieve with oils. Acrylics, most likely. If it was an oil painting, someone had punched up the color saturation when preparing the image for printing.

The attached article seemed to be about techniques for hunting bears with bow and arrows. Lionel very much doubted that the artist who'd created such a pastoral wildlife scene had imagined his (or her) painting being licensed to illustrate a treatise on how to kill forest creatures.

The target audience for articles of this sort was likely composed of people who could prosper in a future without power, or vehicles, or supply chains, or social order. Lionel and Phyllis did not fit into that category.

The failure of civilization probably wouldn't resemble the dark predictions of Hollywood. But—however the breakdown manifested itself—survival would become an unending struggle.

Brutal.

Terrifying.

Lionel wanted no part of anything like that, and he didn't want Phyllis to experience even the glimmerings of such a frightening world.

If the nuclear missiles flew, or if the Russians used their weapon to demolish America's infrastructure, there were two bottles of Seconal in the medicine cabinet. More than enough to see Lionel and Phyllis quietly into whatever world came after this one.

He prayed things would not come to that. Although he couldn't imagine how it might work, there might still be a diplomatic solution, or the Russian weapon might fail, or something…

But—if the dogs of war were loosed upon America—Lionel and Phyllis would go out together. Holding hands.

There might still be time for one last watercolor. He was picturing a glorious sunrise behind the lighthouse on Cape Elizabeth.

A farewell, and a final tribute to the world he had known and loved.

FORTY-ONE

Corvus
(Expiration of Deadline: 6 Hours / 29 Minutes)

Handsome Dan kept one eye on the changing altitude readout in the top right-hand corner of his display. "Main engine shutdown in five... four..."

Right on the mark, Paul Keene flicked a trio of paddle switches to the *off* position. The three Aerospike rocket engines ended their final burn.

Assuming that NASA's numbers were correct, and Dan hadn't boogered his calculations, the *Corvus* should now be at the same altitude as the ISS and moving quickly toward the closest point of approach.

Everything depended on geometry and the accuracy of the Keplerian elements provided by Houston. Even if the *Corvus* had been equipped with radar to track the position of the station, they wouldn't dare turn the thing on.

Nothing would advertise the approach of the *Corvus* more clearly than an unknown radar transmitter appearing suddenly in proximity to the ISS. You couldn't pull off a covert infiltration if you rang the bell on the way in the door.

The Reaction Control System thrusters began firing. Paul doing his pilot thing.

Short jets of gas erupted from nozzles in the nose and leading edges of the wings as Paul nursed the very last of the fuel to make the upcoming flyby as close and as slow as he could manage.

Their metaphorical firetruck was still going to barrel past the scene of the blaze without stopping, but the speed differential would (hopefully) fall somewhere within the range of survivability.

After a disappointingly short interval, the RCS thrusters sputtered and died.

Paul lifted his hand from the control stick. "That's it, guys. As good as we're gonna get."

Handsome Dan checked his screens. The numbers were not at all encouraging, but maybe they'd be good enough.

He thumbed his intercom switch and gave his best imitation of a bored flight attendant. "Ladies and Gentlemen, we've reached our cruising altitude of one million, four hundred and seventy-five thousand feet. The Captain has turned off the Fasten Seatbelt sign. This is a non-smoking flight. Federal law prohibits tampering with or disabling the smoke detectors in the lavatories."

No one laughed.

The next ninety seconds or so were devoted to unbelting themselves from their respective seats and removing the cargo webbing from the gas canisters.

Paul and Dan hadn't worked in microgravity since their final shuttle flight, almost a decade earlier. Their movements were noticeably clumsy. Garrett—whose most recent expedition to the ISS had been only a year ago—was considerably more agile.

They had just finished disentangling the last canister when Garrett spotted the station. "There she is!"

Sure enough, the ISS was now visible through the cockpit windows. A distant star, growing rapidly.

"All right guys, we're up," said Paul. "Detach and prepare for egress."

All three men disconnected their external oxygen hoses and umbilical cables. They were now cut off from the intercom system, and the suits—which hadn't been designed for EVA work—were not equipped with internal radios.

Paul cracked the seal on the cockpit door and the remaining atmosphere gushed out into the vacuum; crystals of ice blossoming on the windows as the escaping air expanded.

The ISS was about a half-mile away and the *Corvus* was closing the range at a little over 30 feet-per-second. That left maybe a minute and a half until the closest point of approach, and Dan started to wonder if they'd be ready in time.

All they had to do was get out the door, tether one gas canister to each man, and be in position before the flyby. But everything takes longer in microgravity and tying a knot with suit gloves was no simple feat.

The exaggerated lethargy of their movements might have seemed funny if the station had not been bearing down on them like a freight train.

They were ready with ten seconds to spare.

Through the cockpit windows of the *Corvus*, they watched a (newly frosted-over) indicator light on the instrument panel.

When the light blinked red, all three men threw themselves into the abyss, trusting vector mathematics and inertia to carry them diagonally toward their goal.

The realization struck Handsome Dan at the precise nanosecond that his boots shoved him away from the *Corvus*. This was—by any measure he could imagine—the dumbest idea he'd ever had. And that was in a lifetime of impressively stupid ideas.

There was a tug when the short working line that tethered the gas canister to his suit went taut. The canister jerked along in his wake, a few kilos of mass yo-yoing at the end of its leash until the tether's cycle of alternating slack and tension dampened itself out.

Hopefully, the spastic perturbations of the canister hadn't thrown off his trajectory too much. There would not be any do-overs. If he missed the station, he couldn't go back and try again.

The absurdity of the situation was staggering. Here he was, soaring through the heavens like a middle-aged superhero with a pot belly and a walrus mustache; on a secret mission to rescue the daughter of his best friend, and save the world from a bunch of nutcases with a no-shit death ray.

Definitely not his best idea.

Time was playing tricks on his mind. First, the ISS seemed to be frozen in position, impossibly far away and coming no closer. Then, suddenly it was careening toward him with frightening speed, looming in the faceplate of his helmet—improbably large and dangerously close.

Garrett would land first. Paul would arrive maybe a half-second later.

Handsome Dan performed an eyeball analysis of his own approach to the onrushing station and did a rapid mental calculation.

Well, *damn...*

Cupola Module
International Space Station

The movement caught Sarah's attention.

Something outside the windows. Motion out there, where nothing should be moving.

She made a shushing sound to catch Rutger's attention and then spoke softly. "Quick! Check this out!"

Her fellow astronaut looked around, eyes searching until he spotted the object of Sarah's interest.

A figure in a bright blue spacesuit, already past the cupola windows now and receding rapidly. The suited person was waving his or her arms—an oblong bundle trailing along on a length of strap.

It wasn't an American EVA suit, and it didn't resemble anything Sarah had seen the Russians use. In fact, it didn't appear to be an EVA suit at all. It had the slimmer lines of an IVA suit, meant for intravehicular activity within a pressurized spacecraft.

There was no indication of a Manned Maneuvering Unit backpack, or any kind of propulsion unit for controlled flight. Just some unidentified person out there, in a suit that was clearly not designed for extravehicular work.

As Sarah watched, the space-suited stranger dwindled into the distance and vanished from view.

"Something's happening," said Rutger.

It seemed like the most unnecessary statement Sarah had ever heard.

Node 1 Exterior
International Space Station

Garrett made a good landing. He grabbed a handhold on the side of the Node 1 Connector Segment and allowed his joints to absorb the impact, so the recoil didn't bounce him off the station.

A split second later, Keene landed with considerably less skill. The older astronaut fumbled and almost missed the handhold he was going for, managing to hook it at the last possible instant with his left hand.

Garrett had no attention to spare for Keene's struggles. There was a more immediate problem.

The knot on the end of Garrett's tether had come loose. His gas canister was getting away from him.

If the three canisters had been identical, he could have let this one escape. The other two would have been adequate to carry out the plan.

But this canister was not the same. It was marked with a small dot of yellow paint, easy to overlook amongst the caution decals.

General Christopher's orders had been unmistakable. The marked canister had to make it onto the station.

Unlike the others, this one wasn't full of fentanyl gas. This one contained the payload for a mission that Paul Keene and Dan Conway knew nothing about.

That payload had to get aboard the ISS. All other considerations were secondary.

Garrett was scrambling to recover his canister when Handsome Dan missed the station entirely.

Dan's trajectory was not off by much. Just a fraction of a degree.

A couple of feet. Enough to put his fingers a few inches beyond range of any available handhold.

There was a moment where Garrett could have saved the man. A tiny sliver of a second in which he could have abandoned the payload canister and grabbed for Handsome Dan's outstretched glove.

Garrett recognized the opportunity and the choice that it embodied.

Handsome Dan recognized it too.

Garrett could see the man's face through his helmet visor, only a few feet away. His groping hand within reach, if only Garrett would grasp it.

Garrett went for the canister.

By the time he had a grip on the thing, he'd already begun to despise himself.

What kind of amoral bastard would put his orders above fundamental human decency?

He had just done something he'd never imagined possible. He had betrayed a member of his own team. Condemned a good and honorable man to an undeserved death.

"I'm sorry," Garrett whispered.

The words were nearly inaudible even within the tight chamber of his helmet, but they resonated like thunder in that empty place where—until just a few seconds earlier—his soul had resided.

The corners of his eyes prickled with the unfamiliar sting of tears. "Oh God... Please forgive me...."

His unheard plea was meaningless, and he knew it. The only man who could grant absolution was a speck in the distance, irretrievably receding into darkness.

Garrett had been through his share of life-or-death situations. He'd always been able to master his fear. Never allowed it to paralyze his thoughts or his muscles.

Now, he was discovering that regret and self-loathing had the power to do what fear had never accomplished.

He was rooted in place. Unable to think. Unable to move. Unable to do anything but stare in the direction of the man he had abandoned.

An immeasurable time later (hours? weeks? seconds?), he felt pressure on his left shoulder. Something pulling at him.

His only response was to tighten his grip on the handhold.

There was a thump, and then a voice.

Keene had brought his helmet into contact with Garrett's and was talking to him through conduction. His speech was muffled but understandable.

"Where is Dan?"

The words were clear, but Garrett's mind didn't want to think about what they meant.

Keene repeated himself. "Where is Dan?"

"Gone..." murmured Garrett.

"What do you mean, *gone?*"

"He—"

Garrett lost interest in finishing the sentence. After some interval—he had no idea how long—he became vaguely aware of movement around him.

There was another thump of touching helmets, and Keene's voice came again. "Let go."

"What?"

"I need to get you into the airlock," said Keene. "Let go of the handhold."

There was no conscious intent to relinquish his grip, but Garrett must have done so. He found himself turning. Moving. Being maneuvered toward the airlock entrance by Keene.

And then, they were in the airlock, Keene pulling the outer door closed. Dogging it shut. Coming back for more helmet-to-helmet talk.

"Floyd, you've got to snap out of it! We need to move!"

"Gone..." moaned Garrett.

"I know he's gone. Dan was the best friend I ever had, and there will be time to mourn him later. But not *now*!"

Garrett said nothing.

Keene's next words came on like gunfire: loud and hard. "Goddamn it, Colonel! Get your head in the game! We've got a mission to carry out! If you get my daughter killed, I'll jettison your sorry ass into space!"

Only one word of Keene's outburst cut through the fog in Garrett's head.

Mission.

A word of almost mystical significance. For the military professional, it was an incantation of the greatest imaginable power, invoking loyalty, commitment to duty, and personal honor.

It shattered the spell that had frozen Garrett's thoughts.

He didn't magically stop despising himself. His honor was tarnished beyond any hope of cleansing, but none of that mattered. His mission was not complete. He had not yet discharged his duty to his service, his nation, or his planet.

He shook his head to clear away the last of the cobwebs, oriented himself, and turned to locate the Airflow Sensor and the Atmospheric Pressure Sensor among the mass of wiring and piping that lined the airlock bulkheads.

Each sensor was connected to a slender telemetry cable by a twist-and-lock style bayonet jack. Neither device was concealed or protected by anti-tamper measures. These were equipment status monitors, not burglar alarms. The engineers responsible for designing the Quest Airlock had never dreamed that uninvited visitors might try to sneak in the back door of the ISS.

Garrett disconnected both sensors, then double-checked that he was disabling the correct devices.

After he was certain he had done things properly, he nudged himself toward the control box and initiated the pressurization cycle.

The lighted tattletale panel inside the lock remained unchanged as the pressure in the airlock rose toward atmospheric normal for the station. Unless one of the Russians happened to be close enough to see or hear the door open, they'd have no warning that the airlock was in use.

When the lock was pressurized, Garrett and Keene spent several uncomfortable minutes bumping around the cramped compartment, going through the freefall contortions needed to slither out of their spacesuits.

The process took longer than either of them expected, and it might have been impossible if Handsome Dan had been crammed in there with them.

With spacesuits off, both men wore the muted blue-gray mission coveralls favored by Russian Cosmonauts. The coveralls were far from a perfect disguise but would hopefully avoid attention if a Russian happened to catch sight of them through an open hatchway.

Around their necks, Garrett and Keene strung respirator masks for use when fentanyl was flowing through the ventilation system.

A final check of their dart pistols, and each man reached for a gas canister. Garrett grabbed the one with the tiny spot of yellow paint and nodded to signal his readiness.

Keene un-dogged the inner door and swung it slowly open.

The Unity Node was empty. No surprise party of armed Russians, waiting to ambush the intruders.

Garrett followed Keene through the hatchway. As he was turning to close the airlock door behind himself, the lights in the Unity Node went dim.

Something—and Garrett knew with visceral certainty what it was—had just placed an enormous drain on the station's power grid.

FORTY-TWO

Kiev, Ukraine
(Expiration of Deadline: 5 Hours / 51 Minutes)

Kiev was an ancient city—arguably one of the oldest on Earth.

Archeological evidence has confirmed the presence of Cro-Magnon settlements on the site as early as the Upper Paleolithic period. Neolithic artifacts mark the location as a center of the prehistoric Cucuteni-Trypillia culture, which flourished during the warming phase after the last Ice Age throughout the regions now known as Moldova, western Ukraine, and northeastern Romania.

At a time when a hundred people and a dozen dwellings constituted a significant focal point of civilization, the area which became Kiev may have supported as many as 3,000 structures with up to 40,000 inhabitants.

Over several centuries, the population of the area expanded, contracted, and expanded again. Cyclical episodes of burning and devastation occurred at intervals of about 60 to 80 years, the reasons for which are a subject of continuing debate among scholars.

Whatever the cause, the intentional destruction of settlements tapered off sometime during the Bronze Age. Relieved of episodic cycles of arson and obliteration, the large village at the site of Kiev gained in size, population, and importance, becoming what many anthropologists consider one of humanity's earliest cities.

By the early Iron Age, the tribes around Kiev were cultivating their lands, practicing animal husbandry, and developing principles of civilization. They formed trading relationships with the Scythians, the settlements of the northern Black Sea coast, and (probably) the eastern provinces of the Roman Empire.

The city was sacked by the Vikings in the ninth century; besieged by the nomadic Pechenegs a few decades later; destroyed entirely by invading Mongols four centuries after that; and then destroyed yet again during the Second World War.

Each time, the ancient metropolis rose from the ruins to be rebuilt, larger and grander than it had been before.

From stone ax, to spear, to sword, to artillery, to aerial bombardment, the city had been burned, hacked, and blasted by nearly every implement of violence conceived by man.

But never—until now—had it been struck by a wavefront of invisible energy that penetrated roofs, walls, and other barriers like x-rays through tissue paper.

The pulse came on at the speed of light and was gone just as quickly, wiping out the tools of technocentric civilization as it passed.

Everywhere the wave of energy touched, vehicles died. Traffic lights, streetlamps, and light fixtures went dark. Loudspeakers, headphones, and earbuds fell silent. Refrigerators, air conditioners, and freezers ceased to function. Televisions, computer monitors, and cell phone screens went black. Elevators stalled between floors. Decorative fountains stopped spraying water into the air.

Surgeons in hospital operating rooms shouted for light, but there would be nothing brighter than candlelight until the sun rose again.

The blackout was instant and terrifying in its thoroughness.

A city that could trace its lineage back to the dawn of the Stone Age was suddenly given a bitter taste of that ancient and unwelcome era.

FORTY-THREE

The armored doors slid closed. President Roth and Lily, flanked by their respective Secret Service agents, began the elevator ride down to the bunker.

The official acronym was *PEOC* (short for *Presidential Emergency Operations Center*), but it had been dubbed "the bunker" by Ronald Reagan and the unofficial title had stuck.

Built for Franklin D. Roosevelt in 1942 and upgraded periodically during the Cold War, the PEOC was a fortified cylindrical refuge three levels below the East Wing of the White House, capped by a forty-foot blast shield layered with high-tensile ferroconcrete, steel plating, and Kevlar.

Equal parts bomb shelter and military command center, the underground facility housed self-contained life support systems, living quarters, office spaces, a communications complex, and an operations center that duplicated the functions of the Situation Room.

According to certain internet rumor mills, the bunker was engineered to withstand a direct nuclear blast, and it was supposedly stocked with sufficient provisions to keep the president, his family, and his favored political cronies alive for years while the rest of the country lay in radioactive cinders.

Crackpot theories to the contrary, there were no super-secret preparations to keep government fat cats basking in subterranean luxury after the annihilation of the American people. The PEOC—and the other protected facilities at Raven Rock, Pennsylvania; Cheyenne Mountain, Colorado; and Mount Weather, Virginia—were intended to keep the government functioning long enough to coordinate retaliatory nuclear strikes, and lead the final defense of the nation.

If America were destroyed, James Roth and everyone he cared about would die shortly thereafter. They might last a few weeks (or even a couple of months) longer than people without such heroic protections, but death would come soon enough in a world gone to nuclear ruin.

So, this trip down the armored elevator was not a ride toward ultimate safety. It was a battening down of hatches for a storm that none of them were likely to survive.

The president wondered again if this was the right thing to do. Maybe it was best to give in to Polichev's demands. Allow the United States to be disarmed and pray that the coming global dictatorship would be relatively benign.

Could he override his doubts and instincts? Make himself surrender his nation's defenses into the hands of a foreign power? How could he reconcile that with his oath to preserve, protect, and defend?

Even if he could force himself to swallow so bitter a pill, could he—in the few hours remaining before the deadline expired—build a majority coalition across both sides of the aisle? He'd have to convince political allies and opponents alike that submitting to Russian hegemony was in the best long-term interests of the American people.

If he were going to try, he'd have to begin immediately.

The decision was made for him as soon as the elevator reached its destination. The doors slid open to reveal General Christopher standing in the vestibule outside the entrance to the PEOC.

The general held out a briefing folder. "Just in, Mr. President. All channels of communication with our embassy in Kiev were chopped off a few minutes ago. NASA confirms a high-intensity electromagnetic surge from the ISS at approximately the same time."

President Roth accepted the folder. "EMP attack?"

"It's got all the earmarks, sir."

The president skimmed the top page of the brief as he walked toward the massive steel doors of the bunker. Polichev was either smoothing the way for a full invasion of Ukraine or signaling to the world that no one could stop him. Not even the United States.

The deadline had not expired yet, and the Russians were already carving out their new empire. Punishing their perceived enemies.

And with that realization, President James Everett Roth finally accepted his place in History.

He knew what he had to do.

FORTY-FOUR

341st Missile Wing
12th Missile Squadron, Silo G-08
Southwest of Simms, Montana
(Expiration of Deadline: 5 Hours / 36 Minutes)

Air Force Captain Susannah Quaid (known to the enlisted missile crew by the hated nickname of Suzy Q) glanced over her penciled notes in preparation for copying them in ink to the Combat Crew Commander's logbook.

"I can deal with the soldier flies," she said. "And the brown ticks, and the digging wasps, and the seventeen kinds of spiders. It's the acorn weevils that are making me bat shit. Can't pour a bowl of Lucky Charms without checking for weevils."

Her Deputy Commander, First Lieutenant Kurt Waller, straightened a row of binders on the metal shelf between their consoles. "Maybe the Lucky Charms are the problem, ma'am. Have you thought about trying a cereal made for grown-ups? Your marshmallow sugar bombs might be attracting the weevils."

"It's not the Lucky Charms."

"Don't be so sure about that," said Waller. "Never any weevils in *my* cereal."

Quaid spotted and corrected a spelling error in her penciled notes.

"I'd rather have weevils than that dry-ass organic wheatgrass crap you eat. When the insects won't touch your food, that should tell you something, Lieutenant."

"Whatever you say, Captain," said Waller.

Quaid looked up from her clipboard, taking in the row of black and white security monitors, each screen showing the LGM-30G Minuteman III intercontinental ballistic missile from a different angle.

The bird was right where it always had been: 79,432 pounds of solidified Armageddon, nestled safely in its armored concrete silo. Not a rivet, weld line, or fleck of paint was changed, but the missile seemed different to Quaid now. It had somehow been transformed by unfolding events. The idea of launching that monster was no longer comfortably hypothetical.

Through all its wars, escalations, and international crises, the United States had never before been to DEFCON 1. To the best of Quaid's knowledge, no president in history had held his finger this close to the big red button.

In the bottom right corner of each security monitor, a digital readout showed the local time. Ticking off the seconds until the Russian ultimatum expired. Maybe ticking away the final seconds of the world as Quaid had always known it.

And she couldn't say a word.

She wanted to discuss her thoughts with Waller, talk about what was happening, and what *might* be happening in the next few minutes or hours. But that topic was—by long unspoken tradition—off limits for missileers on watch.

When they were down in the silo, missile officers could chat about training, logistics, politics, sports, families, food, drinking, cars, house problems, random trivia, and just about anything else, but it was taboo to even speculate about whether they might be ordered to turn the keys. (Those shiny harmless looking little metal keys that could unleash the dogs of hell.)

So, Quaid cleaned up her log notes, prattled on about Montana's apparently endless catalog of pest insects, and stayed clear of the only subject she actually wanted to address.

She thought about breaching missileer protocol by bringing up the topic anyway. The prohibition was social, not regulatory. She couldn't be prosecuted, or put on report, or even reprimanded for violating the unofficial taboo.

But breaking that unwritten rule might come across to Waller as a weakness of character. He might think she lacked the mental fortitude to keep her cool in the run-up to a possible launch. And he might share his doubts with other people in the squadron.

It was possible, of course, that Waller was just as eager to broach the subject as she was. He could be sitting there, trying to think up some way to bring the conversation around to *that-which-must-not-be-discussed.*

If so, maybe he'd give her some kind of signal.

"You know where else I've been finding acorn weevils?" Quaid asked.

Waller was spared the need to answer by a loud metallic warble. It was the attention signal from the National Command Authority Circuit.

As they'd practiced countless times in drills, Quaid and Waller both reached for their message binders.

The warbling tone chopped off and a man's voice came from the speaker box. "Hat Trick, this is Quick Draw with a Red Priority Tripwire Message in four parts. Stand by to authenticate."

Quaid flipped to the red section of her binder and knew that Waller was doing the same.

When the voice spoke, they both copied the alphanumeric code digits into authentication blanks on the cover sheet of the red section.

"Kilo. Bravo. Tango. X-ray. Niner. Lima."

At the end of the sequence, Quaid's sheet read, 'K B T X 9 L' in large block capitals.

The voice repeated the entire authentication sequence and Quaid copied the characters again, ignoring her first entries in case she'd misheard or incorrectly copied one or more of the characters. The result was identical the second time around. 'K B T X 9 L.' No mistakes.

She stood up and began working through the combination on the Combat Crew Commander's safe. "I copied six digits in valid sequence."

"Concur," said Waller, standing to open the Deputy Commander's safe. "Six digits in valid sequence."

Quaid muffed the combination on the first try and had to start again. Her hands weren't trembling, but her thoughts were racing so hard that she had trouble concentrating.

She swung open the heavy little door and reached in for the 'waffle,' an opaque plastic cartridge the length and breadth of a credit card but significantly thicker. She bent the cartridge sharply, snapping the brittle plastic in half to reveal a thinner more flexible plastic card within. On this thinner card were printed three letters.

Quaid extracted the flexible card and compared it to the first three letters of the authentication signal. 'K B T.' A perfect match.

"I authenticate part one," she announced.

Waller compared the card from his own waffle to his writing in the binder. "I authenticate part two."

Quaid pressed the transmit button on the National Command Authority Circuit speaker box, something she'd never done outside of training drills. "Quick Draw, this is Hat Trick. Authentication confirmed. Standing by to copy."

She released the button and sat down with her binder, ready to transcribe the letters and numerals of the prelaunch order.

"Holy fuck!" she said to herself.

The voice blared out of the speaker box again. "Hat Trick, this is Quick Draw. Message part one as follows. Bravo. Alpha. Echo..."

Susannah Quaid began to write.

FORTY-FIVE

International Space Station
(Expiration of Deadline: 5 Hours / 31 Minutes)

It was almost over.

Paul Keene hovered inside the hatchway of the Kibo Module, keeping lookout while Garrett went about the business of connecting a gas canister to the life-support system. Three or four minutes more, that was all they needed.

Time enough for Garrett to finish his various bypasses, and cross-connections, and whatever. If things went according to plan, the Russians would be unconscious before they realized that the station had been invaded.

Not that *anything* had gone according to the plan.

No one had planned for the ISS to do an unscheduled re-boost. No one had planned for arriving at the station without fuel for braking maneuvers. No one had planned for the insane flyby rendezvous. No one had planned for Dan missing the station and zooming off into the great beyond.

Paul didn't want to think about Dan now. Later (after Sarah was safe) he could let himself feel the loss of his friend. Allow himself to mourn. To face the emotions that he was keeping walled off in his heart. But not until then.

All they needed were a few more minutes... Just...

Shit!

He recognized the woman from the prelaunch briefing. One of the cosmonauts, Lieutenant Colonel Anya Malikova, sailing toward him from the Destiny Module.

Paul leveled his dart pistol and took aim. She spotted him before he could squeeze the trigger.

With the agility of someone long accustomed to microgravity, the cosmonaut did a swim-flip turnover that put her facing in the opposite direction and shoved off an equipment cabinet with both feet. Then, she was flying away from him, shouting in Russian. *"Vzlomshchiki! Vzlomshchiki!"*

Paul took off in pursuit, drawing a bead on the cosmonaut as he flew. In the close quarters of the module, the twang of the dart pistol spring was much louder than he expected. Far louder than he remembered from the practice shots he had taken prior to launch.

Loud as it was, the powerful spring did its job—burying a dart in the woman's lower back—pumping the cosmonaut full of quick-acting tranquilizer.

Malikova lost muscle control (or consciousness) almost immediately. She slammed into a bulkhead like a sack of potatoes, rebounded, and floated limply near the middle of the module.

Paul grabbed a hatch coaming to stop his motion, re-cocked the dart gun, and kicked off back toward the entrance of the Kibo Module.

"Garrett, you need to finish what you're doing right now! We're about to be neck-deep in hostiles!"

Taihang Mountains
Henan Province, China

Major Gao Xiantu of the People's Liberation Army Rocket Force oversaw the operation carefully. He watched his crew go about their appointed tasks, saw the men working with the quick deliberate movements of well-reinforced training.

Hauled out of its tunnel lair high on the mountainside, the enormous Dongfeng 5 ballistic missile had been lifted from its horizontal cradle and raised into firing position by the trailer's erector gantry. Sitting upright on the concrete pad outside the tunnel's mouth, the two-stage missile was now being fueled.

The DF-5s were old, nearing the end of their operational lives and gradually being phased out by the solid-fuel DF-41s. Gao had fully expected to see this aging beast retired someday; towed down the winding mountain road to be disassembled and salvaged for its components and constituent materials.

Practice exercises and political indoctrination aside, he'd never imagined himself standing under the stars, watching plumes of vapor rise from the fueling hoses as unsymmetrical dimethylhydrazine and nitrogen tetroxide coursed into the weapon's propellant and oxidizer tanks.

Down in Xinxiang, his wife and daughter would be sleeping in the family's too-small apartment on Jiaowei Road. His Xiǎo yāojing (little goblin) would be snuggled deep under her butterfly quilt like a baby rabbit nestled in its burrow. A tiny whisper of a girl with gigantic dreams for the future. Slumbering peacefully in the belief that her father and his fellow soldiers would keep China safe from all enemies.

Chinese families were supposed to value sons over daughters. A lot of families regarded the birth of a girl child as—perhaps not quite a tragedy—but certainly a disappointment. Not Gao. That tiny goblin face had stolen his heart from the very first.

She expected him to come home in a few days at the end of his duty rotation, like he always had before. Climb down off the imaginary wall that he guarded and return to the role of husband and father, where his responsibilities as a warrior were reduced to battles with the spiders who occasionally invaded the apartment's bathroom.

His little girl had no idea what he was doing now. No suspicion that her protective bàba was busily unshackling a five-megaton demon that would incinerate countless people and begin the immolation of humankind.

Gao's feelings were a seething maelstrom of fear, pride, shame, and confusion. This dreadful and unthinkable task was his duty. His honor as an officer and as a Chinese citizen demanded that he carry out his orders with every gram of skill and professionalism he could muster. But in the deep recesses of his inner being, he had never believed that this moment might come.

Still... What kind of soldier only followed commands that came without consequence? What kind of man turned away when faced with difficult and painful obligations?

He would do this awful thing, knowing that he couldn't possibly predict the outcome for his planet, his country, or his family. He would obey his orders.

Even as the UDMH and N2O4 gushed into the rapidly-filling tanks of the missile, he continued to hope that the final launch order would not be issued. That this terrible night would not end with Gao's old (but still-potent) engine of doom rocketing toward the dark clouds on its way to inaugurate the final war of his species.

Because hope, as fragile and tenuous as it might be, was the only thing that Gao Xiantu had left.

Kibo Module
International Space Station

Maybe he'd missed a step.

Maybe he'd attached one of the jumper wires in the wrong sequence or clipped it to the wrong terminal point.

Maybe—in the rush to complete the job—he'd bypassed the Solid-phase Microextraction Sampler before cutting out the Photoionization Detector.

Or maybe there was some minor hardware or software variation between this Oxygen Generation System rack and the model that Garrett had trained on.

The cause was irrelevant.

What mattered was the result.

Garrett completed the final connection, sliding the quick-release collar of the gas canister hose over one of the fittings on the air scrubber manifold.

"Ready to go!" he said. "Masks up!"

He settled his respirator mask over his nose and mouth, checked the fit, turned on the air supply, and took a couple of breaths.

When he was sure that air was flowing into the mask, he opened the valve on the gas canister and aerosolized fentanyl began pumping into the ISS life support system.

The hiss of flowing gas was expected. The shrieking alarm siren and flashing tattletales were not.

Damn it!

What had he done wrong?

Garrett realized that it didn't matter.

He reached for the other canister. The one with the tiny spot of yellow paint.

Nauka Module
International Space Station

Volkov snatched an emergency mask from a bulkhead rack, pulled the clear plastic hood over his head, and activated the unit's catalytic oxygen generator.

Syomin, Levkin, and Dmitri grabbed emergency masks of their own.

Volkov drew the Makarov from the holster on his belt. As he worked the slide to chamber a round, he glared in Dmitri's direction. "I *told* you we should have killed them!"

He nodded toward Levkin and Syomin. "You two have your orders. Dmitri, draw your weapon and come with me."

Volkov propelled himself out of the module with Dmitri trailing behind.

As one accustomed to having his orders followed, Volkov took it for granted that his subordinates would obey his commands.

He was not watching when Dmitri diverted through a hatchway and vanished from sight.

North Pacific Ocean

Four hundred feet below the waves, the nuclear ballistic missile submarine USS *Nevada* glided through the waters south of the Aleutian Islands.

The sub's official motto was *"Silent Sentry"* and she very nearly lived up to those words. The eighth boat of the legendarily quiet *Ohio* class, the *Nevada* was well into her fourth decade of operation. Despite her years, the sub's electronics, engineering plant, and acoustic suppression measures had been periodically updated throughout her service life.

While she was no longer at the cutting-edge of submarine technology, few sonar sensors could detect her acoustic signatures at any appreciable range, and her 20 Trident II missiles made the *Nevada* a hidden and ceaselessly mobile nuclear arsenal.

The sub's commanding officer, Captain Barry Campbell, sat drinking tea at the wardroom table, beneath a bronze plaque emblazoned with the second (unofficial) motto of his boat: *"You pays your money, and you takes your chances."*

That time-worn idiom was both a reference to the casinos of USS *Nevada's* namesake state and an acknowledgment of the principle that all human endeavors have the potential for unexpected consequences.

A caffeine addict like most military professionals, Campbell was experimenting with hot tea as a substitute for coffee. The uncounted cups of Navy java he had downed over the years were starting to exact their toll on his stomach. He was in search of an alternative means of ingesting the legal stimulant in large quantities, and he couldn't picture the CO of a ballistic missile sub swilling Red Bull like a seventeen-year-old X-Box commando.

In his ongoing research, he'd tried everything from Lipton tea bags to exotic Asian blends. So far, nothing had turned out to be as good as the coffee.

The subject of his current experiment had been recommended by his sister-in-law. The name was *Jumpy Monkey*, which struck Campbell as unnecessarily silly. But it was supposed to have as much caffeine as coffee and—with a little doctoring—the flavor was not too bad. He might be able to get used to this one, if it packed enough wallop to keep him moving.

He was taking another swallow when the phone emitted a quiet bleep.

Campbell pulled the receiver out of its cradle and lifted it to his ear. "Captain speaking."

The voice on the other end belonged to the Communications Officer, Lieutenant Worley. "Morning, Skipper. We've got an FDM coming in, with an X-ray Two-Zero suffix."

"Very well," said Campbell. "On my way."

He returned the handset to its cradle, chugged down the rest of the tea, and got to his feet.

FDM was short for Force Direction Message. The incoming data bundle would contain targeting packages for the *Nevada's* missiles. The X-ray Two-Zero suffix was comm-speak for "x 20," meaning every weapon in the submarine's missile tubes.

National Command Authority was planning to empty the magazine, not holding anything in reserve for a second strike.

Campbell did not doubt that every missile on his boat would be aimed at some city or military base in Russia. President Roth was setting up a preemptive attack that apparently included every weapon in the American stockpile.

The next communication USS *Nevada* received would be an Emergency Action Message containing the final order to launch. Your basic doomsday scenario.

You pays your money, and you takes your chances.

Maybe Campbell wouldn't have to cultivate a taste for tea after all.

Unity Node
International Space Station

Malikova's body floated near the center of the Unity Node, turning languidly in the air.

Paul hoped the woman's unconscious form would serve as a distraction for approaching hostiles. If nothing else, she might partially block sightlines into the alcove where he had positioned himself.

The recess was too shallow to hide in, but it gave him at least partial concealment. Maybe enough to let him get off a good first shot.

Not a perfect ambush site by any stretch of the imagination. The station's designers had planned for a wide range of contingencies. Understandably, creating defendable positions for firefights had not been on anyone's list of engineering priorities.

Paul checked his weapon, making sure there was a dart in the chamber, and it was ready to fire.

He wouldn't have to wait long. The ISS couldn't sustain human life without a source of breathable air. Someone would come to check on the life support system pretty damned fast.

He glanced back toward the entrance to the Kibo Module. Where was Garrett? The fentanyl plan was blown, and the Russians were going to be here any second. What was Garrett waiting for?

Paul gave a low whistle that was muffled by his breathing mask. "Garrett, get your ass up here! I'm gonna need some—"

He cut himself off.

Somebody was coming.

Elbow steadied against the bulkhead, Paul sighted past Malikova's body, aiming for the approaching figure. A man in the blue-gray coveralls of a cosmonaut, head covered in the clear plastic shroud of an emergency respirator hood, some sort of handgun in his outstretched fist.

Again, Paul recognized a face from the prelaunch briefing. Colonel Pavel Volkov, leader of this vicious little band of cutthroats.

Paul squeezed the trigger. The twang of the spring was no quieter the second time around, but the dart flew straight and true.

If not for the Russian man's respirator, the shot would have hit

Volkov just below the larynx and the fight would have been over. Instead, the dart ricocheted off the catalytic oxygen generator of Volkov's emergency hood.

Paul Keene survived the next couple of seconds through a combination of physics and dumb luck. The impact of the tranquilizer dart jammed the oxygen generator unit into Volkov's windpipe with the force of a throat punch. The shock of the blow made the Russian's first bullet go astray. Finally, the recoil of the shot acted like a reaction thruster, spinning the man half around.

The bullet must have struck one of the cable bundles, because the lights in the Unity Node began flickering on and off erratically. Paul's eardrums shrilled with the aftereffects of the muzzle report—almost deafening in the enclosed module.

There was no time to reload his dart pistol. He launched himself toward the intruder, bumping against the still-revolving Malikova woman as he passed. The unexpected contact altered Paul's direction of motion, throwing him off his planned trajectory.

The lights strobed wildly, flaring from brilliance to darkness and back again in drunken sequences with no discernible pattern. Malikova's body revolved and rebounded, limbs flailing, throwing shadows that loomed, jerked, disappeared, and reappeared with surreal unpredictability.

Between the visual chaos and the ringing in his ears from the gunshot, Paul lost track of Volkov's position for half a second.

That was all it took.

The man was upon him. Grabbing the front of Paul's coveralls; yanking the handgun around for a point-blank head shot.

Volkov was younger, better trained, better armed, and accustomed to moving in microgravity.

Paul's only advantage was desperation. Not the panic of a human struggling to stay alive, but the wild and furious abandon of a parent fighting to save a child.

His adrenal glands threw open the floodgates, dumping a deluge of epinephrine into his bloodstream. The buzz of surging adrenaline was louder in his ears than the ringing from the gunshot.

He made no conscious decision. His muscles seemed to act on their own volition. His right hand flew up and around with a speed that was altogether unfamiliar to him, crashing the unloaded dart pistol into Volkov's cheek.

There was a flash and the thunder of another gunshot close to Paul's ear as Volkov got off a second round.

Paul's left hand seized the upper sleeve of Volkov's coveralls, fingers ratcheting closed on thick fabric. His right hand swung the dart gun again, and struck a blow at the Russian's head, trying to bash the man's brains out. He didn't quite succeed, but Volkov's pistol went spinning away into the leaping and heaving shadows.

Paul brought the dart gun in to club the Russian again. But Volkov snatched him in close and there was an explosion of pain as the cosmonaut smashed his forehead into the bridge of Paul's nose.

Dazed and half-blinded, there was no chance to recover before Volkov followed up the head butt with a fist to Paul's temple.

Paul somehow managed to hang on to Volkov's sleeve.

The two men remained locked together, Volkov hammering his fist into Paul's head and neck—Paul struggling to process what was happening—his thoughts unable to regain traction under the continued pummeling.

The motions of their thrashing limbs imparted unpredictable vectors of inertia—sending the combatants gyrating through the alternating light and darkness, bouncing off of bulkheads and the ever-present body of Malikova.

One of their tumbles brought the back of Paul's head up against the metal lip of a hatch coaming. A hard crack that nearly put his lights out for good. Then, Volkov's hands were on his throat. Clenching like a vise. Constricting with a strength beyond Paul's imagining. Choking the life out of him.

It was over.

Over...

The dart pistol floated from Paul's relaxing fingers. All thoughts of fighting gone. His will to survive dwindling. Spark fading.

The buzzing in his ears grew louder. Lurching shadows charging forward to engulf him. Swallow him. Subsume him.

Then, something...

His fingers brushing against something.

An unfamiliar shape.

Paul's hand closed over the shape automatically, a pistol grip form sliding into his palm, finger coming to rest on...

A trigger...

Not the dart gun.

Not Volkov's handgun.

He had no idea what it might be.

Didn't care.

He pulled the trigger.

Volkov's body convulsed. Back arching. Muscles firing involuntarily. Contracting with irresistible and agonizing force. Paroxysms of uncontrolled spasms ripping through the Russian man's anatomy in wave after wave. Pain, upon pain, upon pain, arcing through him with the suddenness of a lightning strike.

If Paul's brain had been functioning properly, he would have recognized the thing in his hand as the military-grade Taser hanging from Volkov's belt. He might have even spotted it as a design that was illegal in the United States and Western Europe. Prohibited for being overamped to the point of lethality.

But in this moment, Paul knew none of that. His mind processed a single idea. When he pulled the trigger, the crushing hands on his throat went away. Left him alone.

He pulled the trigger again.

And again.

And again.

Until the darkness that had been threatening to devour him did just exactly that.

Nauka Module
International Space Station

Levkin tapped the icon to bring the capacitor arrays online. He was rewarded with the expected squeal as the first bank of brick-sized components began building up to a firing charge. Once initiated, the sequence was automated. As each of the five capacitor banks crossed the seventy percent charge threshold, the software started charging the next bank.

That left nothing for Levkin to do except guard the weapon, so he took up a position to cover the door, pulled his Makarov, and chambered a round. If the prisoners had somehow escaped from the Cupola Module, they were probably coming here.

Syomin hovered near the master control screen. One by one, the status tattletales at the left edge of the display flipped from amber to green.

In the targeting map that formed the main section of the screen, a view of the Pacific Ocean scrolled toward the West Coast of the United States.

FORTY-SIX

International Space Station

Sarah and Rutger were both startled by the clank of retracting dogs. The hatch of the Cupola Module swung open. Dmitri floated in the hatchway, fear visible on his face through the plastic of his respirator hood.

Sarah adjusted her own emergency mask. Well, let the bastard be afraid. Between the atmospheric contamination alarm and whoever had flown past the cupola windows in the IVA suit, things might be turning against Team Russia.

Screw 'em! She hoped they were shitting themselves.

"What do you want?" growled Rutger. "Volkov send you to finish us off?"

Dmitri ignored the jab, turning his attention to Sarah. "They're going to destroy your capital!"

Sarah tried to pour all the derision she was feeling into her voice. "What do you care? I mean, that was your big plan, right?"

"Syomin and Levkin are powering up the weapon!" said Dmitri. "We don't have time for this!"

This brought a snort from Rutger. "There is no *we*, Dmitri. You're playing for the other side, remember?"

Dmitri sighed. Then, he pulled the 9mm Makarov from his belt

233

and held it out to Sarah, grip-first. "You can shoot me when it's all over. Right now, we have to move!"

Sarah accepted the offered handgun. Son of a bitch! Maybe D *was* switching teams.

She checked to see if the Makarov was loaded. It was. "Where's Volkov?"

"Out searching for you," said Dmitri. "He thinks you've escaped."

Sarah nodded and handed the pistol to Rutger. "You guys go after the EMP weapon. I'm gonna take down the Beta Gimbals. See if I can cut off the power to that damned thing."

The three of them pushed off: Rutger and Dmitri heading toward the Nauka Module, and Sarah toward the Z1 Truss Dome.

Elsewhere

Darkness.

Fathomless. Unchanging. Infinite.

No...

Not quite unchanging.

Graduations of shadow. Shifting curtains of opacity.

Amid churning tendrils of blackness, Paul Keene began to creep toward consciousness.

Unbidden, his eyelids slid open a crack, admitting smears of shape, light, and color that his visual cortex was not yet ready to interpret.

He became aware of a high-pitched whistling sound. The warble of the Radar Warning Receiver in the cockpit of his *Tomcat*... The bleating of his kitchen smoke alarm... The whine of the *Kickstart* jet's turbines spooling up...

Or...

The lingering result of Volkov's pistol going off next to his ear.

Cognitive processes reasserted themselves; fragments of memory reassembling as his brain regained conscious functions. Shooting

Malikova. The fight with Volkov. Vice-like fingers crushing his throat. The back of his head slamming into something.

And Sarah...

The thought of her name nudged Paul closer to full awareness.

There was some kind of job that he needed to do. Something important involving Sarah.

His eyes came into focus and he spent a few seconds taking in his surroundings. He was drifting, revolving slowly through the air amidst flickering stuttering lights. The Unity Node.

It took him a few more seconds to get his bearings and figure out which hatchway led back toward the Kibo Module.

That way...

He reached for a handhold but missed—his muscles not yet fully back under control.

He caught it on the next rotation and allowed his joints to absorb the inertia of his movement. When he was properly oriented, he kicked off in the direction of the Kibo Module.

He was going to need help from Garrett.

Z1 Truss Dome
International Space Station

Small as the compartment was, the Z1 Truss Dome saw so little use that it had become a storage cubby for the ISS crew. Any tool, device, or instrument that was not needed on a regular basis would eventually end up here.

It reminded Sarah of Fred Flintstone's overflowing closet from the cartoons she had watched as a kid. Whenever the hapless caveman opened the closet door, all manner of junk would fall out, burying him under an avalanche of furniture, sporting equipment, clothing, and bric-a-brac.

The last item to come careening out was always a stone bowling ball, which unerringly homed in on Fred's big toe like a Neolithic guided missile.

The Z1 Dome was just as densely packed as Fred's closet, but the items were not jammed in at indiscriminate angles. Each article had been fitted carefully into place with the precision of a real-world Tetris game.

If Sarah had cared at all for the condition of the stored items, getting into the dome cubicle would have taken her a while. But protecting unused equipment and supplies from accidental damage was the last thing on her mind.

She burrowed in with abandon, snatching out articles and tossing them over her shoulder until the air behind her was a three-dimensional debris field of pinwheeling ricocheting objects.

It took her only a couple of moments to reach her goal, a Guidance, Navigation, and Control laptop mounted to the rear bulkhead. Sarah unfolded the keyboard and tapped the start button.

The display blinked and stuttered before it reluctantly came awake. Readouts from the boot-up routine scrolled down the screen.

This unit was slower than the ones Sarah was accustomed to. An older model and it hadn't been powered up in a while, so it was a bit on the balky side.

Sarah didn't need the thing to play resource-gobbling video games or compute Pi to a million decimal places. All she wanted was access to the PHALCON menu, and that didn't require much in the way of processing capacity.

Even with the GNC laptop dragging its digital feet, it would take her only a minute to rotate the solar arrays away from the sun. Then, figure another thirty seconds or so to override the failsafes and shunt high voltage DC power to the low power controllers that drove the Beta Gimbals.

She'd fry those suckers good.

Then, let Volkov's assholes try to fire their weapon without main power. They'd be lucky if the station's batteries were good for one shot at ten percent strength. She'd pull their fucking teeth all right. You bet your ass!

She tabbed through to the Tier 2 GNC interface, where the menus for Power, Heating, Articulation, and Lighting Control were kept.

Shit!

It was grayed out!

All the icons were visible on the screen, but every one of them was ghosted. Not selectable.

Someone had locked her out of the whole power management system. They'd locked *everybody* out. If Sarah couldn't get in with full PHALCON privileges, then nobody could get in.

The bastards were a step ahead of her.

Again.

Damn it! What was she supposed to do now?

There had to be something else. Some other way to shut down the EMP weapon. There just *had* to be.

But what if there wasn't?

What if her belief in that possibility was nothing more than bullshit magical thinking—drummed into her head by action movies and adventure novels, where the good guys always pulled off a Hail Mary play at the last conceivable second?

What if all that she, and Rutger—and even Dmitri—could do was to throw themselves at armed adversaries and be gunned down with no hope of accomplishing anything?

Well… So what?

If that was how things were, so be it.

She'd been a fighter pilot a lot longer than she'd been an astronaut, and a warrior didn't throw in the towel just because the cause was hopeless. If Sarah was going to die, she wanted to be fighting alongside her friends when it happened.

She backed out of the Z1 Truss Dome and plunged into the cloud of discarded articles, searching through the jumble of items for anything she might use as a weapon.

Kibo Module
International Space Station

Paul Keene was not prepared for the sight that waited for him in the Kibo Module.

Garrett was right where Paul had left him, next to the Oxygen

Generation System rack, still busily working away. But the Air Force man was no longer fiddling with the life support system. He had taken apart one of the gas canisters and was working on the apparatus that had been concealed inside.

Fatigued and battered as he was, Paul felt an instantaneous flare of anger. "Is that what I think it is?"

Garrett's fingers moved over the device he was assembling. He didn't look up. "It's Plan B."

"A bomb? You brought a fucking *bomb*?"

Garrett's attention never wavered from his task.

Paul began mentally sizing up the younger man. Trying to decide if (beat to shit as he was) he had any chance of taking Garrett out. His dart gun was long gone, not that Garrett would give him a chance to reload the thing.

"You don't have to do this," Paul said. "I've already taken out two of the Russians. We can—"

Garrett cut him off. "You had a good plan, Paul. Sorry I screwed things up. But we're the only people in a position to destroy the weapon."

Paul reached for the pouch on his belt, half-numb fingers feeling for one of the tranquilizer darts. "I did not bring you up here to kill my daughter!"

"I have no intention of killing your daughter," said Garrett. "If we do this right, we can get her out of here safely."

Paul's hand closed around a dart, but his muscles relaxed a fraction. "Keep talking…"

Garrett looked up from the bomb. "Timer is set for ten minutes and locked. Nobody can change it without the passcode. I tuck this thing out of sight a little closer to the Nauka Module; then we get the hell out of here. There's a Soyuz docked at Node 3 and I can shortcut the emergency preflight. You find Sarah. We'll *all* be out of the blast radius before the timer hits zero."

The relief that flooded through Paul's body was so sudden and palpable that it nearly made him dizzy. "You really mean that?"

"I mean it," Garrett said. "Let's—"

Before he could utter the next word, a blur of silver shot past Paul's face. The flying object, whatever it was, struck Garrett in the side of the head and sent him spinning. Trailing a fog of red mist as he cartwheeled sideways.

Paul caught a quick glimpse at the silver object. Some kind of handleless knife blade, driven deep into Garrett's left temple. Blood still spraying from the wound as the man's body twitched and shuddered with the random firings of nerve death.

Paul jerked his head around to see Anya Malikova floating in the open hatchway. Improbably hanging on to some shred of consciousness, despite the gas and the tranquilizer dart, like one of those surgery patients who inexplicably wakes up under heavy anesthesia.

In her extended hand was a knife handle with no blade—the other half of whatever had just killed Floyd Garrett.

Malikova muttered something, her speech thick with sedation and a strong Russian accent.

Perhaps Paul heard wrong, but the word sounded like "*Checkmate.*"

He had no idea what that might mean, and he didn't care. He dove through the air toward the cosmonaut, the half-forgotten dart still in his fingers.

Neither of them was in any shape for a fight, but they went after one other like a pair of punch-drunk boxers in the twelfth round. They were a tangle of leaden limbs and uncoordinated movements, each trying to get in a telling attack.

In the scuffle, Malikova ripped the respirator mask from Paul's face. That might have been her moment of triumph, but that instant of distraction gave Paul the opening he needed. He brought his hand around hard, stabbing the dart into the cosmonaut's side, just below her ribs.

The second dose of tranquilizer pumped into the woman's bloodstream just as Paul got a lungful of air laced with fentanyl.

Both of the combatants lost consciousness within seconds.

A few yards from where Paul's limp body floated, the bomb did slow-motion pirouettes in the air.

Unseen by anyone, the digits on the timer reached nine minutes and thirty seconds and continued to count backward toward zero.

FORTY-SEVEN

United States Strategic Command
Offutt Air Force Base, Nebraska

The Global Operations Center was buttoned down and ready for war.

Eighty feet beneath the General Curtis E. LeMay headquarters building, the GOC was the nerve center for USSTRATCOM and the locus of America's nuclear command and control system.

Depicted as the infamous "War Room" in too many Cold War thriller films to count, the subterranean citadel had never been used for its ultimate intended purpose: to launch and prosecute a nuclear war.

The GOC was staffed by officers and enlisted personnel from every branch of the U.S. military, supported by representatives of the various intelligence organizations. Together, they (and decades of predecessors) had overseen numerous acts of conventional warfare and antiterrorism actions of many kinds, but they had never done that singular and unthinkable thing for which this underground command center had been constructed.

From his raised chair in the middle of the operations floor, Air Force General Scott Mercier watched his people go through their last-second equipment tests and communications checks.

It was about to happen.

The moment he had never expected to see was about to happen. Not a training exercise. Not a simulation. The real thing. A full-scale nuclear strike, against an adversary that was fully capable of destroying the United States.

On the far wall, between two enormous geographic display screens, hung the circular emblem of the U.S. Strategic Command: an armored gauntlet clutching an olive branch and three red lightning bolts superimposed over the globe of the Earth. Below the seal, in embossed capital letters, was the USSTRATCOM motto. *"OUR BUSINESS IS PEACE."*

Just below this hopeful pronouncement was an illuminated status board, and the "DEFCON 1" enunciator blazed like a baleful white eye.

What Mercier wanted more than anything in the world was for that bright white enunciator to go dark. To cease its glaring proclamation of the destruction that was minutes (or seconds) from commencing.

He got his wish, but not in the manner he had imagined.

In his mind, the status board would wink from the white of DEFCON 1, to the red of DEFCON 2, to the yellow of DEFCON 3, to the green of DEFCON 4, and finally the blue of DEFCON 5. U.S. military forces scaling back to their ordinary levels of readiness, and the GOC team returning to the more prosaic business of trying to combat organized terror groups.

What actually happened was something else.

The glowing white DEFCON 1 enunciator went dark, but so did everything else.

All over the operations floor, light bulbs and display screens lost power. Redundant electrical systems and backup power supplies should have kicked in immediately.

They didn't.

Poised as it was on the brink of launching a massive nuclear strike, the United States Strategic Command Global Operations Center was plunged into darkness.

Looking Glass

Approximately 116 miles to the south, the U.S. Navy Boeing E-6B Mercury aircraft known as *Looking Glass* was passing over Holton, Kansas at 40,000 feet.

The plane's official designation was ABNCP, short for Airborne Command Post. The *Looking Glass* code name had come about because the aircraft was a flying nuclear command and control center, with capabilities and functions designed to 'mirror' those of the USSTRATCOM Global Operations Center.

If the GOC was ever destroyed or otherwise taken out of service, *Looking Glass* was standing by to assume control of America's nuclear forces.

Apart from war games and exercises, that situation had never occurred before. *Looking Glass* had never actually assumed command and control duties for U.S. strategic nuclear assets.

Until now.

Rear Admiral Cynthia Norris, the current Mission Commander, had trained, studied, and prepared to take the ball if the GOC ever went down. But—all preparations aside—she hadn't expected it to happen. The GOC had backups and failsafes on top of backups and failsafes. Short of being taken out by a preemptive strike, everyone expected STRATCOM's Global Operations Center to stay up and functional at least through the first round of ICBM launches.

Of course, when the shit hit the proverbial fan, nothing *ever* quite went the way your training had led you to expect.

Her first indication of trouble came over the intercom, from the Communications Systems Officer.

"Mission Commander, this is COMMO. We've lost communications with *Home Plate*."

Admiral Norris sat up straighter and keyed her intercom. "Say that again?"

"Mission Commander, this is COMMO. The Global Operations Center is down. All channels, all frequencies. No traffic whatsoever."

The admiral took a breath, then squeezed her intercom transmit button again. "This is Mission Commander. I understand that the GOC is down. Stand by to patch me in to NCA."

She released the button and spoke under her breath. "Okay, Cindy. You've got the ball. Better get ready to run like hell."

And somewhere up beyond the clouds, about 280 miles above the Earth, the International Space Station swept eastward toward Washington, DC.

Zvezda Service Module
International Space Station

As battle plans went, it wasn't much, but it was the best that Rutger had been able to come up with on short notice.

Dmitri—armed with the Taser—positioned himself to one side of the Nauka Module hatch. Rutger took up station a few meters back, with the Makarov aimed in the direction of the hatch.

On Rutger's signal, Dmitri would pull the dogging handle and push the hatch open, keeping to the side as Rutger started firing 9mm rounds through the widening gap.

Maybe Rutger would get lucky and hit Syomin or Levkin, or (*Please, God!*) that infernal weapon. Even if the bullets didn't hit anything vital, the Russians would dive for cover, giving Rutger a chance to take more careful aim at the machine.

Dmitri would be ready to zap anyone who came within range of his Taser.

Not a strategy worthy of von Clausewitz, but it was simple enough that it might actually work.

Rutger checked that the Makarov safety was off, then gave Dmitri the nod.

Dmitri pulled the dogging lever.

It didn't budge.

The Russian cosmonaut frowned, braced his feet against a

bullhead support rib, and applied some muscle to the lever.

Nothing happened.

Levkin and Syomin had done something to jam the dogging lever in place. Tied it down, maybe, like Sarah had done when she'd tried to depressurize the Columbus Lab.

Dmitri was tensing his shoulders for another go at the dogging lever when station lights went dim for a second.

The EMP weapon had just fired again. It was starting! The EMP attack against America was starting!

Dmitri released the handle. *"Chort!"*

It was the Russian man's favorite expletive. As Rutger understood it, the literal translation was "the devil!" but the spirit of the expression was something closer to "shit!" or "damn!"

The curse might have been meant for the jammed dogging handle, or for the fact that Dmitri's countrymen had begun their destruction of the United States, or a general complaint to whatever gods there might be. Rutger had no idea, but one thing was clear to him: they weren't getting through that hatch.

He had a mental image of Sarah's nylon strap holding down the dogging lever of the Columbus Laboratory hatch. That was enough to give him an idea.

"Hey, D… Can you depressurize the Nauka Module? Like Sarah did for the Columbus Module?"

As the Maintenance Lead for the Russian Orbital Segment of the station, Dmitri knew the Russian systems intimately.

He shook his head. "No. The Columbus Module has those two big depressurization valves, in case there's a fire in the lab. The Nauka Module doesn't have that feature."

"Can we punch a hole through the hull and let their air out?"

"We'd have to go EVA. It would take us hours. America would be a third world country before we could get suited up. We'd…"

He trailed off in mid-thought and a strange look came into his eyes. He kicked off from the hatch and flew toward an electrical junction box on another bulkhead.

When he arrived at the box, he tripped the latch and opened the cover.

"We can't depressurize the module," he said. "But we can make them *think* it's losing pressure."

He located a particular wiring pigtail and traced a green and white wire to a snap connector. He popped the wire connector out of its insulated socket and looked around to Rutger. "Get ready. They're going to come out of there fast!"

Rutger took aim on the hatch again and nodded.

At least the first part of it went according to plan this time.

Dmitri worked his cross-wiring magic, and suddenly the depressurization alarm was screeching, and red lights were flashing on both of the Caution and Warning panels in the Zvezda Module.

It happened fast, just as Dmitri had predicted. The previously immobile dogging lever flipped up and the hatch jerked open.

Rutger squeezed the trigger. The Makarov bucked in his hand, the muzzle report painfully loud in his ears, the recoil swinging him to the side.

As he struggled to reorient himself on the hatch, out of the corner of his eye, he saw that his first round had taken Levkin in the chest. There were two more gunshots in quick succession, neither one of them from Rutger's weapon.

Rutger was facing the other way when Syomin shot Dmitri. Rutger didn't see his Russian friend tumbling backward from the impact—spraying blood as he went.

Rutger didn't see the second impact either.

The ceramic slug hit him just behind the left ear and did just what its designers had intended. On contact with the hard surface of his skull, the frangible bullet shattered, sending dozens of ceramic fragments and splinters of bone rocketing through his brain.

For an infinitesimally brief fraction of time, all the pain in the universe came simultaneously to focus within the confines of the Dutch Astronaut's head. Overloaded by a torrent of conflicting synaptic signals and the violent shredding of uncountable neural pathways, his primary visual cortex interpreted his death spasm as an explosion of colors that no human eye has ever seen.

But it was Rutger's ears that registered the very last sensory experiences of his life. The sounds of a metal hatch slamming closed, a dogging lever clanging into position, and the false depressurization alarm continuing its meaningless scream.

Kremlin Defense Center Complex
Moscow

The master display screen was gargantuan enough for one of those oversized American cinemas.

Polichev's gray leather observation chair was on the opposite side of the cavernous room, perched behind a waist-high frosted glass barrier on the first balcony level above the operations floor.

He was twenty meters or so from the screen, and—given its ludicrous dimensions even from this distance—the gigantic display seemed more like cultural braggadocio than a legitimate use of technology. As if the architects of the defense complex had tried so hard to convey the impression of Russian military power that they had strayed into self-parody.

If the screen had been half that large, Polichev could have seen it perfectly well from his balcony vantage point. But, for the moment, he was more interested in what the display was depicting than in any pseudo-Freudian interpretations of overcompensation.

The screen was locked to the targeting display from the EMP weapon: a circle of shaded topographic map that enclosed several million kilometers of the United States. The footprint was continually moving in synchronization with the orbit of the ISS, always showing the section of territory within the space station's line of sight.

Target icons were scattered around the map, each one marking the location of a city, a military installation, or a major piece of infrastructure. The vast majority of the markers were green, but the icons for Kennedy Space Center and Offutt Air Force Base were red.

The marker over Fort Campbell, Kentucky flipped to red. The U.S. Army's 101st Airborne Division, the 160th Special Operations Aviation Regiment, the 5th Special Forces Group, and their associated support facilities had all been rendered powerless.

With one shot from the pulse weapon, Russia had dealt a serious blow to America's military. Although Fort Campbell didn't qualify as a strategic asset, its loss would impact America's ability to wage conventional warfare, not to mention hindering their ability to maintain control when social order broke down in the aftermath.

The icon for Fort Knox went red, followed by the marker for the electrical power generating facility near Harrodsburg, and then Wright Patterson Air Force Base. One after another, the dominos were falling.

Polichev took a swallow of black tea from a crystal and silver glass engraved with the crest of the Russian Federation.

The footprint of the ISS swept eastward, destroying as it went. Moving toward Washington D.C., where the EMP weapon would chop the head off of the legendary American serpent.

In minutes, the government of Russia's greatest adversary would be—in both the figurative and literal sense—powerless.

Lieutenant General Belyakov of the GRU approached Polichev's chair and rendered his usual head nod of respect. "Good evening, Mr. President. I have information for your immediate attention."

Polichev took another sip of tea and motioned for the general to continue.

"The Americans are not bluffing, sir. We have confirmation from two separate operatives within their command and control loop. They're in the final phases of a full-scale nuclear strike. The pre-launch command has already been authenticated. The final launch order will go out any second!"

With a barely repressed sigh, Polichev lowered his tea glass. "I have studied the American president," he said. "I've watched every speech the man has made since he was the freshman congressman from Louisiana's Second District. I know what he eats, what films he enjoys, what music he listens to, and how many times he has voted against defense spending or spoken out against American military intervention. This is a man who quotes Mahatma Gandhi and Frances Crowe. He has no stomach for war."

Polichev turned back to the gigantic display screen where another power station flipped from green to red. "Calm yourself, General. By the time I finish this tea, the Americans will no longer be a problem."

General Belyakov leaned in closer to the president's ear and lowered his voice. "If you're wrong, sir..."

Polichev didn't take his eyes off the screen. "I am not wrong, General. And I'm sure that you have duties elsewhere."

The general started to say something, decided to keep his mouth shut, and turned to depart.

A few meters behind Polichev's plush leather chair, his stone-faced Lead Bodyguard stood with his back to the wall—observing everything but saying nothing.

Functional Cargo Block
International Space Station

The station lights dimmed again as Sarah slipped past the hatch threshold into the Functional Cargo Block. She moved quietly and cautiously, staying close to bulkheads. Taking advantage of any cabinets, equipment, or other features that might offer concealment. If any of the Russian hostiles were in the Zvezda Service Module, she didn't want to be spotted through the open hatchway.

Probably, the Russians were barricaded inside the Nauka Module with their EMP device again. But at least one of the bastards had emerged for long enough to exchange gunfire with Rutger and Dmitri.

Sarah had heard the shots. It would have been nearly impossible to avoid hearing them in an enclosed volume as small as the ISS.

As she pulled herself slowly toward the hatchway, the lights went dim again and then returned to normal intensity. That goddamned EMP weapon was still in business, so she had a fairly good idea of who had won the gunfight.

Rutger and Dmitri had carried a 9mm and a Taser, neither of which had apparently made much of a difference.

Sarah was armed with a meter-long steel rod, about the diameter of her thumb. The packing sleeve it had come in labeled the rod as a replacement part for Dextre, the two-armed telemanipulator robot used for repairs and maintenance to the exterior of the station.

It was the closest thing to a weapon that she'd found among the jumble of gear from the Z1 Truss Dome. She might be able to use it as a club, or maybe throw it like a spear, assuming that she could get close enough to one of the hostiles without having her ass shot off.

Nearing the entrance to the Zvezda Module, she noticed that the air in the hatchway held an odd mist-like quality. Hardly noticeable, like the thinnest imaginable fog.

It was blood. A cloud of droplets. Innumerable tiny globules of the precious stuff of life.

Sarah drew up short. She wasn't squeamish by nature, but she had no desire to pass through a vapor of human gore. There wasn't much choice, of course. Her friends were in there somewhere.

She peeked around the edge of the hatch coaming. There was more blood on the other side. Not tiny droplets, but spheres the size of marbles and golf balls drifting around the Zvezda Module.

Rutger was dead. Sarah didn't have to look very closely to see that. But she couldn't tell about Dmitri. He was curled up in a ball, turning lazily in the air.

There were no Russian hostiles in sight.

Sarah grabbed the lip of the hatch coaming and propelled herself through the mist of blood, not caring that it dotted her hair, face, breathing mask, and coveralls with red stigmata as she passed.

As she entered the module, she became aware that Dmitri was singing softly to himself, or perhaps chanting in the kind of singsong voice that Sarah associated with nursery rhymes or poetry meant for small children. Soft, melodic, and almost inaudible.

His eyes were closed, and his arms were wrapped around his midsection, where blood was still flowing from some kind of stomach wound.

Sarah allowed herself to go past him, then she rebounded off the far end of the module and redirected herself toward a First Aid box mounted on one of the side bulkheads.

She tripped the latches and rifled through the contents, searching for (and finding) a large sterile wound dressing. Disturbed by her search, packages of gauze and rolls of medical tape went bounding around the module.

Dressing in hand, she pushed herself toward her injured friend, ripping open the plastic-coated paper wrapping as she went.

The lights in the module dimmed again and then returned to full brightness.

Fuck!

She reached Dmitri. Getting his arms loose to put the dressing in place turned out to be easier than she was expecting. There didn't seem to be much strength left in his muscles.

As she worked, the wounded cosmonaut's half-mumbled words became clearer.

"Kotenok, malen'kiy kotenok..."

He took a ragged breath.

"Malen'kiy seryy khvost..."

Another breath.

Sarah recognized "seryy" as *gray* and she thought that "kotenok" might mean *kitty,* or *kitten.*

Something about a little gray kitten?

Sarah felt the tears welling in her eyes. "Can you hear me, D? I need you to hang on. You're gonna be okay, but I need you to hang on for me."

Dmitri's body shuddered, and then came one last exhalation.

His muscles went slack as the final spark of life went out of him.

Sarah didn't know how long she hung there, hands pressing a bandage against the wound that no longer mattered.

She had failed. Not just at rescuing Dmitri. At *everything.* And now, her country (and the world) would pay the price of her failure.

The station lights dimmed again.

Kibo Module
International Space Station

Six and a half minutes.

That was how long Paul Keene had been out. He wasn't really sure why he was conscious now. The fentanyl might have easily kept him under for another thirty or forty minutes.

Maybe the station's life support system scrubbed enough gas out of the air to dilute it below the effective level. He didn't know.

But the timer on the bomb reached three minutes as he was trying to pull his mind into focus. The digital readout continued its backward march toward zero.

Three minutes?

He had to get moving!

It took a major act of concentration to make his muscles obey his brain. He ached all over; his thoughts were muddled, and his limbs felt heavy from the effects of the fentanyl.

He missed the slowly turning bomb on his first grab, but he caught it on the second try.

Paul used his feet to get a push off from an equipment rack and sailed toward the hatch on his way to the airlock. His aim was not good. He had to use his free hand to ward off a collision with the lip of the open hatchway.

In the Harmony Node on the far side of the hatch, he had to correct his course again and make the ninety-degree turn to get him headed through the Destiny Module.

His movements were as unsteady as his thoughts. The Destiny Module was only about thirty feet long, but he had to make three adjustments to his trajectory to stay on track.

Ahead of him, the lights in the Unity Node were still flashing on and off at crazy intervals.

As Paul approached the node, he saw what seemed like movement amid the chaos of light and shadow.

Paul felt an instant and instinctive dread that it was Volkov stirring around. The vicious son of a bitch didn't have the common decency to stay dead.

But—as Paul drifted closer—he saw that it wasn't Volkov.

It looked like…

"Sarah?"

She came out of the flaring-jerking darkness. It was Sarah all right—her face speckled with blood, her eyes streaming tears, her hands streaked with gore.

"Oh, my God! *Dad?* What are you doing here?"

Paul felt a heave of blind panic. All of his worst fears were suddenly and finally coming true. He tried to wave Sarah off with his free hand. "You have to go, Sprite! There's no time! Take the Soyuz at Node 3 and get off the station!"

She gave no sign of having heard. "Dad, is that a bomb?"

Paul heard his voice climb to a near scream. "Listen to me, Sprite! There's still time to save yourself!"

Sarah reached for the bomb. Laid hands on it. Tried to take it from his grasp.

"Sarah! What in the hell are you doing?"

She looked into his eyes. Her face, tear-stained and blood dotted though it was, carried a calm resignation that was at opposite ends of the spectrum from Paul's rising hysteria.

Her grip on the bomb became more insistent. "Dad... I *need* this. I have a job to do now."

"Stop it, Sprite! You can't—"

She lifted one hand away from the bomb and touched Paul's cheek. "You've carried the ball as far as you could," she said. "Now, it's my turn."

Paul looked at his daughter—*really* looked at her—for the first time in years. Maybe for the first time ever.

There was fear in Sarah's eyes. But there was also dedication and determination; a fierce internal drive to accomplish the mission. To do what had to be done, regardless of the danger. Regardless of the personal cost.

Paul knew that look.

He'd seen it in the mirror, in his own reflection. In the eyes of people like *Handsome Dan* Conway, and *Shooter* Sullivan, and *Hozer* Miller. Every one of the best combat pilots he'd ever flown with.

It wasn't a decision.

He didn't choose to relax his fingers, to release the bomb into Sarah's hands. But suddenly she had possession of the dreadful thing, and she was turning away.

Paul followed her into the Unity Node and the wildly flashing lights.

He knew what she intended to do when she opened the door to

the Quest Airlock. She wasn't going to flush the bomb out into space. She was going to carry it out there. Deliver it to the target.

Paul felt a resurgence of his panic. "No, Sarah! You can't!"

She touched his cheek again and smiled. "I've got it, Dad. You can let go, now..."

Then, she ducked into the airlock and closed the door, leaving Paul behind.

Quest Airlock
International Space Station

There was just over a minute left on the timer when Sarah got the inner airlock door properly sealed. She wasn't wearing a spacesuit and there was nowhere near enough time to find one and suit up.

She didn't need one for what she had in mind.

She positioned herself for what was coming next and slid back the cover that protected the Emergency Depressurization switch. She steeled herself and tapped the blinking red button.

The outer door flew open, and the escaping atmosphere propelled Sarah into space amid clouds of expanding air turned to vapor.

Bomb held tight to her chest, she hurtled through the void—skin contracting with the sudden cold—eyes going glassy as her body tried vainly to adjust itself to conditions of vacuum that no mammalian form of life could survive.

Inertia carried her toward the Nauka Module at the far end of the station.

If the experience had lasted much longer, her death would have been unimaginably more painful. But there wasn't time for any real unpleasantness. Just as the burning in her lungs and the pressure inside her body was crossing the boundary from shock to pain, the timer of the bomb reached zero.

Nauka Module
International Space Station

There it was!

Mikhail Syomin watched the American capital slide into the footprint of his weapon.

Yes! Now, the world would see Russia's greatest enemy reduced to less than nothing!

His finger stabbed at the flashing icon on his targeting display.

If he touched the glass of the screen, he never felt it.

The bulkhead under his feet imploded, the metal fracturing and erupting inward as the heat and shockwave of the bomb he'd never seen ripped through the thin outer skin of the station.

Syomin's flesh was pierced by a thousand minuscule pieces of shrapnel and then seared by the fireball that consumed the oxygen in the Nauka Module.

His charred and lifeless body was sucked out through the enormous hole torn through the hull of the ISS.

Somersaulting like a dizzy five-year-old, Syomin's mortal remains whirled away into the infinite night, intermingled with scorched and broken pieces of the weapon that had once been called *Moon Song*.

FORTY-EIGHT

Presidential Emergency Operations Center
Washington, DC

Every eye in the room was on him. President Roth could feel the weight of their collective gazes on his skin. Every man and woman in the PEOC, watching their leader and waiting for him to take the final step.

If he turned his head quickly, he knew that he'd see their gazes quickly averted.

It was time. No. It was past time. U.S. and Chinese nuclear forces were poised at hair-trigger readiness, standing by to empty the silos and missile tubes on the president's order. An order he should have given five minutes ago.

There was no reason to delay. Every second of hesitation brought another American target into the crosshairs of the Russian EMP device.

But no one in all of history had issued the command he was about to give. Not even Harry Truman.

When Truman had authorized the bombing of Hiroshima and Nagasaki, he might have understood that he was authorizing a massive humanitarian travesty, but he had not been faced with a guarantee of massive nuclear reprisal.

Truman had not been loosing the four horsemen upon his world. And Truman had not been risking the survival of his species.

President Roth swallowed hard. His fingers toyed unconsciously with his wedding band. "May God forgive me for what I'm about to do."

He took a breath and opened his mouth to speak the words that would—in all likelihood—bring an end to humanity's fragile and imperfect attempt at civilization.

General Christopher raised a hand. "Just a second, Mr. President. We've got an incoming video teleconference request from NASA. Urgent priority."

The president released the breath and nodded.

General Christopher tapped the 'Accept' icon on the VTC unit, and Flight Director Harper appeared in a video window on the big screen.

There was a weary smile on her face. "Mr. President, I've got the International Space Station on relay. Permission to patch it through?"

Again, the president nodded.

"Put 'em on," said General Christopher.

A second teleconference window popped up next to Harper's. This one contained Paul Keene, floating at an odd oblique angle in microgravity.

Battered. Bleeding. Exhausted. Looking like death on a cracker. "The hostiles are down, sir. The EMP weapon has been destroyed."

President Roth's knees gave way so suddenly that he practically fell into his chair. "Say that again?"

"The threat has been eliminated," said Keene. "It's all over, Mr. President."

The somber aura of the operations bunker was shattered by whistles and wild cheering.

Hats and papers went flying into the air. Military men and women abandoning professional decorum in sweet and welcome relief.

At that moment, James Everett Roth—President of the United States, Commander in Chief of the U.S. Military, and (arguably) the most powerful man on Earth—discovered that he had peed himself a little.

Not much. Only the tiniest little bit. Not enough to show. Barely enough to feel the dampness in his boxer shorts and recognize that he had done it. Just enough to underscore his human frailty, and the unworthiness of *any* national leader to be the custodian of weapons that could destroy the world.

And that small instant of self-awareness took away any temptation to use the weapons now aimed at the Russian Federation. There would be sanctions. There would be payback. But he would not perpetrate a global holocaust to punish the enemies of the United States.

He looked toward the video screen where Paul Keene's image still floated, making eye contact electronically across the hundreds of miles that currently separated the space station from the White House. "Thank you, Mr. Keene. I don't believe I'm exaggerating when I say that you have saved the world."

When Paul Keene responded, his voice was ragged with emotion. "Not me, Mr. President. The real hero was my daughter. And I'm sorry she can't be here to take her bows."

Apogee Launch Systems
Mojave, CA

Amy Spicer followed Gil Lawson through the steel door and into the hangar.

"This is the assembly area," said Gil, "where the *Corvus* was built."

His evident delight in showing off a large empty rectangle of white-painted concrete floor was entirely out of proportion to its lack of features. There was some interesting looking equipment here, but it was all shoved up against the walls and not currently in use.

Gil walked across the open floor, heading toward a set of stairs at the far end of the hangar.

He might have caught Amy's less-than-amazed expression out of the corner of his eye. Or, he might have intuited her response, because he glanced over his shoulder and gave Amy a knowing look. "Don't worry. I didn't bring you here to show you an empty hangar. We've got footage of the assembly process. Mating the *Corvus* with the *Kickstart*. Design graphics. Recordings from simulator runs. Enough B-roll for ten news studios. Plus, I shot video of the launch with my iPhone. Not professional quality, but you're literally going to be the only journalist in the world with a recording of the launch."

Amy grinned. "Fantastic!"

Gil reached the stairs and started climbing. "You're going to be interviewing General Byrd, who's in charge of this circus. Also, the pilot of the *Kickstart*, and some of the *Corvus* ground crew. I'm trying to get you two minutes with the president, but that's probably not going to happen."

Following Gil up the steps, Amy tried to keep her eyes off of his butt. The man did look good in a pair of jeans.

"When do I hear more about this Paul Keene guy?" she asked. "It sounds like he's the *real* story."

At the top of the stairs, Gil opened a door and held it for Amy. "You're going to do more than hear about him. We've got a satellite relay set up with the ISS. You're going to be interviewing him over video chat in about five minutes. A Space Force Public Affairs guy is standing by with a camera to record."

Amy stepped past Gil into the office of Paul Keene. The far wall was covered with photographs, plaques, and framed awards. On a desk was some kind of oversized metallic laptop, and a guy in a Space Force uniform was futzing with a professional-grade video camera on a tripod.

The butterflies in Amy's stomach went from fluttery to full-out frenzy. "He's going to talk to me? Really? Seriously?"

"Really," said Gil. "Seriously."

"I need a mirror!" said Amy. "I've got to check my hair and makeup before I go on camera."

She had done herself up with more than usual care, in preparation for what she hoped would be the first edition of the Spice Report with a massive audience. But she wanted a last-second check that she didn't have lipstick on her teeth and that her hair wasn't doing something freaky.

"You look perfect," Gil said. "*Amazing.*"

Amy felt her cheeks go warm. "Really?"

Gil looked into her eyes. "Really," he said. "Seriously."

Olimpiyskiy Prospekt
Moscow

President Polichev spared no attention for the city sliding past the bulletproof windows of his limousine. Moscow was beautiful at night, but he had no eyes for architecture glistening with late evening dew or the light mist that threw halos around every streetlamp.

He held the secure phone clamped tight against his ear. "He said *what?*"

There was a hesitation before Ivan Gusev answered. "Please, Mr. President. I'm only relaying the message…"

Polichev's grip on the phone tightened. "Tell me again what the American President said. I want to hear his exact words."

"Please, Mr. President… I…"

"*Tell me!*" shouted Polichev.

"He said you can… shove your ultimatum and your Pax Russica up your… uh… *ass*, sir! He also said we should be thankful he hasn't turned Moscow into a radioactive parking lot."

"Bring me the American Ambassador," Polichev growled. "I want him in my office in ten minutes!"

Gusev hesitated again. "Uh… Sir… They've recalled their ambassador."

Polichev didn't hang up the phone. He threw it into the floorboard and stomped on it, shattering the glass screen, and cracking the plastic casing. Crunching microchips and electronic components.

He was still grinding the unfortunate device under the heel of his shoe when the Chauffeur made an abrupt left turn, departing the main thoroughfare.

Up the block—visible under the streetlamps and the light of the crescent moon—was a large crowd of protesters. Hundreds, maybe thousands of them, spilling off the sidewalks into the street. All marching toward the Kremlin.

Perhaps they would have taken their demonstrations straight to the gates of the famous walled complex, braving the teargas and the guns of the Kremlin Regiment.

Or perhaps they would have congregated in one of Moscow's many parks and vented their anger through chants and rhetoric-ladened speeches made through bullhorns.

Neither of those scenarios played out because the crowd found another way to express its rage.

The chauffeur drove toward them, slowing when he reached the fringes of the gathering. He reduced his speed to a crawl as the throng parted reluctantly to admit the limousine.

Polichev didn't start paying attention to the world outside the windows until the car was already surrounded.

Suddenly becoming aware, he tried to catch the chauffer's eye in the rear-view mirror. "What are you doing?"

The limo braked to a stop, and Polichev's stone-faced bodyguard turned around in his seat. "Tatyana will be five next Wednesday," he said.

Polichev glared back at the man. "Who the fuck is Tatyana?"

"My daughter," said the bodyguard. "You arrogant svoloch! You nearly threw her life away, and you don't even know her name."

Polichev drew a breath to scream at his insolent underling, but the bodyguard climbed out of the car, leaving his door open. The chauffeur followed the bodyguard's example, a move that could only have been planned in advance.

"Wait!" shouted Polichev. "Where do you think you're going?"

Neither man looked back. They walked away, melting into the crowd.

It took Polichev only a half-second to recognize the vulnerability of his situation. He scrambled over the seat back into the front of the car, slamming and locking both doors.

There were no keys in the ignition. The chauffeur had taken the keys with him!

Protesters began pointing toward the limousine. Gesturing toward Polichev.

He'd been recognized.

Suddenly, the mob was focused on the stopped vehicle. Irate faces just on the other side of the windows. Fists, stones, and bottles pounding against the roof, doors, and bulletproof glass.

The racket rose to deafening levels, but even that paled beside the throaty snarl of this enraged swarm of humanity.

Abandoned without phone, weapon, or friend, Leonid Polichev cowered before the fury of his constituents. He was flung from one side of the car to the other as the mob began to rock the limousine on its suspension.

The left tires came off the ground and the crowd redoubled its efforts, rolling the vehicle on to its side like some great wounded beast.

Polichev slid down the seat and slammed into the interior door panel and unbreakable window as the side of the car became his floor.

They didn't seem to be getting in. For all their screamed threats and the fearsome power of their wrath, the car's armor and bulletproof glass were keeping them at bay.

Polichev felt the first stirrings of hope. Someone would come for him. Police, or the Kremlin Regiment, or a detachment from his personal protection detail.

Someone would come.

And someone *did* come.

But it wasn't a rescue mission. It was a self-appointed deputation of protesters. They brought cans of petrol and they doused the limousine with liter after liter of the stuff.

The fire caught with a *whoomph* that drowned out the shouts of the crowd.

And it turned out that the armor could not protect Polichev after all.

FORTY-NINE

International Space Station

Keene wriggled backward into the left seat of the Soyuz and began sorting out the straps of the safety harness.

Belting himself in was more challenging than it should have been. His body felt like one gigantic injury. Every laceration, sprain, welt, and bruise seemed to have merged into a contiguous mass of abused tissue.

His soul was in no better shape.

Sarah and Dan were gone. Losing either of them would have been devastating. Losing *both* of them felt like taking a mortar round to the chest. The pain was more than he was ready to deal with, and he'd barely begun to process their deaths.

He hurt in so many places—emotionally and physically—that every movement (and every decision) required a deliberate act of will.

His current defensive strategy was to concentrate on minutia. Keep his brain distracted by inconsequential thoughts and useless observations. Expend enough mental bandwidth to keep his grief at arm's length until he had the safety and privacy to face it directly.

Like puzzling out the unfamiliar arrangement of straps and buckles that made up the safety harness. Examining the layout of the

Soyuz.

The capsule was foreign to him. Literally. It clearly carried DNA from its origins in the Soviet Union of the 1960s. Cold War design ethics continuing to linger more than three decades after the fall of the Warsaw Pact. Engineering influences that were not just from another culture, but from another time.

As an astronaut of the shuttle era, Keene had never hitched a ride with a non-U.S. mission. His training had not included practice time in Soyuz simulators. He hadn't drilled in Russian emergency procedures, or even the methods and processes of a routine flight. He hadn't learned the minimum Russian vocabulary and syntax required to integrate with a Roscosmos flight crew.

Which made this alien craft as incomprehensible to him as the control room of a submarine.

In the Commander's seat to Keene's right, Anya Malikova was ticking off the pre-launch procedures. She worked from a checklist strapped to the thigh of her suit, communicating only when necessary, speaking in a lifeless monotone to Mission Control Moscow. (And to Keene, not at all.)

The cosmonaut moved like a robot; her actions mechanical, face devoid of human emotion. Probably her way of holding grief and regrets at a safe distance.

Keene couldn't imagine what must be going through the woman's head.

With Polichev out and Acting President Kuznetsov (or maybe it was Kukurov?) stepping in, the Russians were tripping over themselves to be conciliatory.

Sorry about all that nasty world domination business! Let's forget all that and be friends, okay?

There would be formal apologies, diplomatic concessions, reparations, probably financial compensation for the people killed and the infrastructure destroyed.

But what did any of that mean for Malikova? What was she heading home to? Not a hero's welcome, to be sure.

Possibly a show trial and a prison cell, depending on how hard Moscow wanted to kiss Washington's ass. Maybe a bullet in the back of the head, or a fatal traffic accident, or a freak tumble down a long flight of stairs.

Or maybe just a life of shame and obscurity in a country that preferred to forget her existence.

Sarah had mentioned Anya Malikova in a few of her emails. Keene had gotten the impression—not of a friend, perhaps—but certainly of someone whom Sarah had liked and respected. Someone Sarah had described as quick to smile. Gentle. Humorous. Superbly competent.

That version of the woman no longer seemed to exist. If anything of her former persona remained, it was her competence. She appeared to know exactly what she was doing at the controls of the Soyuz.

After an exchange with MCC Moscow, Malikova flipped up the safety cover of a protected rocker switch and toggled it. There were a number of muted metallic bangs as the docking latches disengaged.

Then, the spacecraft was backing away from the station. Leaving the ISS unmanned for the first time since Expedition One, the original full-time crew, had come aboard in 2000.

In three and a half hours, the Soyuz would be on the ground somewhere in the deserts of Kazakhstan. (So long as nothing went wrong during the transit, or the deorbit burn, or separation of the descent module, or reentry, or parachute deployment….)

Keene wondered what the chances of an "accident" might be.

Under normal circumstances, not too high. The Soyuz design had a long history of successful flights with an impressive safety record.

But Keene and Malikova were both embarrassments to a Russian president who was fighting to distance himself from his predecessor, while dodging as many uncomfortable questions as possible.

How much simpler might things be if the only remaining witnesses were both tragically killed before they could speak to the press, or testify before any investigative bodies?

It wouldn't be difficult to arrange.

The sweet spot for a Soyuz reentry was around 120 meters per second. Much slower than that, and the descent module would come in too steep. Atmospheric friction would overwhelm the heat shield and the capsule would be incinerated, along with its passengers. A bit faster than 120 meters per second would ricochet the vehicle off the atmosphere and send them streaking out into deep space, never to return.

A relatively minor error in delta-v could make the difference between a successful landing and a messy death.

One tiny *oopsie* from Mission Control Moscow would do the trick. For that matter, Anya Malikova could do it herself. If she held the main engine burn just a few seconds too long, she could permanently forestall whatever unwelcome future waited for her on the ground.

Keene's chances of getting home alive were dependent on two different entities, either of which might be better off if he never made it back to Earth.

He thought about that for a few seconds. Tried to figure out what (if anything) he could do about it. And decided that he didn't give a shit.

If Malikova wanted to burn across the sky like a Roman Candle, Keene would go along for the ride. *Let 'er rip.*

Several minutes of silence passed as the Soyuz continued drifting away from the station.

When the range reached the safety threshold, a tattletale on the control panel illuminated and MCC Moscow began speaking in Russian again.

Malikova gripped the twin joysticks, twitching the righthand control several times. In response, the thrusters of the Reaction Control System fired in a series of short bursts, and the nose swung around to starboard.

"More rudder," said the cosmonaut in accented English. "Less *stick.*"

She seemed to be talking to herself, but her voice broke on the last syllable and she started to cry, so quietly that Keene could barely hear.

TWO WEEKS LATER

FIFTY

**Apogee Launch Systems
Mojave, California**

To an inattentive observer, the décor of Paul's office might have seemed unchanged.

The brag wall was still filled with photos, magazine covers, diplomas, and awards celebrating the accomplishments of Paul Xavier Keene, retired Navy fighter pilot, former astronaut, wildcat aerospace engineer, protector of kittens, and all-around nice guy.

His desk was still lined with framed pictures of his daughter, but—as someone with a sharp eye might have noticed—the ratio was reversed. Only a couple now showed Sarah as a little girl. The rest depicted her as an adult, mostly wearing flight suits or her Navy uniform.

Front and center was a copy of her ISS mission photo, Sarah broadcasting the confident (but not cocky) grin that all astronauts seem to learn.

Paul's attention wasn't on the brag wall, or the photos of his daughter.

With Gil Lawson hovering at his elbow, Paul was going over rough design blueprints for the successor to the *Corvus*, a longer and sleeker design that Paul had dubbed the *Sprite*.

Gil tapped a section of the blueprint. "Right here, see? We shift the whole latching mechanism to the dorsal hardpoint on the *Kickstart*. Keep nothing but the capture lugs on the *Sprite*. Cuts down on parasitic mass and eliminates the wiring for the micro-switches and solenoids."

Paul swatted Gil's hand away from the blueprint. "You want the job or not? Lead Flight Engineer. Your own office. All the Frosted Pop-Tarts you can eat, and the occasional flight into Low Earth Orbit."

"That depends," said Gil. "Can my band practice in the hangar during off-hours?"

"Not a chance!" said Paul. "But I'll bump your starting pay by five percent if you promise never to play any of your so-called 'music' within two hundred yards of the perimeter fence."

"I don't know..." said Gil. "What kind of Pop-Tarts have you got?"

"Any kind you want," Paul said. "Except chocolate. Those suckers are nasty."

Gil nodded. "I can live with that."

There was a tap at the door, and an administrative assistant showed a visitor into the office.

It was Paul's old pal, Beancounter, the knuckleheaded bureaucrat from the FAA's Office of Commercial Space Transportation.

The idiot marched over to Paul's desk and dropped a large manila envelope on top of the *Sprite* blueprint. "I'm afraid your request for a launch testing permit has been rejected, Mr. Keene. Title 14..."

He faltered as he got a look at the bruises and bandages on Keene's face. Then, he realized that Paul was smiling.

Beancounter frowned. "Did I say something funny?"

Paul tried (and failed) to stifle his grin. He reached for the envelope. "Not at all. You were saying?"

Less sure of himself now, Beancounter tried to pick up the thread of his announcement. "Chapter III, Subchapter C, just like I told you..."

He paused again because Paul was chuckling now.

"Our engineers have reviewed the drawings and specifications for your vehicle," the bureaucrat said. "They have serious doubts about whether the thing will even fly."

That was all it took.

Paul Keene threw his head back and brayed with laughter. He laughed so hard that tears begin to course down his ravaged cheeks.

He literally laughed until he cried.

When Keene finally got a grip on himself, he rose from his chair—still grinning—and threw the pencil-pushing son of a bitch out of his office.

CODA

Space Launch Complex 3-E
Vandenberg Air Force Base, California

There were no camera crews jockeying for angles to cover the launch. No journalists primping or memorizing clever sound bites for stand-up shots with the Atlas V booster in the background.

Just the ground crew, working through pre-launch checklists, and the rocket gleaming like a silver-white lance under floodlights in the predawn gloom.

In the twelve years since the recapture of the (now retired) ISS, public interest in the space program had dwindled to a level approaching zero. It was a cycle that NASA had encountered and endured multiple times. Land on the moon once, and you're gods. Land on the moon twice, and you're repeating yourself. Land on the moon three times, and people are watching reruns of *I Love Lucy*.

The long-promised manned Mars mission would likely rekindle the public's interest for a while, if and when it ever came to fruition. In the meantime, the lack of enthusiasm for space travel was somewhere between the post-Apollo doldrums and the resounding apathy that had followed the end of the shuttle program.

The "final frontier" still had its aficionados, as evidenced by the small crowd of onlookers gathered in the viewing area for the launch. But the aluminum grandstands were at less than one percent of their capacity. The people braving the early morning chill were the same bunch of hardcore rocketheads who showed up for every launch from Vandenberg.

Unlike their less informed (or less imaginative) counterparts among the general populace, the spectators understood that today's launch was different; something that press releases and PR videos had utterly failed to communicate to the average guy on the street.

Atop the Centaur second stage of the Atlas V, concealed by the bulbous carbon fiber cone of the payload faring, was the space probe *Inspiration.*

The offspring of a joint project between Jet Propulsion Laboratory, Roscosmos, and the European Space Agency, *Inspiration* was visually similar in design to *Voyager 1* and *Voyager 2*. But the *Voyager* probes had no propulsion systems, apart from their attitude control thrusters. Their speeds derived from the inertia of their initial launches, supplemented by various gravity assists from planetary "slingshot" maneuvers during their respective transits through the Solar System.

By contrast, *Inspiration* was outfitted with an electromagnetic drive engine fed by electrical power from six radioisotope thermoelectric generators.

Each of the RTGs contained 24 pressed spheres of plutonium-238 oxide, capable of generating 2,400 Watts of thermal energy (the decay heat of the isotope). The shell of each generator was lined with silicon-germanium thermoelectric couples, which converted radiant heat from the plutonium into electrical current.

The conversion process was not efficient. Less than 50% of the thermal energy was captured and converted, with the remainder being dissipated as waste heat from the RTG's cooling vanes. But what the arrangement lacked in functional economy, it made up for in simplicity and longevity.

The power generation system had no moving parts, and the half-life of the plutonium was 87.7 years. Even accounting for the gradual degradation of the thermocouples, the RTGs would continue producing useful levels of electrical power for the better part of a century, and most of that energy would go into the EmDrive.

Inspiration's ancestor, *Voyager 1,* had taken thirty-five years to cross the heliopause and depart the Solar System. *Inspiration* would overtake the older probe and leave it behind in just a little over eighteen months.

Traveling under a constant acceleration of one one-thousandth of a gravity, with no need for reaction mass, the probe would not merely coast through interstellar space. It would continue gaining speed for as long as the radioisotope thermoelectric generators held out.

When it blew through the heliopause at 595,000 meters per second, *Inspiration* would be the first and only manmade object to reach any appreciable fraction of the speed of light, and the probe would still be accelerating.

The electromagnetic engine that made this extraordinary feat possible had been dubbed the Koltsov Drive, in honor of the researcher who had lost his life in testing the prototype, and thereby brought his world to the precipice of annihilation.

The late Doktor Yevgeny Koltsov had never intended for his beloved EmDrive to become an engine of destruction. He had seen only its potential for opening the door to the boundless riches of the universe.

At 5:02 AM Pacific time, under a sky turning pink with the approaching sunrise, the countdown reached zero and the Atlas V booster shook itself awake. The RD-180 rocket engine of the first stage belched fiery exhaust and bellowed like a mechanical dragon, utterly drowning out the wild cheers of the onlookers.

In keeping with the dreams of the man who had made it possible, the interstellar probe *Inspiration* began its journey to the stars.

The End

AUTHOR'S NOTE

Readers who've served in U.S. Air Force missile silos or aboard U.S. Navy ballistic missile submarines will recognize that my descriptions of certain communications technologies and command and control methods are not in alignment with real-world techniques. It's difficult to describe this topic accurately without straying into (A) areas for which I have no professional training, and (B) material that is either sensitive or classified in nature. As the story doesn't require close adherence to actual nuclear C2 measures, I've opted for a genericized approximation rather than a faithful depiction.

ISS experts will recognize that I've taken some liberties with my descriptions of onboard systems and procedures. I drew from the best documents and resources I could lay hands on, including the *NASA International Space Station Familiarization Astronaut Training Manual*, the *NASA Reference Guide to the International Space Station*, *www.nasa.gov/station*, and *www.nasa.gov/iss-science*, along with inputs from technical advisors named in the Acknowledgments page of this book.

Despite these sources—in the field of manned space flight—I am (at best) a layman who's not afraid to ask stupid questions. My lack of expertise has undoubtedly resulted in many errors of which I am unaware. In addition to these unintentional mistakes, I've injected some that were less accidental in nature. Specifically, I've pared down some of the more complex technical descriptions and communications procedures, as well as the NASA command structure in the interests of clarity and pacing. This is, after all, a novel and not a technical manual.

As I mentioned in the Acknowledgments page, Abolfazl Shirazi (Ph.D Fellow, Astrodynamics & Machine Learning) was kind enough to create detailed simulations of ISS orbital patterns for this book. I therefore have the data to know that the final track of the station over the United States is not consistent with the actual movements of the ISS. I needed a trajectory that allowed the station to threaten specific targets in a certain order, so the one described in the climax of the book is straight out of my imagination.

I've also taken the liberty of stationing Paul Keene's old F-14 squadron in Pensacola, which—as any naval aviation buff will tell you—was never home to Tomcats, except for the F-14D currently on display at the

National Naval Aviation Museum. I needed Paul there for story purposes, and it didn't seem like too drastic a departure from reality.

Paul's space shuttle mission, STS-136, is loosely based on an actual flight that was scheduled but scrubbed before launch. Had STS-136 flown as planned, the real crew would have included Commander: Frederick "Rick" Sturckow, Pilot: Barry "Butch" Wilmore, Mission Specialist 1: Randolph "Randy" Bresnik, and Mission Specialist 2: Patrick "Pat" Forrester.

If their mission had not been cancelled, *Endeavour* would have flown 26 times, carrying a total of 158 crew members into orbit, made 13 visits to the ISS, visited Mir once, deployed three satellites, and completed approximately 308 days in space.

I decided to recast STS-136 for this story, because the shuttle deserved to fly one more mission, even if only in the pages of fiction.

Unfortunately, the scariest parts of this novel are based on real world technologies and emerging threats. If you feel like spending a few sleepless nights, or if you just enjoy an occasional infusion of nightmare fuel, some of the sources I drew from were:

1) Dr. Peter Vincent Pry - Executive Director - EMP Task Force on National and Homeland Security (2021) *The Russian Federation's Military Doctrine, Plans, and Capabilities for Electromagnetic Pulse (EMP) Attack.* Report Presented to the House Armed Services Committee

2) M. Schneider - National Institute for Public Policy (2017) *The Emerging EMP Threat to the United States.* United States Nuclear Strategy Forum Publication No. 0006

3) H. White, P. March, J. Lawrence, J. Vera, A. Sylvester, D. Brady, P. Bailey - NASA Johnson Space Center (2017) *Measurement of Impulsive Thrust from a Closed Radio-Frequency Cavity in Vacuum.* Journal of Propulsion and Power Vol. 33, No. 4

4) B. Corbett, J. Price, A. Corda, Y. Agassis, W. Sessions (2014) *Flux Compression Generator.* United States Patent No. US 8,723,390 B2

5) J. Foster, E. Gjelde, W. Graham, R. Hermann, H. Kluepfel, R. Lawson, G. Soper, L. Wood, J. Woodard (2008) *Report of the Commission to Assess the Threat to the United States from Electromagnetic Pulse (EMP) Attack.* Report Presented to the House Armed Services Committee

6) G. Baker III, Professor Emeritus - James Madison University (2015) *Joint Hearing on 'The EMP Threat: The State of Preparedness against the Threat of an Electromagnetic Pulse Event'.* Testimony Before the House Committee on National Security and the House Subcommittee on the Interior of the House Committee on Oversight and Government Reform

7) C. Fowler - Los Alamos National Laboratory, L. Altgilbers - U.S. Army Space and Missile Defense Command (2003) *Magnetic Flux Compression Generators: A Tutorial and Survey*. Electromagnetic Phenomena, V.3, No. 3 (11)

8) Edward E. Conrad, Gerald A. Gurtman, Glenn Kweder, Myron J. Mandell, Willard W. White - Defense Threat Reduction Agency (2010) *Collateral Damage to Satellites from an EMP Attack*. DTRA-IR-10-22

9) E. Savage, J. Gilbert, W. Radasky (2010) *The Early-Time (E1) High-Altitude Electromagnetic Pulse (HEMP) and Its Impact on the U.S. Power Grid*. Report R-320 Prepared for Oak Ridge National Laboratory

10) J. Gilbert, J. Kappenman, W. Radasky, E. Savage (2010) *The Late-Time (E3) High-Altitude Electromagnetic Pulse (HEMP) and Its Impact on the U.S. Power Grid*. Report R-321 Prepared for Oak Ridge National Laboratory

11) D. Stuckenberg, R. Woolsey, D. DeMaio, E. Rockwell (2018) *Electromagnetic Defense Task Force 2018 Report*. Air University Press - Curtis E. LeMay Center for Doctrine Development and Education

I must also cop to a bit of artistic license with the layout of the West Wing of the White House, as well as playing around with place names at various points in the story.

If (or when) you encounter blunders not described in these notes, it's a safe assumption that they resulted from some similar decision or oversight on my part.

As always, I throw myself on the mercy of the court.

— Jeff Edwards

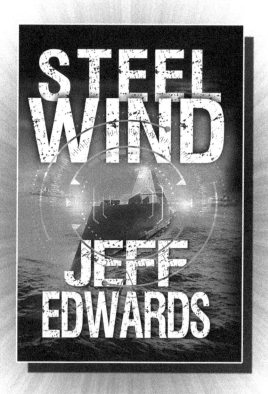

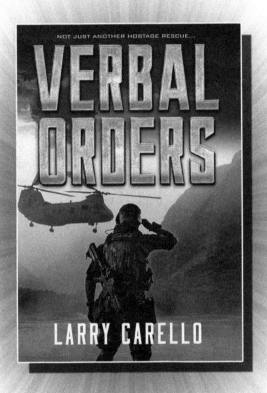

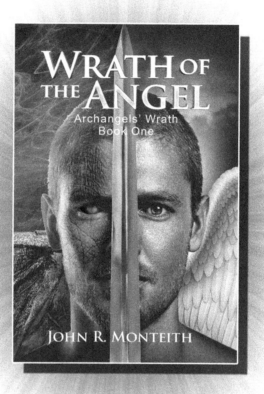

**THE THOUSAND YEAR REICH MAY BE
ONLY BEGINNING...**

ALLAN LEVERONE

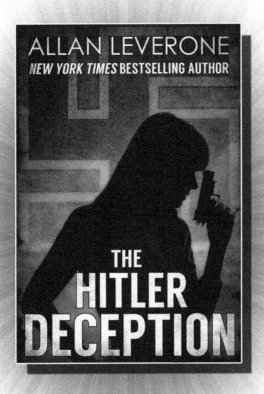

A Tracie Tanner Thriller

www.braveshipbooks.com

TRIBE. LOYALTY. LOVE

JOHN THOMAS EVERETT

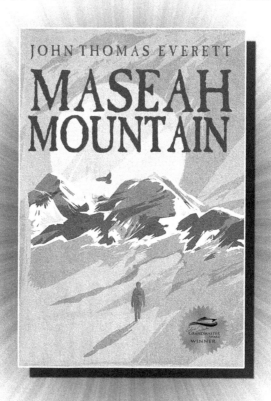

A tale of survival, adventure, and self-discovery.

www.braveshipbooks.com

CPSIA information can be obtained
at www.ICGtesting.com
Printed in the USA
LVHW090541180621
690505LV00011B/210/J